When the Captain spoke next his voice was unexpectedly gentle.

'You should get some sleep, my lady. You have had a hard day and we'll be back on the road early. I give you my word that you will come to no such harm again.'

The memory of the Captain's body on hers as they had struggled on the ground came back to Aline in a flash, along with the words she had screamed at him and the manner in which he had countered her assumption. He had said she was safe from…*that*, but could she trust him?

As if he was reading Aline's thoughts, the Captain unrolled the blanket and wrapped it snugly around her shoulders. 'You need have no fear for your safety in any respect whilst you are in my charge. I *will* keep you safe.'

AUTHOR NOTE

FALLING FOR HER CAPTOR takes place in an unspecified country, though I have tried to keep as close as possible to an accurate portrayal of life in Medieval Europe.

Women in the Middle Ages were not usually able to inherit titles or land unless they had no living brothers able to take the role. As such, Aline's unfortunate brother had to be bumped off years before the events in FALLNG FOR HER CAPTOR take place to allow her this opportunity.

Of course there were many powerful women who were determined to take their destinies into their own hands—notable examples include Eleanor of Aquitaine and her daughters Matilda and Eleanor of Castile.

Cauterisation of wounds was commonplace, but extremely painful and likely to lead to further infection. Suturing was also carried out, and horses' hair often took the place of thread. I wish I had known that at the time I wrote the chapter. I'm sure Bayliss wouldn't have begrudged a couple, and Aline's dress might have been saved...

FALLING FOR
HER CAPTOR

Elisabeth Hobbes

Published in Great Britain 2014
by Mills & Boon, an imprint of Harlequin (UK) Limited,
Eton House, 18-24 Paradise Road, Richmond, Surrey, TW9 1SR

© 2014 Claire Lackford

ISBN: 978-0-263-90989-0

Elisabeth Hobbes grew up in York, where she spent most of her teenage years wandering around the city looking for a handsome Roman or Viking to sweep her off her feet. Inspired by this, she took a degree in History and Art History.

These days she holds down jobs as a teacher and a mum. When she isn't writing she spends a lot of her spare time reading, and is a pro at cooking one-handed while holding a book! She is less successful at vacuuming in the same way, and would like to publicly apologise to her husband for the dust.

Elisabeth's other hobbies include skiing, Arabic dance, fencing and exploring dreadful tourist attractions—none of which has made it into a story yet. She loves historical fiction and has a fondness for dark-haired bearded heroes.

Elisabeth lives in Cheshire with her husband, two young children, and three cats with ridiculous names.

This is Elisabeth Hobbes's stunning debut novel for Mills & Boon® Historical Romance!

DEDICATION

For all the ladies who helped me cast Hugh.
I hope you're pleasantly surprised. x

Chapter One

'This is the third proposal you have rejected this year, Aline, and the fifth in total. When are you going to do your duty and choose a husband as you are required to do?'

The Duke of Leavingham and High Lord of the Five Provinces settled back in his chair with a frown. Lady Aline returned his stare, ignoring the muttering of the assembled knights and nobles. Her eyes fell again on the ornately decorated parchment lying on the table.

'My lord, if the offer was from the Count himself I would consider it. On behalf of his son, however, my answer is no. The boy is only nine years old!'

'Most women would consider themselves honoured to be allied with such a wealthy and respected family,' replied the Duke sternly.

Aline's cheeks reddened. The room felt much warmer. 'My lord, the terms of the proposal are generous, indeed, but there are those here who believe rule of Leavingham should not pass to a woman. Would you prefer it to pass to a child instead?'

A shaft of watery sunlight broke through the clouds and Aline's eyes drifted to the window as she half listened to the murmurs of agreement. She straightened her shoulders and brushed back a strand of ash-blond hair.

'My lords,' Aline said, addressing the assembled council, 'I know I must marry, and I will. If my brother had lived to be heir the husband you chose for me would barely have mattered—however, the man I marry will rule not only Leavingham, but also the whole of the Five Provinces. I will not make that choice lightly.' Silence hung in the air. Aline walked round the table and knelt. She took hold of her grandfather's hands and raised her face modestly. 'Please, Grandfather, don't force me to accept him.'

The old man peered at her with his lips pursed. Aline held her breath as she stared into the grey eyes so like her own.

'No, you need not accept *this* proposal,' the High Lord said finally. 'But you are running out of time. You are my last living descendant. When I named you heir I pledged you would be wed by your twentieth birthday. Remember that is barely six months away. I suggest you find any future offers more appealing or I will make the choice for you. You may leave us.'

Aline curtseyed to the assembled men and left the room, her heart beating rapidly at her narrow escape. The atmosphere in the council chamber had been stifling and the unexpected summons had made Aline more agitated than she had expected. She ran up the winding staircase to her chamber and rapidly changed into her riding gown. In the stable yard her groom would be waiting patiently with horses. The prospect of missing one of the few chances for freedom before autumn turned to winter was almost unbearable.

She sped down the stairs and through the smaller of the castle's two halls, fastening the clasp of her riding cloak around her neck as she went. Rounding a corner, she almost collided bodily with a large man coming in the other direction. She jumped back with a gasp of surprise as his hands reached out to steady her. Sir Godfrey, her friend since childhood, grinned down at her.

'Very decorous behaviour, Aline! But I doubt your grandfather would approve,' he remarked.

Usually Aline would respond with a lighthearted retort, but after the morning's audience she found she could not summon the energy.

'You know I give him no cause for disapproval,' she replied defensively. 'I read all the dusty old histories and treatises on diplomacy I am tasked with learning. I am a gracious hostess and a dutiful, modest lady of court. I play every part he expects. There is nothing he has asked of me that I have not done!'

'Apart from accept a suitor.' Godfrey smiled.

'Men whose proposals speak only of the power they will gain, or the dowry I will provide—' Aline snorted '—and today a child! Would you be so eager in my place?'

The young knight held his hands out in mock supplication. 'Aline, I'm only teasing. I'm sorry. You're right to wait for the right man, for you and for Leavingham. Your parents would have been proud of you—your brother, too.'

An ache clawed Aline's heart at the mention of her family. Six years after the influenza that had claimed them she still missed them dreadfully. Her fingers moved instinctively to the necklace she always wore: a smooth amethyst set into a filigree of silver—the legacy of the mother who had followed her husband and son to the grave after barely a year.

'You do want to marry, don't you?' Godfrey asked, linking his arm in Aline's as they strolled into the chilly morning air.

Aline shrugged. 'Whether I want to or not is immaterial. I have no choice. You heard what my grandfather said: I am running out of time. I lost any chance of marrying for love when I became heir. Now all I can hope for is to at least like my husband!'

Godfrey laughed. 'My wife was not my first choice, but we are happy. You will be, too.'

Aline said nothing, though the prospect seemed increasingly unlikely.

They had reached the archway leading to the stable yard and said their farewells. Aline watched as Godfrey returned to the castle, only slightly regretting that when *she* had been his first choice she had said no.

The sky had lightened as Aline made her way round the inner wall to the stable yard and stopped in surprise. Instead of her usual groom, a younger man held the reins of two horses.

'Greetings, my lady,' he said with a sweeping bow.

'Where is Robert?' Aline asked him cautiously.

The man raised his eyes to Aline's, pushing a lock of sandy-coloured hair from his face. Now that she had time to study him she saw his face was familiar, and Aline recalled that she had seen him around the stables once or twice over the past few weeks.

'My name is Dickon, my lady. Robert apologises that he cannot attend you today but an unexpected malady of…how shall I say it?…a delicate nature has left him unable to move far from the privy.'

Aline laughed, instinctively liking him, though doubt crept into her mind. Robert had been her escort for as long as she remembered; he had been the person who'd lifted her onto her first childhood pony and was well trusted to accompany her alone. Riding in the company of this young man would be highly improper. Her grandfather would have plenty to say if he ever found out.

'I'm not sure… Perhaps we had better not ride today,' Aline began.

The groom tipped his head to one side and his lips twitched into a half smile. 'If you wish—though I for one would be sad to miss such a fine day. Especially when I had thought my only company was to be horseflies and the saddle-grease pot!'

A well brought up and respectable lady would send for a maid to accompany them, but none rode as swiftly as Aline did and she so wanted an exciting day. Dickon's steady brown eyes were watching her earnestly. The memory of the morning's audience with the council sped through her mind and a spark of rebellion that had been growing since Godfrey's teasing flared inside her.

'We'll go,' she announced.

Dickon helped Aline onto her grey mare, a broad smile on his tanned face as he put his hand out to steady her. Side by side they trotted through the wide streets of the city to the main gate, talking idly of their plans for the day.

Aline was used to riding far and fast, and she was delighted to discover Dickon well matched and equally fearless. They galloped far across the moorland, daring each other on to greater speeds. By late morning they had come upon a small village, where an alewife stood at her gate, broadcasting her wares. In unspoken agreement the riders dismounted and bought a flagon, drinking down the cool liquid gladly.

Wiping his mouth on his sleeve, Dickon spoke. 'If you would care to wait here and finish your drink, my lady, I will buy lunch in the market.'

Aline watched him depart. There was a swagger in his step that caused her pulse to quicken. Unbidden, her mind drifted back to her conversation with Godfrey. Like all highborn women, she knew her husband would be the first man to bed her. In moments of honesty she admitted that she was curious. Sometimes, watching other couples in the court laughing and dancing, she longed so much for someone to seize her up in an embrace that the sensation was almost painful.

She spotted Dickon as he appeared from behind a hut, his saddlebag slung carelessly over his shoulder. Bowing again, he held out an arm for Aline. They walked together through the village, Aline acutely aware of the nearness of Dickon's body. She was glad when they returned to the horses and she could push such inappropriate thoughts away.

The sun had started to descend before they stopped again. The purple heather had begun to thin and clusters of trees appeared, providing some welcome shade from the sun. Aline had been happy for Dickon to choose the route and they had ridden close to the borders of the province. Now, as she dismounted, Aline's stomach fluttered uneasily at being so far from the castle with only one groom for security.

After tethering the horses to a tree she scratched them between their eyes while Dickon unloaded his pannier. He handed Aline a goblet of cool wine and she drained it thirstily, pushing her worries to the back of her mind. The day was unexpectedly warm, so they removed their cloaks and sat lazily against the trunk of a tree, sipping the wine and picking at bread and cheese. Dickon was easy company, though the talk never moved much beyond horses and amusing snippets of gossip about the goings-on of the castle staff.

Dickon refilled Aline's goblet once more and she lay back in the warm heather, eyes closed, sleepily enjoying the chance to leave behind her duties and her lessons. Somewhere not too far away a horn sounded and she idly wondered who it might be. She tried to pull herself upright to see but found her body felt heavier than usual. Her head started to swim. She looked up to find Dickon staring at her.

'It didn't taste strange in the slightest, did it, my lady?' Dickon said, his mouth twisting into a smile but his eyes cold.

The look on his face terrified Aline more than anything she had ever experienced. Something was deeply wrong.

'What do you mean, "taste strange"?' she asked, alarmed to hear that her voice sounded a long way off and not her own. Dickon leaned over and picked up the goblet from Aline's side. She flinched as his hand brushed her arm.

'The wine, my lady. I put rock-poppy juice in your cup. Not the most sophisticated drug, but effective. It paralyses the drinker quickly and sleep follows soon after,' he explained.

'What do…?' Aline tried to make sense of what the man was saying but she was finding it hard to concentrate. 'What have…you…done?'

'I just told you—I've drugged you,' Dickon explained matter-of-factly. 'The Duke of Roxholm has paid me very well to hand you over to him. In a short while a number of his guards will be here to take you to the Citadel of Roxholm.'

He sat back on his heels.

'I will, of course, try to defend you from their "surprise" attack, but unfortunately I will be no match. I will be found with some minor but alarming-looking injuries, wandering near Leavingham Keep, dazed and with a ransom letter, some time this evening.'

With growing alarm Aline tried again to sit up. 'You filthy traitor. You will hang...for... this...' she tried to snarl, though her voice barely broke the silence surrounding them.

Dickon's response was a smirk. 'Ah, my lady, so fierce! Do you think I would tell you any of this if I thought there was a chance that might happen? I shall be far overseas by the time your fool of a grandfather has negotiated your return.' He knelt down beside Aline and spoke softly in her ear. 'I'm sorry we have to part like this. But, as attractive as you are, the price I was paid is even more so.'

He started to run his fingers through Aline's hair, pulling the combs out and unwinding the long braid. Aline tried to push him away but her arms felt weighted and numb. She gave a scream that in her head sounded loud and piercing but which came out as half gasp, half sob.

'Still,' Dickon continued, as though he had heard nothing, 'I imagine we have some time before my associates arrive. We may as well say our goodbyes thoroughly. I've been longing to do this since I first saw you.'

With one hand pulling at the laces of Aline's bodice Dickon moved closer, so that his wine-scented breath was warm on her face. Aline had not thought she could be any more horrified, but at his touch she felt as though hot knives were being drawn across her skin. She tried again to scream, but before she could cry out his lips were crushing her own and his tongue was forcing them apart.

Instinctively Aline bit down hard. The groom pulled away with a cry of surprise, a trickle of blood leaking down his chin. He grabbed a handful of Aline's hair and jerked her head sharply to the side, then wiped his mouth with the back of his hand.

Aline cried out at the pain that shot through her head, but again found that her voice was no more than a mewl. She glared at him, her face full of hate but her eyes pleading with him to stop.

'Lady Aline,' Dickon reproached her, 'your modesty is charming but I know you find me desirable. I've seen it in your eyes so don't be coy. We must take our pleasure while we can.'

Dickon moved so swiftly he was astride her almost before Aline realised, one knee forcing its way between her legs, the weight of his body crushing the breath from her chest. His mouth worked roughly down her neck while his arms pinned her own to the ground. By now Aline's body felt leaden and the blood was pounding in her ears. She could no more fight his assault than she could prevent the wind from blowing.

She made one last futile effort to throw her assailant off, kicking her legs wildly, but the effort sent her head reeling. Her vision began to blur. From what seemed like a great distance she heard the sound of hooves, followed by raised voices. A shadowy figure loomed above them; a dagger glinted at Dickon's neck.

'Get off the lady now or I'll slit your worthless throat,' a harsh voice snarled.

The pressure of Dickon's body lifted from her and Aline drew a rasping breath. Two figures spun like puppets before Aline's heavy eyes: the groom in his rough brown jerkin and a black-clad man. Her last memory was of piercing blue eyes flashing in her direction, before darkness closed over her and she was lost to the world.

Chapter Two

Aline was dragged slowly back to wakefulness from dreams of violence and fear. Her stomach was on the point of revolting, her head felt heavy, and her limbs were tender and bruised. She opened her eyes but closed them again hastily as a sharp spasm of pain burst across her brow. She swallowed with difficulty through a throat that was dry and raw.

A steady rocking informed her that she was in a moving vehicle, though she could not tell what. Gritting her teeth in readiness for the anticipated pain, she forced her eyes open again. It was less painful this time, and when her vision cleared she pushed herself with shaking arms to a seated position. Immediately an icy wave of nausea crashed over her. She lunged forwards and vomited into a bucket that someone had thoughtfully placed within her reach, clutching the rim as her stomach emptied itself violently.

'Rock-poppy juice will do that to you, milady.'

The voice was male, and at the sound Aline's memory attacked her with images. Instinctively she hurled herself back into a corner with a gasp, her hands curling into fists.

'Who…? Where…?' Aline asked in a voice far from controlled. She bit down hard on her lip in an attempt to control her chattering teeth.

A young man sat on a wooden chest, a short sword lying across his lap. He looked no more than eighteen, his hair cropped short in the manner of a soldier. His face was not the one she feared to see, and Aline felt her legs go weak with relief.

'Would you like something to drink?' the boy asked nervously, passing her a leather-covered bottle.

Gratefully Aline gulped the weak ale, taking in her surroundings as she did so. The vehicle was a small cart, long and wide enough for a couple of tall men to lie comfortably. The upper half was covered with fabric stretched over a wooden frame. The only light came from a gap in the rough spun curtains at the rear. It was not the sort of place anyone would think to look for her.

'You…you aren't helping me, are you?' Aline asked, her heart sinking.

'I'm sorry, Lady Aline, but no,' the boy replied. 'We have orders to take you to Roxholm.'

Aline sagged back down onto the mattress as she attempted to make sense of her memories. Her stomach heaved with mounting disgust as she felt again the weight of Dickon's body on hers and the scraping of his mouth over her throat and breasts. She rolled onto her side and drew her knees up to her chest, wrapping her arms tightly about her body with a soft groan.

'Are you cold, my lady?' the boy asked kindly.

Aline shook her head, but her stomach lurched and another cold sweat enveloped her. An image flashed before her eyes of two men fighting. Was this boy her rescuer? It seemed unlikely somehow.

The boy stuck his head through the curtains. 'She's awake,' he called.

Presently the cart jerked to a halt. The boy jumped down from the cart, leaving Aline alone. After a few minutes a grey head appeared through the flaps of the curtain and with a curt nod motioned at her to come out.

Aline climbed out on shaky legs to find three men waiting. Two were dressed in rough brown tunics and leather cloaks: the young man who still held his sword, and an older man who must be at least fifty and was holding a crossbow pointed at her. The third man was clad in a black leather greatcoat. He held no weapon but stood with his legs planted apart and arms folded. Dark brown hair fell in a mess of tangled waves about his face, the ends brushing against the collar of his coat.

'Lady Aline, I was starting to fear you would never wake!'

His voice was deep and unexpectedly refined. When his blue eyes met her own Aline felt a jolt run through her body as though she had been slapped. The memory that had eluded her finally dragged itself into her mind. *This* was the man who had wrenched Dickon off her.

'We're stopping here for a while,' he said. 'The horses need water.' He rummaged in a basket strapped to the cart and produced a small loaf of bread. He held out a chunk in her direction. 'Eat this—you'll feel better with food inside you. Stay where you are and don't move.'

The older guard brushed past her into the cart and returned with the bucket and a bulging sack that he passed to the young guard. 'Get the chicken plucked,' he ordered. He walked over to the stream and began to swill out the bucket. The boy stared at Aline nervously, then pulled a scrawny fowl from the sack and turned his attention to it.

Aline sat on the step of the cart and nibbled the bread, surreptitiously studying her surroundings. Faint sunlight barely broke through the trees, so they were deep in the woods, though on a rough track. The sun was low in the sky, so she reasoned they had been travelling for an hour or two. With luck they were still within the borders of Leavingham. Maybe she could hide in the woods and evade discovery, then she might be able to make her way back home, or at least wait until rescuers came. Surely she would have been missed by now? Or would Dickon delay his discovery to allow his accomplices longer to escape?

Aline finished her bread and stood up. She stretched, arching her back and rolling her head. Out of the corner of her eye she could see the young guard had paused in his task and was watching her. She put her hands to her head, as if dizzier than she truly felt, then with a weak cry staggered slightly, allowing her knees to buckle. If she seemed anything other than weak and helpless her plan would not work. The boy dropped his bird and moved forwards anxiously to catch her before she fell. He helped her to sit down again.

She cast her eyes downwards modestly and with a shy smile whispered to him, 'Please sir…' *a nice touch,* she thought '…I need to…umm…I have to…the woods…'

The lad's forehead wrinkled in confusion

and then, as he understood what Aline meant, he blushed deeply. He glanced over to where the older guard was filling the bucket in the stream. The man in black was standing by the horses, poring over a parchment, and had his back to them both. The young guard nodded in the direction of the undergrowth. Aline walked to where he had indicated but to her dismay the boy followed close behind.

With her best attempt at an innocent smile she turned to the lad. 'Oh, thank you, but you don't have to come with me. I will not faint again. I don't want you to get into trouble for not finishing your task in time.'

He looked back to where the half-plucked chicken lay and relief crossed his face. 'Be quick,' he said.

Aline walked into the bushes, swaying slightly for effect, then lowered herself onto her hands and knees and crawled slowly away. She moved as quietly as possible in what she hoped was the direction they had come from, keeping the track in sight. Every moment now meant the difference between freedom and recapture. If only she could reach a village she might be safe.

Aline crawled to the edge of the woods and then ran along the track. When she reached a bend in the road an idea occurred to her. With fumbling fingers she unclasped her necklace.

For a moment she hesitated, clutching her mother's keepsake tightly, but her necklace was so distinctive that someone searching for her might spot it and know she had come this way. She carefully looped the necklace over a low branch. The silver glinted in the sunlight and surely could not be missed.

She walked back towards the undergrowth into the trees, then hesitated. It might be better to stay on the road; there would be less cover but it would be faster to travel and with luck her captors would not suspect her of leaving the forest.

'I wouldn't advise heading into the woods, my lady. Who knows what wild animals or bandits you might find there?'

Aline turned at the voice, a yelp of surprise bursting from her. The man in black was leaning against a tree, arms folded. He cocked his head to one side and smiled. 'A creditable effort, my lady. I'm impressed, truly,' he said. 'However, I have orders to obey and I can't let your escape attempts stand in the way.'

Aline ran.

She hurled herself into the woods without caring which direction, only knowing she had to get away. Branches and thorns tore at her dress and hands. With a stomach too empty and a throat too raw, every breath was becoming harder to take. Her strength was fading, but still she pushed on. Her pursuer stalked after her, moving at an almost leisurely pace and yet gaining ground with every step.

The trees started to thin out and she found herself in a clearing. Frantically she looked around for anything that might serve as a weapon. Her eye fell on a fallen branch and she picked it up, her other hand grasping at a handful of dirt and leaves. As the man came between the trees she held the branch out as though it were a sword.

'Stay back!' she shouted.

The man threw his head back and laughed, deep-throated and with genuine amusement.

'What will you do if I don't, my lady? Give me a splinter?'

'I mean it,' Aline spat, using all her will to keep her voice firm. 'I'll scream.'

'Scream all you like, Lady Aline. The only people who can hear you are my men, and that would hardly be to *your* advantage.'

He moved towards her and Aline thrust the branch forwards sharply. Her opponent took a step backwards, then abruptly lunged and knocked the branch sideways. Aline threw the handful of dirt in his face, and when he instinctively covered his eyes she ran again.

She had barely reached the other side of the clearing before the man recovered. Picking up the branch, he hurled it hard at Aline. It caught her behind the knees and she jerked forward. Her legs tangled in her skirts and she landed heavily, palms outstretched. Before she could stand the man was on her. He rolled her over and pushed her back, one knee across her stomach, pinning her to the ground. She struggled to push him off, blindly clawing at his face with her nails. Her fingers pulled at the dark mane that flopped over his face, and she screamed all the obscenities she could recall.

Astonishment showed in her assailant's face at the fierceness with which she fought him. With one fluid movement he twisted to kneel astride her, his legs gripped tightly at either side of Aline's waist, pinning her firmly. At a leisurely pace he reached a hand beneath his leather coat and removed a knife from the scabbard at his belt.

A sob burst from Aline's lips at the sight of it. She did not want to die—not here, not like this! But instead of slitting her throat, as she'd expected, the man reached for Aline's skirt. With one swift movement he cut it open down the side. Aline's stomach almost revolted as the memory of Dickon's assault flashed through her mind. She redoubled her efforts to escape, beating against his chest with both fists and flailing wildly with her legs.

'Don't touch me!' Aline screamed, grasping

at his knife. 'I will kill myself before I let you have me!'

Her attacker sat back, genuine surprise flickering momentarily across his blue eyes. His mouth turned down with distaste at the implication of Aline's words.

'You rate your charms very highly, my lady! Don't fear—I prefer my partners to be willing.'

An unbidden sob of relief burst from Aline's throat and her body sagged.

The man's smile faded, replaced by a softer expression. 'I promise you, your honour is safe,' he said solemnly.

Without waiting for a reply he cut a strip of cloth from Aline's dress and, lifting the pressure of his body, rolled Aline onto her front. He pulled her hands behind her back and bound them tightly. Though she dug her feet into the ground, Aline was unable to resist as the man put his arms about her waist and pulled her to her feet.

'Walk,' he instructed curtly. He gave her a gentle prod in the centre of her back.

Hoping to surprise him, Aline launched her body backwards, knocking him off balance. She lashed out wildly, kicking the heel of her riding boot into his kneecap for good measure, and ran screaming as he doubled over with a satisfying grunt of pain.

She had not run more than six paces before he caught her from behind by the neck of her dress. He knelt down and pulled her backwards against his body, his arm across her chest and throat. She felt the scratch of his beard against her neck. With the blood pounding in her throat, she writhed and twisted against the controlled strength in his arms. She had fought her hardest and he had barely raised a sweat!

The man cut another strip from Aline's skirt and bound her ankles together. Aline let fly another volley of curses, bucking wildly. In response the man laughed, unwound the cloth from about his neck and gagged her. He sat back against a tree, cross-legged, and folded his arms as Aline lay writhing angrily on the forest floor. She glared at him, hoping hate was clear in her face.

The man did nothing, indifferent to her anger and clearly prepared to wait as long as necessary for Aline to surrender. She lay still as misery crept over her.

'Good. You are beginning to see sense.' He unwound himself and heaved Aline over his shoulder as if she weighed no more than a bundle of straw. Whistling to himself, he carried her through the woods to the track, seemingly oblivious to the double-footed kicks she aimed at his chest.

After an undignified journey for Aline they reached the cart. Relief flooded the faces of the two guards as the man in black strode towards them. Aline saw that the young guard sported a livid red mark across his cheek.

'Duncan, explain,' Aline's captor said questioningly. The older guard saluted smartly.

'He was stupid. He won't be again,' he answered gruffly.

'Then it's done with,' the man in black said curtly to the youth. 'But if anything like that happens again you answer to me.'

The boy cast a reproachful look at Aline, then mumbled an apology. The man in black climbed into the cart and put Aline face-down on the mattress, turning her head towards his.

'May I suggest you use this time to realise the foolishness of trying to escape, my lady?' he said. He climbed down from the cart. 'Move off,' he shouted, and after a few moments they lurched forwards.

Waves of nausea washed over Aline. She strangled a sob, shut her eyes and concentrated on not vomiting again. She silently cursed Dickon for his betrayal, cursed herself for falling for it and for her clumsy escape attempt, and finally cursed the dark-haired man whose face swam before her eyes.

She did not know how, but she swore that one

day the man would pay for his treatment of her, and she consoled herself by picturing myriad deaths and humiliations for the arrogant swine.

Chapter Three

They travelled for what felt like hours. A brief struggle convinced Aline that her limbs were too tightly bound to give her any hope of freeing herself. The repetitive motion of the cart and sounds of hooves made her drowsy, and she kept slipping in and out of consciousness.

She awoke with wet cheeks, realising she had been weeping in her sleep. Now her mind dwelt further on the people she had left behind. When would anyone even know what had befallen her? It could be hours before Dickon returned to the city with his lies.

As much as that, however, she could not stop dwelling on why she had been taken. But for the gag in her mouth the lack of knowledge would have made her scream. Was she a hostage? The notion seemed ridiculous. There had been peace for many years, so why would the Duke of Roxholm risk disrupting it? But it had to be that, she told herself. Any other alternative was far too horrific to contemplate.

The movement of the cart stopped abruptly and Aline became alert once more. It was colder now, and the muted light coming through the curtains told her night was beginning to fall. They had been travelling for hours, so it was little wonder her body ached from lying on the rough mattress. Her throat felt rough and sore and she would have begged willingly for a drink. Her fingers were cold and numb, though wriggling them caused sparks of pain to shoot up her arms from where the ropes bit tightly into her wrists.

From outside the cart came voices and the clattering of equipment as the men set up camp for the night. Aline tried to twist her body round to see what was happening but all she succeeded in doing was covering her face with her hair and catching her skirt on a loose piece of wood. After minutes of fruitless attempts she gave up and lay still. Her throat tightened at the prospect of being left like this all night and she forced herself to breathe slowly. Finally, as her composure began to crumble, she heard somebody climb inside.

The person came closer and Aline gave a muffled cry as hands touched her shoulders. She was lifted briskly by the arms and pulled to a seated position against the side of the cart, with her legs curled underneath her. Loose strands of hair fell in front of her face, tendrils sticking to the saltwater tracks on her cheeks. The itching irritated her. That it was evidence she had been crying infuriated her even more. She wiped her cheek across her shoulder to move the hair from her eyes and saw who had lifted her upright.

The man in black sat back against the opposite side of the cart, too tall to stand upright. Aline studied her captor properly for the first time. He was well built, and she estimated no more than ten years her elder, though lines were starting to show on his brow and round his eyes. He sat silently, elbows on his knees and chin on his hands, returning Aline's gaze.

Eventually he cleared his throat and spoke. 'Forgive me for not introducing myself before, Lady Aline. I am Hugh of Eardham, Captain of the Guard of Roxholm.'

He paused, as though he expected a response, though what did he expect her to do, given that she was bound and with a gag in her mouth? Aline thought scornfully.

When no reaction was forthcoming he continued. 'I think it is important that we reach an understanding that will make the journey easier for everyone, so let me explain your situation. A message was sent back to Leavingham with your horses and the body of your groom. It states very strongly that the High Lord must take no action until he receives further communication or you will forfeit your life.'

He paused to let his words sink in, watching Aline closely.

'If we have an easy journey it will take us several days before we rendezvous with the rest of my men. Now, I can untie you, and let you travel the rest of the way in comfort, but only if you give your word not to make things difficult for us. Otherwise you will remain as you are. The choice is yours.'

Aline glared at him, any number of sharp responses coming to mind. But her arms and shoulders ached from the unnatural position they had been forced into, and the gag dug into the sides of her mouth. Knowing she had little choice, she nodded. The Captain leaned forwards and removed the cloth from Aline's mouth. As he came close she caught a mixture of scents: horse, leather, and something musky that made her catch her breath.

Drawing his dagger, the man reached around and cut the bindings on Aline's hands and feet. Red weals stood out on her skin, stark against the pale flesh. She rubbed her arms to dull the pain as feeling came rushing back into them in sharp bursts.

The Captain stuck his head out of the cart

and called for wine. Presently someone passed a wineskin through to him and he held it out to Aline. She tried to take it but her hands were numb and she winced in pain, her fingers unable to grip properly. Seeing her discomfort, the Captain knelt next to her and held the wineskin to her lips. It was an unexpectedly kind gesture and Aline paused, suspecting trickery of some sort.

'It is only wine, I promise you. See?' the Captain said. He took a deep draught himself, then held it so she could drink. 'Here…not too fast.'

Aline sipped the cool liquid slowly, conscious of his eyes on her and unsettled at the way his gaze made her heart thump.

'You knew all along I had gone,' she said accusingly. 'Were you just toying with me?'

The Captain shook his head. 'Not toying,' he said. 'I was curious to see what you would do. I meant it when I said I was impressed. It took courage to do what you did. No one is coming for you, however, so while I commend you on your ingenuity in leaving this—' he drew Aline's necklace from the pouch at his waist and let the chain dangle between his gloved fingers '—it was futile.'

Until that moment Aline had held on to the hope that she might be rescued. Now that hope vanished completely. Everything she had tried to do had been in vain. Her eyes began to prickle and she blinked furiously, determined not to let the tears spill once more.

With his eyes never leaving Aline's, her captor gathered up the chain and slipped it away. His eyes travelled downwards to take in the state of her clothing. Aline blushed at how dishevelled she must look: her bodice was still unlaced from Dickon's attack and her shift had slipped to show more of her flesh than was seemly. The telltale heat of a blush coursed over her neck and cheeks. She hoped it was not noticeable in the fading light.

'Take a few moments to compose yourself, then join us,' the Captain said. 'Duncan can find you some salve to ease the pain in your wrists and Jack is cooking dinner. He makes a better cook than he does watchman. If you have any need to attend to that which you did not take care of earlier you can use the bucket round the side of the cart. You will have your privacy, but don't even think of sneaking off or I'll truss you like a chicken and leave you in here until we get to the citadel.'

With a curt nod of the head he left her.

Aline quickly relaced her bodice and pushed a stray comb back into her hair, then climbed from the cart to locate the bucket. They had stopped in a clearing close to the river. Aline knelt on the bank, washing her hands and face in the cool

water and rubbing salve over her wrists. Standing up, she noticed the Captain watching her
and she frowned. Did he think she was about to
jump in and swim for freedom?

The men continued to set up camp while
Aline watched from the low step at the back of
the cart. The older man, Duncan, produced thick
blankets from one of the boxes in the wagon.
Wordlessly he passed one to Aline as she sat
hugging her knees to her chest. The night was
cold, and she shivered in spite of the warm blanket. Though she had been asleep or unconscious
for most of the afternoon she felt fatigue start to
creep over her and she stifled a yawn.

The Captain strode over and Aline eyed him
coldly. Before she could protest he had taken
hold of her hands. He pushed her sleeves up, running his thumbs lightly over the flesh.

'Is this less painful now?' he asked brusquely.

Aline nodded. The salve had eased the sting
and the redness had all but disappeared.

'Good,' he said.

Abruptly he left her, and walked round to the
front of the cart, then returned bearing a set of
iron cuffs linked with a long chain. Aline drew
an angry breath as she realised their purpose.
He passed the chain through the spokes of the
cartwheel, then fastened the manacles round her
wrists. The chain was long enough to give her

freedom to move close to the fire or lie down, but ensured that she could not try another escape attempt.

'So men of Roxholm break their word quickly!' she spat at him.

'I plan to sleep tonight—not sit up making sure my charge doesn't walk away again. You will have your liberty in the morning,' he answered.

The condescending tone of his voice made Aline's blood boil but she bit back a retort, knowing that there was nothing to be gained by provoking him.

'I want my necklace back,' she demanded instead.

The Captain shook his head. 'No. I think I'll keep that for the time being. Maybe if you behave yourself over the next few days…'

The Captain was still holding on to her wrists, so she pulled her hand away from his sharply. He gave a deep, appreciative laugh, as though he respected her rebellion, and bowed before leaving her. Aline pulled fretfully at the cuffs, eventually succeeding in easing her sleeves under the metal. The material provided some shield from the sharp edges, leaving the only injury to Aline's pride.

The night wore on slowly.

The three men sat close to the fire, playing

dice and sharing a jug of ale. They ignored Aline, who sat watching from her position on the step, thinking miserably of home. Later Jack brought her a bowl of surprisingly good stew, thick with barley and sorrel. Her appetite returned with a vengeance and she ate greedily. The boy hovered over her, smiling shyly at how well the meal was received. His eye was beginning to turn a lurid colour from the thump Duncan had given him.

'You should find some comfrey for your eye… it must hurt,' Aline told him.

The boy gave her a rueful smile and brushed a hand across his swollen cheek. 'If you had succeeded in escaping we would all have been dead men—the Captain included. I think I got off lightly really.'

They both looked over to where the Captain sat cross-legged and his meaning was clear. Aline shivered and followed his gaze. The Captain had removed his leather greatcoat and was clad in a light tunic. He wore a look of intense concentration on his face as he sharpened his dagger in slow, methodical strokes. An odd fluttering curled about Aline's stomach as she noticed the way his muscles moved. A traitorous voice whispered in her mind that if he ever smiled properly this man would be very handsome. She mentally hushed the voice, annoyed that she had noticed at all.

The Captain became aware that he was being watched and turned to stare at Aline. She held his gaze boldly. He put down his whetstone, picked up a rolled blanket and walked over to where she sat.

'May I join you, my lady?'

Aline shrugged, a twinge of embarrassment causing her heart to miss a beat. He took her empty bowl and gave it back to the young guard with a jerk of his head.

'Thank you, Jack,' he said pointedly.

The lad took the hint and went back to his companion. Aline moved to turn her back on the Captain, disinclined to talk, but the question that had gripped her heart since she had awoken got the better of her.

'What does the Duke want with me?' she asked, trying to keep the anxiety from her voice.

The Captain folded his arms across his broad chest and shook his head. 'That I cannot tell you, I am afraid. My lord has not shared such information with me.'

A thought that had been shouting for Aline's attention resurfaced. 'You said a message was sent with the *body* of my groom. What happened to him?'

'He betrayed you and tried to violate you, but you care how he died?' The man raised his eyebrows in surprise.

'I didn't say I cared. I said I wanted to know what had happened!' Aline snapped.

Her fury must have hit a target because the Captain's expression softened, then became serious.

He sat down next to her on the step, his shoulder brushing hers, and set his jaw. 'As you must have guessed by now, he worked for my lord. He had been a groom in the citadel, then a criminal under sentence of death. He was offered a pardon in exchange for working his way into your household and bringing you to us.'

'What had he done?' Aline asked. Her hands curled into fists at the thought of how easily Leavingham's security had been breached.

'His crime? I am not sure. I did not play any part in choosing him,' the Captain explained. 'My only part in the affair was to meet him and escort you to Roxholm. We were to send him back to Leavingham alive, but battered. He had to keep up his story of heroically defending you against us.'

He paused and a strange look crossed his face that Aline did not fully understand. She wondered briefly if he was holding something back.

The Captain continued his tale. 'He must have believed he was a dead man once his task was done, or maybe he took exception to my timing, because he produced a knife and attacked me.

I had to act in self-defence. I do not regret his death, though, given what he was preparing to do. Neither should you.'

Aline exhaled deeply and her shoulders sagged as she felt the tension leaving her. 'Thank you for telling me,' she said. 'And thank you for…' Her voice tailed off as her mind played out the memory of Dickon's mouth and hands roaming across her unwilling body. Her mouth twisted into a grimace.

When the Captain spoke next his voice was unexpectedly gentle. 'You should get some sleep, my lady. You have had a hard day and we'll be back on the road early. I give you my word that you will come to no such harm again.'

The memory of the Captain's body on hers as they had struggled on the ground came back to Aline in a flash, along with the words she had screamed at him and the manner in which he had countered her assumption. He had said she was safe from…*that*, but could she trust him?

As if he was reading Aline's thoughts, the Captain unrolled the blanket and wrapped it snugly around her shoulders with a smile. 'You need have no fear for your safety in any respect whilst you are in my charge. I *will* keep you safe.'

He walked back to the fire, wrapped his own blanket around his body, and lay down, arms crossed over his chest. He was soon snoring gently, as though he had no cares in the world, and as though he had *not* just calmly told her of the death of a man and left her chained in the dark!

Aline climbed off the step and lay on the bed-roll placed for her on the ground. His body had been warm next to hers and the air was chilly in comparison. She wrapped her blanket tighter and curled into a ball, hating him and doubting she would find such peace herself that night.

Chapter Four

As Aline had expected, she slept badly that night. The blanket did little to keep out the chill and damp and she lay awake, resentfully watching the silhouettes of the sleeping men round the fire. Every time she almost found a comfortable position the manacles dug into her wrists and dragged her back to consciousness, and more than once she found herself stifling a scream of frustration. As a result, her slumber had been light, every sound waking her in a fog of confusion. A soft grey dawn was already replacing the moonlight before exhaustion defeated her discomfort. Unable to keep her eyes open any longer, she fell dreamlessly into a true sleep.

A gentle pat on the shoulder roused Aline to consciousness. She lay with her eyes closed, ignoring it as best she could. A slightly harder shake of her shoulder caused her to let off a stream of angry obscenities.

She opened her eyes to find Jack staring at her, open-mouthed. She glared at him through her tangle of hair and his face took on an injured expression. A stab of remorse pricked Aline's conscience, quickly replaced by irritation for being soft-hearted. Didn't she have every reason to curse? She was stiff and cold, never mind being held against her will. The lad really should learn not to take things so personally.

She sat up, wrapping the dew-damp blanket around her shoulders, and rubbed her eyes sleepily.

The Captain strolled over to where Aline sat. He knelt down facing her, unlocked the cuffs and gathered up the chains. 'Time we were moving, my lady. I let you sleep as long as I could.'

'How kind of you!' Aline looked him up and down with exaggerated care. His hair was damp and he had changed his tunic for a fresh one, over which he wore a sleeveless jerkin of soft leather. He looked well rested and Aline immediately hated him for it. 'Did your consideration extend to bringing some clean clothes for me?' she asked haughtily.

The Captain had the grace to look uncomfortable. 'Alas, no. Though there is fresh water if you would like to wash before we leave, and Duncan will find you some breakfast.'

Aline longed for a bath, but had to content

herself with a quick rinse of her face and teeth in cold water. She pulled the comb from her hair and plaited it into a long braid. Duncan brought her over a hunk of bread and a mug of warm, honeyed ale. The bread was old, but dipped in the sweet liquid it was possibly the most welcome meal she could remember.

The Captain left Aline unrestrained, as he had promised, and she dozed, soothed by the rocking of the vehicle as it sped along.

During the afternoon she sat towards the back of the cart, staring out through the curtains. Duncan and Jack alternated between driving the cart and riding the brown mare but the Captain rode his own mount possessively. The animal seemed remarkably suited to his owner: a chestnut stallion with glistening flanks and an assured gait that Aline could not help but admire.

They kept to forest tracks as much as possible, though as the ground became swampier they were forced back onto roads. Any hope Aline had of being able to attract aid was soon dashed, and pangs of homesickness gripped her as they left her home further behind.

Whenever passing through settlements was unavoidable the Captain would hitch his horse to the cart, climb inside and sit opposite Aline, his dagger unsheathed, ready should he need to silence her. He would hold her gaze intently.

as though he were a cat watching a mouse, his blue eyes boring into her. After the third time he paused as he climbed out, and gave Aline an unexpected smile.

'I trust that you are not finding the journey too disagreeable, Lady Aline?'

It was the first time he had spoken to her since setting off other than to issue terse instructions. Caught unawares, she felt disinclined to be sociable with him. 'Would it matter if I was?' she replied bitterly.

The Captain looked taken aback by the venom in her voice, his smile vanishing instantly. He nodded curtly before climbing down. Aline watched him with curiosity through the opening, wondering why her reaction had surprised him.

It was late afternoon before the Captain signalled the cart to stop. Other than the chunk of bread at sunrise and an apple at midday Aline had eaten nothing, and her stomach was starting to complain. Jack walked over, carrying a bag, and handed it to her. She examined the contents: a bundle of rosemary, mushrooms and a handful of onions. He produced a knife and held it out expectantly.

'Isn't it enough that you have kidnapped me without expecting me to cook for you?' Aline said haughtily, pushing the bag back at him.

The Captain looked over from where he was

unsaddling his stallion. 'If you don't help then you don't eat. Though I suppose a lady as fine as yourself has little experience of such menial tasks.'

Aline bit back her first impulse to retort angrily and smiled sweetly, replying in a voice that dripped honey. 'On the contrary, my grandfather ensured that my education covered a wide variety of subjects, Captain. He said a true leader should be able to serve his people in any way. So do not assume I am unskilled because I am well born simply because you are not.'

She sat down, drew her legs under her gracefully and began speedily to peel the onions. The Captain pursed his lips and Aline couldn't tell whether he was angry or laughing as he hefted the saddle over his shoulder and walked off.

Jack cooked dinner, frying the vegetables then simmering them in ale, and the four travellers sat together, eating companionably.

'Particularly well-sliced onions, my lady,' the Captain remarked drily, tipping his mug of ale at her in a salute.

Despite herself Aline smiled back, and returned the gesture with her own mug.

That night, when the Captain took her hand and affixed the manacle to her wrist, Aline stared into his eyes, refusing to look away.

'You know I have to do this,' he told her.

Was that a hint of apology in his voice? Aline wasn't sure. She nodded silently as she held out her second arm. The Captain ignored her hand and instead fixed the other manacle round the wheel of the cart. The act left her with double the freedom she had had the previous night. Aline looked at him quizzically.

'It's colder tonight, Lady Aline. You should sleep closer to the fire,' the Captain explained. He held his hands out to help her stand.

'I can manage without your help,' Aline said stiffly, pulling herself to her feet.

The Captain rolled his eyes and dropped his arms, though he picked up her bedroll and moved it closer to the fire.

'Sleep well, my lady,' he murmured softly, before walking to the far side of the fire.

Aline drew her blanket around her shoulders. She stared into the flames until her eyes began to sag and slept peacefully for the first time in two days, the voices of the three men lulling her to sleep.

It came as a surprise to Aline that the fear and anger she had been feeling was gradually being replaced by boredom. For much of the next day Aline dozed on the straw pallet. It was late afternoon when the cart drew again to a halt and she woke to the sounds of an argument.

'…wasn't here before.'

'That was nine days ago. Things change, Jack. So, it appears, must our plans!'

Aline listened for more but the voices moved further away.

Duncan pushed his head through the curtains and beckoned Aline out. About half a mile ahead was a fair, with stalls and tents covering the route through a small hamlet. The Captain was standing by his horse, adjusting the saddle. In brief terms he explained to Aline that Duncan and Jack would be stopping to replenish supplies. He walked the horse closer to Aline.

'You and I will be taking a detour, my lady. I can't run the risk of you drawing attention to us. Mount up.'

He offered his hand for Aline's foot. She pointedly ignored it, instead gathering her skirts in one hand and reaching her foot into the stirrup. She swung her leg over the horse with ease and settled herself into the saddle. With one hand she patted the animal's neck to calm him.

'You may lead on,' she instructed.

The Captain let out a bark of a laugh. 'This fellow is far too good to waste on a walk. We ride together.'

Before Aline could protest the man swung up behind her, reaching around her waist to take the reins. He wheeled the horse around and set off at a trot across the marsh.

Aline sat stiffly, holding on to the front of the saddle. She was acutely aware of where the Captain's arms brushed against her body, and the way his breath touched like feathers on the back of her neck. Trying to avoid more than the minimum contact with him, she found herself unable to catch the rhythm of the animal and once or twice slipped sideways in the saddle. The third time it happened the Captain caught her with one hand round her waist before she fell.

'Relax—he'll pick up on your fear,' he instructed her.

Aline bristled at the implication. 'I'm not scared of the horse,' she snapped, glancing over her shoulder. 'I could ride him perfectly if I was in command of him and not sharing a saddle with *you.*'

'So what are you scared of?' the Captain asked, smiling.

Aline twisted around in the saddle to face him. Could he really not know?

'I was drugged and nearly violated by someone I thought I could trust. You pinned me bodily to the ground and drew a dagger on me. You left me bound and gagged for hours, then chained me to a cartwheel like an animal.' Her voice began to crack and all her frustration, fear and anger threatened to overwhelm her. 'I am here against my will. I have no idea what awaits me at the end of the journey and you feign puzzlement that I am uneasy with such...such...closeness!' she said angrily.

The Captain pulled the horse to a stop and dropped the reins. Slowly and with care he drew his arms away from Aline and let them fall to his sides. He looked at her, his eyes narrowing as though he suspected trickery.

'What that brute tried to do to you was deplorable. I meant what I told you before. You are under no threat from me, or my men.'

Aline raised her eyebrows.

He tilted his face down and then he shook his head. 'Lady Aline, any man would freely admit you are a very attractive woman, but I'm no defiler. You have my word that all we are doing now is riding.'

Aline looked up into the Captain's eyes. Her throat tightened as she stared into the icy blue depths. A fluttering in the pit of her stomach whispered that it was not fear that sent her stomach tumbling at his touch, but rather some new sensation she was reluctant to name.

'Thank you,' she said hesitantly.

The horse tossed its mane, impatient at the delay, and the riders both looked away. The moment had ended almost as soon as it had begun, but something had taken place that Aline did not quite understand.

The Captain reached round Aline once more to take the reins. He was careful to avoid touching her more than he needed to, and Aline smiled to herself at the small gesture. She buried her hands in the horse's mane to hold on and adjusted her seat. She had been on horseback since an early age, and riding was one of her greatest pleasures. She soon found herself rising and falling to the rhythm, responding to the movements of the man and the creature.

As they reached open ground the Captain gave a jab with his heels. The horse surged forwards and broke into a gallop. Aline held tighter, and in her admiration for the animal almost forgot where she was and with whom she was riding.

Once they had bypassed the village Aline supposed that the Captain would head back to the road as quickly as possible. However, he seemed in no rush as he headed further away, spurring the horse on even faster than before. Twice they jumped a stream, and Aline laughed unconsciously with exhilaration. She was genuinely sorry when they finally joined up with the road. They slowed to a trot and continued until they reached a small clearing. The Captain brought the horse to a standstill and dismounted. He held out a hand to Aline. She hesitated momentarily then took it and climbed down.

'We'll camp here tonight. Jack and Duncan should be along soon with supplies,' he told her.

Aline found a flat rock and sat down, her legs outstretched. The Captain reclined on his elbows, his long legs crossed at the ankles, watching Aline as she rewound her dishevelled hair. He opened his mouth to speak, then looked away. Aline felt no compulsion to speak, though her earlier anger had subsided. If he wanted to make idle conversation then let him be the one to start it.

Finally he spoke. 'His name is Bayliss. The horse, I mean. In case you were wondering.'

'Oh,' Aline replied, nodding. Impulsively she added, 'Thank you for telling me. Next time you take me for an unwished-for expedition I'll know what to call him.'

'Oh, now, Lady Aline!' the Captain exclaimed, sitting up. 'Don't try to deny you enjoyed this afternoon! You might dislike my company, but I'm a good enough judge of horsemanship to see that you were having a wonderful time!'

He caught sight of the smile playing on her lips and his eyes lit up as he realised she was teasing. Aline saw she had been right: when humour took him he *was* handsome.

They were both lost in their own thoughts,

but peaceful in each other's company, when the cart drew near and stopped. The Captain walked round to the back and began to investigate the contents of the boxes and bags it contained. Once he had gone, Jack pulled a bundle of cloth from the bench underneath the driver's seat.

'My lady, we saw this and I thought you might like it,' he said as he offered it to Aline, his cheeks flushing.

Aline unfolded the cloth to reveal a deep blue dress with wide sleeves and a belt of brown leather. Red embroidered flowers decorated the neck and sleeves. Aline ran her fingers lovingly over the stitching.

'I'm sorry, it isn't as fine as you're used to,' he stammered, blushing even redder.

'Jack,' she said, standing up and taking his hand, 'thank you. It's beautiful.'

At that point the Captain came from the back of the cart. He pulled up short at the scene in front of him, his eyebrows shooting up in surprise. Aline dropped Jack's hand guiltily.

The Captain's glance fell on the dress, lying over Aline's arm. He pulled it from her and held it up. Then he turned to the youth, an expression of disbelief on his face.

'Jack? Do I understand clearly what you have done? We are in the process of abducting the heir to Leavingham, trying to be discreet, and you go buying her a *dress*?'

'I thought… I didn't… She needs…' the boy spluttered, his voice beginning to crack.

'No! You *didn't* think,' the Captain bellowed, bundling the garment and throwing it to one side.

Furious at his behaviour, Aline stepped in front of Jack protectively. 'He didn't mean any harm,' she declared, in as firm a voice as she could muster.

'Stay out of this, my lady!' the Captain shouted.

He tried to sidestep round her, but she moved again to stand in his way.

The Captain balled his fists and Aline feared he might strike her. She drew a sharp breath.

At the sound he ran his hands through his hair, gripping his skull. He gave a growl. 'Save me from soft-hearted women!'

'Captain…my lord…I—' Jack protested, but the Captain cut him off with a wave of the hand and a snort of annoyance.

'*What* did he call you?' Aline interrupted in astonishment.

The Captain's eyes blazed as he looked at her. 'Nothing you were intended to hear, my lady. Though I am sure Jack will be more than happy to answer your questions in my absence. I'm going to scout the area. We're in wolf country now.'

He turned and stormed off through the trees, swiping at the undergrowth with his fist.

Duncan ambled up the road. He rolled his eyes at Jack.

'I told you he'd do that.'

Aline stooped to pick up the dress and turned to Jack, who was standing as though rooted to the ground. 'Jack, you called him "my lord." What did you mean?'

The two men exchanged a glance.

'Duncan, tell me!' Aline ordered. 'Please,' she added.

Jack opened his mouth but Duncan spoke first. 'Of course there is no reason why you should know, but I'm surprised he hasn't told you. He calls himself Captain but he's really Sir Hugh of Eardham. He's Duke Stephen's cousin, and second in line to the throne.'

Chapter Five

Sir Hugh! Aline winced as she thought how she had taunted him by calling him common born.

Duncan smiled at her expression.

'You didn't suspect? *Ha!* He'll be most put out when I tell him his innate nobility didn't shine through,' he crowed.

'And who are you two? The Lord Chancellor and the Keeper of the Duke's Keys?' Aline asked witheringly, still not entirely sure she was being told the truth.

The old man snorted. 'No, my lady, just a couple of soldiers looking for a quiet life.'

'*He* really is a knight, though,' Jack added.

Given the temper in which the Captain had stormed off, Aline was amazed at how indifferent the two men seemed. Just who *was* this man who hid his rank and title and whose men seemed unconcerned at his anger?

'Lad, best get that fire started before the night

draws in,' Duncan barked to Jack, and the boy scurried off.

The old man ambled over to the large rock and sat down, leaning his back against it. He cocked his head towards Aline, who followed and sat alongside him. She folded the blue dress neatly and laid it on the rock, the joy of it crushed by the quarrel. Duncan was following her actions carefully and she gave him a sad smile.

'He'll not mind when he's had the time to stamp his mood off,' the old man said.

Aline didn't need to ask who he meant. They watched as Jack expertly struck a spark with a flint and blew on the flames until they caught.

'Sir Hugh's mother and Duke Stephen's father were brother and sister,' Duncan offered, although Aline had not asked. 'Lady Eleanor fell in love with her father's steward and they married, despite the difference in rank. Oh, I know what you're thinking,' he said, with a wave of his hands to forestall Aline's interruption. 'It sounds unlikely, but somehow they persuaded her father. I think he knew he'd never get any peace from Eleanor until he consented, and of course she was only a daughter. She certainly passed on her strong will to her son!'

It was on the tip of Aline's tongue to ask from whom the Captain got his bad moods, but she held back, eager to hear the rest of the tale.

'Until he was seven Hugh was the only child born to either side of the family. His aunt had baby after baby, but none of them survived more than a few weeks. Duke Rufus—that's Stephen's father—adored his nephew. He decreed that Hugh would become Duke and he was raised as such.'

'The son of a steward?' Aline asked, raising her eyebrows in surprise.

'Aye, that might be strange, but some would say a granddaughter taking the throne would be unusual, too.'

Aline conceded the point with a smile.

'When everyone had given up hope Stephen was born, and overnight Hugh lost his position.'

Aline's heart gave a twinge of sympathy for the disinherited boy. 'As I gained mine when my brother died,' she commented. 'A birth or a death can change so many lives!'

She watched as Jack finished preparing dinner and buried the pot in the flames. Rummaging in the back of the cart, he produced a bottle of wine and three mugs. He broke the wax seal, poured a good quantity into the pot and joined Aline and Duncan. The three companions sat together, peacefully drinking, watching the sun as it set behind the mountains and listening to the distant howling of a pack of wolves.

The old man continued his tale. Aline learned

how everyone had naturally expected Duke Rufus to focus all his affection on his heir. There had been surprise and pleasure when he had continued to treat Sir Hugh as a second son. The boy had had the finest tutors, travelled to other provinces and inherited his mother's land and wealth. The two children had grown up as brothers.

'Rufus died two years back and Stephen became Duke,' Jack interrupted.

Jack and Duncan exchanged a glance, and the younger man suddenly looked wary. 'There were those,' the old man said darkly, 'who would have preferred his older cousin to take the throne as he had once been expected to.'

Aline would have pressed Duncan for more information, but the peace was broken by the return of Sir Hugh.

He strode into the camp and inspected the horses, pausing to stroke Bayliss's soft nose and scratch the carthorse behind the ears. His hair was damp with sweat and he held his jerkin under one arm; his tunic was unlaced at the neck. He had obviously been walking hard.

Determinedly ignoring Aline and the men, he walked to the fire and prodded a couple of stray branches back with his foot. He took the lid off the cooking pot and sniffed the contents, then gave them a stir. Seemingly satisfied, he found himself a cup from the cart and finally joined the three by the rock. His face was stern as he held his cup out to Jack, who filled it.

Eventually he looked at Aline and spoke. 'I see you aren't wearing your new dress,' he remarked, raising his eyebrow.

The statement was so unexpected that Aline burst out laughing. She shook her head, 'No, *Sir Hugh*, I am not.'

At the mention of his title the Captain looked sharply at Jack, who paled, then at Duncan, who merely shrugged.

'Jack, I should have brought your old mother instead of you. She'd have kept a confidence longer,' Sir Hugh remarked sternly, though Aline saw an unexpected glint of humour in his eye. Sir Hugh's gaze travelled to the folded dress. 'I would have chosen green,' he said, half under his breath.

He refilled his cup and held out the bottle to Aline, who declined.

'Jack, you've got a kind heart but a soft head. Fortunately it seems your gift-buying did not attract any suspicion so we can sleep easily tonight.' He turned his attention to Aline, his clear blue eyes regarding her carefully. 'I know that is no consolation to you, Lady Aline. I'm sure you would much rather a rescue party was heading this way. But if you give me your word you won't try to leave I will allow you to sleep unchained tonight. Can I trust you?'

Aline nodded and Sir Hugh smiled, his blue eyes crinkling. He walked to the cart and withdrew the crossbow from the rack underneath.

'For the wolves, my lady,' he explained. 'They won't often approach travellers this low down, but I saw their tracks and it's best to be prepared.'

Feeling uneasy, Aline drew a blanket around her and watched the fire until the sky turned black.

Aline woke with the sun on her face and stretched drowsily, enjoying the warmth, not quite remembering where she was until the sound of voices dragged her back to reality.

Sir Hugh wandered over with a smile.

'I hope you're a good walker. Once we get high the cart will need to be as light as possible and we'll be on foot. Today we cross the mountains and enter my lands.'

'Your lands or the Duke's, my lord?' Aline asked, raising her eyebrow archly. It was the sort of barbed quip she might make to Godfrey, but the flash of hurt and anger that crossed Sir Hugh's face made her regret it instantly.

'No... I'm sorry, I didn't mean...' she began, but he turned and walked off without a word.

'That was unkind, Lady Aline,' Duncan said reprovingly.

He was sitting by the cart and Aline had not noticed his presence. Her cheeks flamed as she stared after the departing Captain, shame at her words flooding over her. He had been friendly, and for no good reason she had rebuffed his attempts.

Duncan came to stand by her side. 'I know you'd not think it, given the way you've met him, but he's an honourable man and plays the hand he's been dealt as best he can,' he said. 'In fact, my advice is that you'll have an easier time in the citadel with him on your side.'

The thought of everything that implied hit Aline like a fist to the chest. 'I didn't ask for advice, Duncan,' Aline said sharply, biting down the fear, 'and I don't need anyone to protect me.'

Duncan folded his arms and stared at her. 'The advice was freely given, my lady, and don't be foolish— everyone needs allies.'

Aline stared at the Captain, now pacing back and forth next to the cart like a restless animal. His dark hair was swept back off his face and three days' growth of beard lent him a rakish air. His expression was belligerent and his reaction stung her unreasonably. So what if his smile caused her throat to tighten? He was rude, bad-tempered and seemed to have no awareness of how to behave towards a lady.

'Trust *him*? I doubt it very much!' she muttered under her breath, wrapping her arms tightly about herself.

By late morning they'd reached the foot of the low mountains that acted as a natural border between the provinces. The road became a steep uneven track, which made for slow progress. As Sir Hugh had predicted, the single carthorse struggled to pull the cart, and the other two were hitched to the front to help, Sir Hugh muttering about how such a task was beneath Bayliss. The travellers loaded themselves up with as much baggage as they could carry and pressed on.

Aline walked between Jack and Sir Hugh, determined to keep up with the pace the men were marching at. Her dress caused her to stumble on more than one occasion, which added to her misery.

'Lady Aline—wait.'

Aline was lost in thoughts of home, and the voice made her jump. Sir Hugh had not addressed her directly since her joke had misfired. He was still clearly offended as he had spurned all her attempts to make conversation.

'Let me,' he said.

He lifted the pack Aline had been carrying

and hefted it with ease onto his back, along with his own.

Aline started to speak, but he cut her off curtly. 'Don't thank me. I want to reach our destination before midnight and we won't if you hold us up.'

He strode on ahead, leaving her standing.

'I wasn't going to thank you,' Aline called after him. 'I was going to tell you not to treat me as though I am incapable!'

He turned back to look at her and cocked his head. 'Then we can all walk faster, my lady.'

His lips curled into a smile and Aline could not tell if it was mocking or not. She stalked past him with her head high and a flounce of her skirts. After that Aline caught him looking at her more than once with something in his expression that she could not identify.

The temperature increased hourly. They'd reached the high point by mid-afternoon, but as they began their descent down through the pass it became uncomfortably hot. The travellers were all irritable and bickering at the slightest provocation when they came upon a tarn, deep and clear, set into an outcrop on the hill. The pool looked so invitingly cool that Aline longed to dive in.

Clearly Aline was not the only one who found the water calling to her, because with Sir Hugh's

consent the men stripped off their shirts and
boots and plunged into the water. Aline stood
by the cart, enviously watching.

Duncan waded to Sir Hugh. The men had a
brief exchange, then Duncan climbed onto the
bank and escorted Aline down to the water, suggesting she swim, too. She had a brief internal
battle about the appropriateness of undressing in
front of her captors and almost refused.

'We'll close our eyes while you get in!' Jack
yelled good-heartedly.

Aline laughed, her resolve wavering. She
glanced at Sir Hugh, but he had turned away
and was wading to the middle of the lake in confident strides. In the end the overpowering heat
and the need to wash away the grime of the past
three days won out over modesty. She discarded
her boots and thick stockings and then, turning
her back on the swimmers, unlaced her bodice
and slipped out of the torn and filthy dress. She
quickly waded into the shallows in her under-
shift.

Ah, the water was wonderful! Revelling in
the sensation of the cool water around her body,
she unwound her hair from its braid. Closing her
eyes, she lay back and floated. For the first time
in days she felt peaceful, forgetting her captivity and the man who waited at the end of the
journey.

* * *

Sir Hugh stood waist-deep in the tarn, watching his prisoner as she lay in the water. Her pale hair drifted around her like a cloud of smoke and her face was serene. It had been an impulse to let the men cool off and a risk to allow Lady Aline to do the same. But then, what harm could it do? The journey had been difficult and she seemed exhausted—a marked contrast to the spirited woman who had so fiercely fought him. Since that first escape attempt she had caused no difficulties, and the likelihood of her attempting anything reckless was slight.

Though he would have denied it utterly, if questioned, he had developed a grudging respect for the woman. Most fine ladies—and if it came to that some men he could name—would have crumbled in such circumstances, but she remained unafraid. Even her swipe at his position had shown spirit.

His mind drifted back to his first sight of her, lying barely conscious and helpless against the odious bastard he'd dragged off her. His fists clenched in anger as he remembered the obscene propositions the groom had made regarding the unconscious woman. Hugh's temper had flared, and when the brute had lunged at him with the knife he had lashed out. The blow he'd delivered had sent the groom's head back against a tree trunk with a crack of the neck, his body falling lifeless to the floor. Seeing it again in his mind's eye, he knew he had been right not to trouble her with those particular details.

Aline was standing now, with her back to him, running her fingers through her dripping hair. Hugh could not tear his eyes away from her. The fabric of her shift clung to her slim form, outlining the contours beneath, yet temptingly veiling them. It had been weeks since he was last with a woman, and he was shocked at the way his heart leaped as he imagined his lips travelling down the slender curve of her spine. The memory of their struggle on the forest floor was vivid. He felt himself stirring at the thought of her body held fast against him, not fighting to escape but with desire matching his own.

She's not for you, he told himself sharply.

He dived under the water and swam a few strokes, hoping the chill would bring him to his senses. Surfacing, he threw his head back to shake the water from his eyes. A ripple of surprise coursed through him as he saw Aline was watching him intently. For a moment they held each other's gaze. A deep blush began to spread across Aline's creamy throat and she glanced away hurriedly. This was too much! Could the woman see inside his very thoughts?

Feeling unexpectedly self-conscious, Hugh

strode to where Aline stood and grasped her tightly by the arm.

'Out!' he commanded. 'We move on in ten minutes.'

She made no protest as he hauled her back to the cart. He left her stroking Bayliss while her shift dried in the heat and strode back to the water's edge. He sent Duncan over with Aline's clothes, unable to look at her himself.

'Just keep your head down,' he heard Duncan advise her. 'Whatever is eating him will pass soon enough.'

Hugh pulled on his boots roughly, refusing to think about the tears that had brimmed in Aline's grey eyes. He insisted that they must get through the mountains and down to a more sheltered area before they stopped for the night. 'The weather is closing in and I have no desire to get caught in a storm without cover,' he snapped.

They travelled silently after that. Aline walked the other side of Jack and kept her eyes fixed on the path, which suited Hugh fine. Once they were on flatter ground, and Bayliss and the mare were unhitched from the cart, he brusquely ordered her into the cart and they sped on their way.

The sun had set by the time they stopped in the shelter of a high rock face. It was still not far enough, but the horses were beginning to stumble on the loose ground. Duncan went to gather wood for the fire, and Jack began preparing dinner. Hugh made some unnecessary adjustments to Bayliss's bridle and saddle, checked the contents of the seat box and kicked the wheels of the cart before he finally admitted to himself there were no more pretexts for ignoring Aline.

'Will you come out, please, my lady?'

There was no response. Hugh cleared his throat and stopped himself in the act of smoothing his hair back. He was about to stalk off when Aline climbed through the curtains. The sight stopped him in his tracks. Her hair was free over her shoulders and she had changed into the blue dress. It was too loose, but Aline had gathered it at the waist with the belt and the billowing folds hinted invitingly at the contours beneath. The wide neckline revealed the delicate hollow where neck met collarbone, soft and oh, so tantalising.

Hugh's scalp prickled and his stomach flipped. He knew he was staring, and that she was waiting.

'Lady Aline,' he began hesitantly, feeling as awkward as a youth propositioning his first bar wench, 'I ask forgiveness for my behaviour earlier. I was rude and it was unwarranted.'

Before Aline could speak a soft whimper of terror broke the silence. They exchanged a glance of alarm. Hugh took Aline by the arm and pulled her round the corner after him.

They both stopped short at the sight before them. Jack had been skinning and boning a brace of rabbits and the scent of blood had attracted a wolf. The animal must have been starving and desperate, because the rangy beast had crept closer into the camp and had now backed Jack against the wall of rock. It paced back and forth in front of him, snarling. Whenever the boy made a move it snapped its teeth and pawed the dirt.

'Get back inside,' Sir Hugh ordered Aline. He pushed her towards the cart before turning to Jack. 'Throw it the bloody rabbit!' he ordered.

The boy was frozen to the spot. He stood holding the carcass as if in a trance, not even aware of the crossbow that lay on the log next to him. The animal was confused by the shout and turned; emitting a low growl, as if unable to decide which man seemed the most likely threat. It turned back to Jack and bared its teeth, transferring its weight as though preparing to attack.

Sir Hugh took his dagger out of its sheath and with a roar crossed the ground between them. He made a feint at the animal. It turned and tensed, then leaped forwards, hitting him square in the chest and sending him flailing painfully to the ground.

Chapter Six

Above all else there was the smell: an intensely sweet stench of blood and rotting meat. Then there was the heat: the wolf's breath, wet and overpowering on his face. A small part of Hugh's mind was amazed that it had registered such an irrelevant detail at such a time, as though his mind was storing up memories while it still had the chance. His heartbeat pounded in his ears, almost obliterating the shouts of alarm and the whinnying of horses that seemed to come from a great distance. The wolf snarled and snapped viciously at his face, its weight pinning him down. Claws scratched at his torso through the thin shirt and he felt searing pain.

Hugh covered his face with his left arm, the leather sleeve of his greatcoat offering some protection. With his right hand he swiped out blindly with the dagger. The animal's fur was too thick to penetrate and the blade had little more effect than a feather. Enraged, the wolf shook its head with a force that knocked the dagger from the man's grasp. Hugh dug his heels into the ground and twisted his body, his hand reaching desperately towards where the dagger lay but falling short. The creature lunged down at him again with a snarl, its grey muzzle wrinkled and teeth bared. Hugh felt a dull pain rip across his chest and he bellowed with shock and anger.

The pain was not yet intense; he knew that would come later—if he survived the attack. He was dimly aware of wetness down the side of his neck, which he knew instinctively must be his blood. At the scent of the blood the beast raised its head and gave a deep, triumphant howl. Waves of panic coursed through Hugh's body. He abandoned his hunt for the dagger and pushed his hands against the animal's chest with the strength he had left. His arms felt heavy and he could barely make his fingers work as they brushed through the wiry fur. The edges of the world became a grey blur. A thought passed through his mind: *What a stupid way to die.*

He closed his eyes, bracing himself for a final assault.

No pain came. Instead he felt heaviness as the animal slumped onto him. It twitched frantically, then lay still. A moment passed as Hugh's brain caught up with the sensations he was feel-

ing. He opened his eyes and craned his neck.
The wolf was lying across his body, a crossbow
bolt protruding from one eye. Spittle and blood
dripped from its open jaws. He raised himself
up onto his right elbow but it gave way immediately and he felt the first true pulse of agony
course through his body.

Hugh collapsed back onto the dirt, his head
spinning, and turned to look in the direction the
bolt had come from. Instead of Duncan or Jack,
as he was expecting, Aline stood white-faced,
with the crossbow reloaded and now aimed menacingly at his heart.

This was the final straw, and a wordless exclamation of disbelief burst from Hugh's aching
lungs. He closed his eyes, blood loss and pain
making him light-headed and hysteria in danger of consuming him. In a moment of clarity he
was struck by the absurdity of the situation. His
own men were next to useless in a crisis and a
woman, *his prisoner*, who for some reason had
saved his life, was now threatening to end it.

Despite Sir Hugh's order Aline had stayed
outside the cart. She had watched transfixed
with horror as the wolf attacked.

Jack had still been frozen to the spot, his earlier whimpers replaced by a keening cry of, 'No…
no…no…no…no!'

Hugh's shriek of pain had broken the trance they'd both been under. At the same time as Jack picked up his boning knife Aline had snatched the crossbow from where it had been lying. Breathing slowly to steady her nerve, she'd taken careful aim and fired. With trembling fingers she'd slid another bolt into place and wound back the string, but there had been no need. Her aim had been true and the beast lay dead.

Now she stood stiffly, holding the weapon at arm's length, uncertain what to do. A noise behind her made her jump. She turned her head, though she kept the bow aimed at the man on the ground. Duncan had returned at the commotion and stood red-faced and panting at the edge of the clearing, his short sword drawn. Jack stood with his knife outstretched, still holding his rabbit, trembling and close to tears.

Aline stared at the Captain, who now lay laughing uncontrollably under the body of the wolf. For a moment she considered the likely outcome if she *did* shoot him. She walked slowly towards him, still holding the crossbow at chest height. Sir Hugh's face changed as she stood over him, doubt and possibly fear in his eyes, his hysteria over as quickly as it had arisen. His chest rose and fell heavily, the muscles straining with exertion.

'What will you do now, my lady?' he asked,

his voice hoarse and slurred. 'What purpose would it serve to kill me? Even if my men don't execute you immediately, how long do you think you would last on your own in the wilds?'

Aline looked deep into the eyes of the man who had captured and humiliated her. With her sweetest smile she aimed her bow and pulled the trigger.

The bolt thrummed close to the Captain's head and stuck in the ground by his ear. Aline had the satisfaction of seeing him jerk in alarm. She lowered the bow and held out a hand; he took it, grunting as she helped him up.

No sooner was he on his feet than his legs buckled underneath him and he slumped forwards with a groan. Aline caught him in her arms. but could barely support his weight. She let the crossbow fall and awkwardly lowered the man to the ground. She cradled his head in her lap as Jack and Duncan rushed forwards to haul the body of the wolf away to the edge of the clearing.

'Get some torches lit,' Sir Hugh ordered weakly, 'and bring one over here. I need to see how bad this is.'

A warm stickiness was starting to soak through Aline's bodice. She tensed, alarmed at how clammy her dress felt. Sir Hugh had been such a short time in her arms before he fell. The man's injury must be serious if the blood was soaking through his clothing so quickly!

Duncan brought a torch and cautiously peeled back the Captain's coat and tunic, both now crimson and sticky. Duncan swore, Jack made retching sounds, and Aline blanched as the flickering light revealed the terrible state he was in.

There were scratches covering his torso, but these were nothing in comparison to those on his chest. Where the wolf had razed him with its claws the wound was shallow, but long. It stretched from his shoulder to finish just over his heart, three ragged gashes in all. The Captain pressed his good hand tightly down to try and slow the blood oozing out. From the controlled sound of his breathing Aline could tell he was fighting hard to remain alert, but she knew he could pass out at any moment.

'Get one of those bottles of whisky quickly and start a fire, Jack,' Duncan rasped. 'I'm going to have to cauterise that before he dies from the loss of blood.'

Sir Hugh let out a deep, wordless moan of protest and closed his eyes.

'What can I do to help?' Aline asked.

'Hold him. Comfort him as best as you can, my lady,' Duncan said kindly. 'I don't know if you understand what is going to happen here, but I have to seal the wound. Be warned: when the knife touches he'll be in terrible pain—more than he is in now. You'll have to be ready. Can you do that?'

Aline nodded dumbly. Sir Hugh began to shake, whether from the knowledge of what he faced or from loss of blood Aline was uncertain. She reached down and smoothed his matted hair back from his face with a trembling hand, then stroked his face gently. She made vague shushing sounds, as though she was comforting an injured animal or a child.

Jack ran across with the bottle of whisky and a leather strap from the carthorse's halter and wrapped it around a thick twig. Duncan picked up the fallen dagger and poured some of the liquor over the blade, then took it to the fire. He balanced it in the flames, his face solemn as he prepared for his task. When he was satisfied the blade was hot enough he nodded to Jack, who held the bottle for Sir Hugh to drink from, then tipped more of the liquid over the injured shoulder and chest.

Sir Hugh swore as the sharp spirit flowed over his injury. Again Jack gave him the bottle, and Hugh took a couple of deep gulps. As an afterthought Jack took a swig, passed it to Duncan, and then to Aline, who took a hesitant drink, glad to feel the sharp warmth in her stomach.

Duncan carried the dagger over and knelt

astride his captain. He nodded his head and Jack pushed the leather-wrapped wood between Sir Hugh's teeth, then leaned across his legs to restrain him. Aline laced her fingers through Sir Hugh's, noting with alarm how cold they felt. She moved his hand away from the wound and gave a reassuring squeeze, which he answered almost imperceptibly with one of his own.

'Ready, lad—my lady?' Duncan asked. 'I'm going to count to three, then I'll do it. One... two...'

Without waiting for the third count Duncan pressed the knife against the largest laceration on the Captain's chest. He held it for a couple of seconds, then quickly removed it. The smell of burning flesh filled the air, assaulting Aline's senses. Sir Hugh bit down on the wood but could not prevent himself from letting out a groan, more animal than human, deep in his throat as his skin blistered.

His hand gave a spasm and his fingers squeezed Aline's so tightly she cried out. His body jerked, then fell still as he collapsed into a deep faint. Bile rose in Aline's throat and she let out an anguished sob, while Jack leaned away and vomited loudly. Duncan removed the wood from the unconscious man's mouth and inspected his handiwork, then smiled grimly at a job well done.

'You both did well. Two more to go,' he told them. 'I need to reheat the blade. Too cool and it won't seal the edges.'

'You can't do that again!' Aline blurted out. 'He'll never survive another shock like that!'

'I don't have a choice,' Duncan told her gently. 'If I don't then the blood loss will end him anyway. How else can I close the wounds?'

Aline looked down at the unconscious man, his face pale and drawn, knowing the old man was right. Then from nowhere a memory surfaced of a visiting doctor from across the seas. He had amazed the whole court when he'd sewn together a deep cut in the leg of her grandfather's favourite horse.

She looked up with bright eyes and asked, 'Do you have a needle?'

She explained her idea to Duncan, who spat out a loud protest. Aline's angry retort was cut short by the slight movement of the head in her lap. Sir Hugh gave a guttural sigh and opened his eyes to see his soldier and his prisoner staring at each other angrily.

'Is it over?' he whispered huskily through cracked lips.

'Hardly started,' Duncan raged. 'This madwoman wants to sew you together like—like a tapestry!'

Again Aline explained her plan, ignoring the

snorts from the old soldier behind her. Sir Hugh
lay silently as she spoke, all the while looking
up at Aline.

'Please, let me try?' she asked.

Sir Hugh held her gaze for what felt like hours
before nodding slowly.

'I'm going to need warm water and clean
cloths,' Aline ordered.

Jack hastened to fill the pot and set it onto
the fire. Duncan walked to the cart and pulled a
leather roll out of a box, grumbling all the while
under his breath, then returned bearing a selection of needles and tools.

Leaving Sir Hugh lying alone, Aline retrieved
her old dress from the cart. As rapidly as she
could she cut it into strips with the dagger, un-
picking the thread that decorated the bodice. She
returned to where Duncan and Jack had posi-
tioned her patient. They had moved him against
the cartwheel and sat either side, supporting his
weight. With a lurching heart Aline saw that the
only way she could reach the wound was to kneel
astride the reclining man.

She gathered her skirts and moved as carefully as she could into position. She reached a
timid hand to his smooth chest, feeling for the
torn flesh.

Sir Hugh managed to smile weakly despite

the pain. 'There are some advantages to being mauled, I see.'

'You flatter yourself, Captain,' Aline said in a voice lighter than she felt. 'I prefer my companions to be less bloodstained!'

The man's face darkened as he obviously recalled when he had said something similar and he looked away.

Aline's slim fingers probed the area where the skin was torn. She noted with relief that the blood no longer flowed so quickly. She had sounded more confident than she felt when describing the procedure; now, faced with actually doing it, she was beginning to lose her nerve.

'This is going to need a lot of stitches and it needs to be well cleaned. Are you sure you want me to do this?' she asked cautiously.

Sir Hugh nodded, his eyes half-closed. Aline took a deep breath and began.

She dipped the strips of dress into the hot water, ignoring the sting in her hands. She cleaned what blood she could from round the wound, ignoring the wincing this caused. Jack passed the whisky bottle to Aline, who drank deeply, then held it to Hugh's lips. Her hair fell across her face and she paused, twisted it into a roll and secured it with a strip of skirt. Knowing she could put the moment off no longer, she took a deep breath and pushed the needle through

Hugh's skin. He jerked and let out a growl, but did not pass out again.

The needle was blunter than Aline would have preferred, and sewing the wound took what seemed like hours. It turned out that skin proved a lot tougher to pierce than tapestry cloth.

The sky was almost pitch-black by the time she was finished. Hugh had remained still after the first few stitches and contented himself with groaning or swearing depending on the depth of the stitch. Now Aline knotted the final thread with a sigh of relief. The Captain had lost a lot of blood, but with luck he would survive if he kept the wound clean. She used the remaining strips of dress to wrap the wound as best as she could, winding it across Sir Hugh's chest and behind his shoulder.

Duncan brought a pile of blankets from the cart and rolled two up for a pillow, then covered Sir Hugh's legs with another, fussing around him until the Captain waved him away irritably. Duncan patted Aline on the shoulder and gave her a smile of approval, then moved off to tend the fire. Jack went to the cart and returned with another bottle of whisky.

The four sat together, passing it between them, any hostility gone for now. They talked over events until they had pieced them together. Though Sir Hugh was exhausted, and weak from the loss of blood and his exertions, he had revived sufficiently to join in the conversation.

Aline was unused to drink that strong, but the warmth spreading through her body was far too comforting for her to care, and she soon found her head spinning. Jack made a further, slightly wobbly trip to the cart and returned with another bottle. He warned her in a slurred voice it was his own brew and would be 'very, very much too strong for a woman.'

Her pride stung, Aline snatched it from his hand. Tilting her head back, she drank defiantly, conscious of Sir Hugh's soft laugh as it caused her to cough abruptly and made her eyes water.

The night wore on and peace descended on the camp. Everyone became preoccupied with their own thoughts as the drink took effect. Duncan sat cross-legged with his back to the cartwheel next to Hugh, singing the same song over and over—something about cheeses and a maiden, though he seemed to know only half the words and was humming the rest. Jack lay on his back a little way off, hiccupping and ranting to the stars about how he should have followed his father into the ironmongery trade.

There would be no getting any sense out of them until the morning, Hugh realised.

Hugh found himself watching Aline as she sat

silhouetted by the firelight. Her hair had come loose and now she tried fruitlessly to wind it up again, her body swaying slightly. He could not make out her features, though he found he could bring them to mind with ease. Despite—or maybe because of—his tiredness and the alcohol muddling his brain he could clearly picture the expression on her face as her fingers refused to obey her instructions.

After the third attempt she gave up and allowed her hair to uncurl down her back. Hugh's fingers twitched as he longed to wind them into the pale tangle and draw her close.

As though she had sensed him watching Aline looked in his direction. Embarrassed at his thoughts, he passed her the nearly empty bottle. She beamed at him hazily before taking a sip and offering it back. He caught hold of her outstretched wrist and pulled her closer. She offered no resistance.

'When we saw the wolf I told you to get inside the cart,' he said sternly. 'Why didn't you do as I ordered?'

Aline shrugged. 'If I had you would be dead now.'

Hugh conceded the point with a nod. 'Thank you for tonight,' he murmured. 'Your shooting is excellent!'

Aline smiled again—and overbalanced. She

ended up with her face close to his and they studied each other in the dying torchlight, neither one moving or speaking. Hugh found his lips parting in anticipation. Aline's eyes closed, her head lolled sideways, and she slumped next to him with a sigh and fell asleep.

'Good night, Aline,' he whispered to her unconscious form.

He tugged the bottle from her hand and drained it, falling eventually into an uncomfortable slumber.

Chapter Seven

Hugh woke the next morning with a pounding behind the eyes that he recognised was the cost of drinking anything Jack had brewed. He lay with his eyes shut, hoping the sensation of nausea would soon pass.

It was barely light. The stillness of the camp was a welcome contrast to the chaos of the night before. Hugh's right arm and shoulder were cold and excruciatingly painful. Something was weighing down his legs. Panic tightened his chest as he pictured himself paralysed. Swallowing nervously, he pushed himself up onto his left elbow to investigate.

Lady Aline, still asleep, was curled against him, one arm flung across his shins and her head resting on that arm. Her hair was tangled and half covering her face, though Hugh could make out the tilt of her nose and a smile on her lips. Lips that he had come so close to tasting last night.

He smiled as he remembered Aline holding the crossbow, wide-eyed and trying to look threatening. Could she ever understand how alluring she had looked at that moment? Come to think of it, did she have any idea what a flash of her eyes could do to a man?

Hugh felt old. Thirty was not such a great age, he knew. With fortune on his side he could have more than that number of years still ahead of him. All the same, he was discovering that a life of drinking into the night and riding all day was long over. His body cried out for a long rest in a soft bed. Images flashed through his mind of who should be sharing it with him and he blinked rapidly to banish them.

Through his closed eyelids he could sense the sky lightening. They needed to move out soon. *One more day,* he thought. Lying near to Aline, he felt his blood chill at the knowledge that the end of their journey together was so close. Impulsively he reached his hand out and tucked a loose strand of hair behind her ear. She frowned, shifting slightly, but carried on sleeping. The serious expression on her face caused his heart to turn over.

He sat up and shook her awake gently. 'Good morning, my Lady Wolfkiller.'

Aline rolled onto her back and stretched her arms above her head, arching her back in a manner that did nothing for Hugh's peace of mind. With a yawn she opened her eyes, then closed them tightly with a groan. Hugh watched with amusement as it dawned on her where she was lying. She sat bolt upright, her cheeks colouring.

'I… How…? Oh!'

Seeing her embarrassment, Hugh looked away and called to Jack and Duncan to wake up. With difficulty he pulled himself to his feet and left Aline to regain her composure. Hugh walked round to the front of the cart and sluiced his face in the water bucket. The coolness went some way to alleviating his headache.

He could no longer put off what he was afraid to see. He took a couple of deep breaths, anticipating the sight of his torn and bloodied body. He pushed the dressing away from his wound. The sight of the scorched and blistered flesh sent his stomach rolling as he recalled the agony of the knife. Aline's stitching seemed to be holding, however. The wound was clean, though it would no doubt be painful for a while to come, and his shoulder felt stiff and sore. All in all, he considered, he had come out of the escapade remarkably well.

His tunic was torn and stiff with blood, so he awkwardly shrugged it off and plunged it into

the water. He wiped himself down, relieved to be
washing away the grime, blood and sweat of the
previous night. He turned and without warning
found himself face to face with Aline, a mug in
her hand, her mouth a circle of surprise.

Aline stopped abruptly at the sight of the half-
naked man standing before her. Only the fact
that he looked as taken aback as she felt stopped
her turning on her heel and running back the
way she had come. Though she had been inti-
mately—many would say indecently—close to
Sir Hugh the previous night, it had been almost
dark. She had been aware of the strength in his
body as she sat astride him, but her only concern
at the time had been to staunch the bleeding and
stitch his wounds. Now she became intensely
aware of what the night had hidden from her.

She had interrupted him in the act of bathing,
and rivulets of water ran from Sir Hugh's hair.
Aline's eyes followed their journey across the
arc of his collarbone to the fine thatch of hair
across his chest, where beads of water clung to
him still. Sir Hugh slowly lowered the wet cloth.
His chest and arms were taut and well defined.
Aline's eyes travelled further downwards to his
lean waist and the line of dark hair leading from
his belly down past the waistband of...

Aline realised with shock where her eyes and

imagination were leading her and forced herself to look upwards, hardly daring to meet Sir Hugh's eyes. She could sense a slow blush creeping across her chest and neck.

'Can I help you, Lady Aline?' Sir Hugh asked pleasantly. 'I hope last night has not taken too much of a toll on you?'

Aline shook her head. He gave no indication that he had seen her staring, though how could he not have?

'I thought…that is… Here. I brought you some ale. Take this—you'll need to drink more than usual today.' She faltered and thrust the mug into his hand.

Turning on her heel, she walked away, desperately hoping that the chill morning air would bleach the colour from her cheeks before anyone noticed how flushed they were.

Hugh appeared a few minutes later. Aline bent over a pile of blankets, rolling them carefully, not trusting herself to look him in the face. From the corner of her eye she could see him watching, his eyes burning into her. She carried the blankets to the cart, passing Jack as he walked Bayliss round to where Hugh waited. Hugh put his foot in the stirrup and stretched up to grasp the pommel. He stopped abruptly with a curse and took a step back.

'Let me help, sir,' Jack offered, taking hold of the bridle.

'I can manage alone,' Hugh growled, brushing away the young guard's hands.

He rolled his shoulders back and reached up again. He swung his leg over the horse and landed heavily in the saddle. Bayliss bucked and for a moment Aline feared Hugh might slip. She crossed the ground between them almost without realising, her arms outstretched. Jack looked at her quizzically and she dropped her hands to her sides. With a fluttering heart she started to climb into the cart.

'My lady!'

At the sound of Hugh's voice Aline felt the breath catch in her throat. She paused and looked over her shoulder.

'It's a fine morning. Why don't you sit with Duncan?' Hugh suggested.

When Aline nodded he raised an eyebrow.

'Good. You're looking rather pale. The air will bring the colour back to your cheeks.' With an innocent smile he dug his heels into the horse's flanks and trotted off, leaving Aline open-mouthed and lost for words.

Despite his insistence to the contrary it was obvious that Hugh could not ride without pain, and progress was slow. By the time they stopped for lunch his face had developed a waxy sheen

Elisabeth Hobbes

95

and his knuckles were white from the effort of gripping the reins.

It was late afternoon before they crossed the hills and made their way through the narrow valley towards Roxholm. As the cart travelled faster Hugh became more frustrated at his inability to control his mount. Finally he called for the cart to stop. Handing the reins to Jack, he climbed from the saddle somewhat awkwardly. He walked stiffly to where Aline sat and held out his good arm. His mouth twisted into a grimace.

'I'm afraid I must trouble you for your place, my lady.'

He sounded weary and his hand was cold to the touch as Aline took it. All the same her skin prickled where he rubbed his thumb across her palm. As Jack began to tether Bayliss to the cart Hugh motioned him to stop.

'Bayliss gets restive if he doesn't get enough exercise. Would you like to ride him, Lady Aline?' Hugh gestured to where Bayliss stood, shifting his weight from foot to foot. 'Unless you don't think you could handle him, that is?'

Aline lifted her chin with a snort and saw the challenge in Hugh's eyes. Without speaking she took the reins from Jack and swung herself into the saddle. Bayliss tossed his head, impatient to move, his breath sweet on the air. A ripple of excitement ran up Aline's spine at the sheer power of the animal. For a split second it crossed her mind that she could turn him about and be gone before anyone could stop her.

She slid a sideways glance at Hugh. He was leaning forwards on the bench, watching her intently. With a nod she snapped her heels and spurred the animal into a gallop, Jack following behind on the mare.

Hugh watched them go, Aline's exhilarated laughter floating on the breeze, and smiled to himself.

Duncan cracked the reins and the carthorse set off. He looked from the path to Hugh, then back to the path, before smiling and shaking his head.

Hugh ignored the soldier's smile for as long as he could bear before finally sighing. 'What is it, Duncan?'

'You're taking a risk, aren't you, sir?' Duncan asked. 'Jack'll never catch her if she makes a break for it.'

'I don't think she would now. We're too far from her lands—she'd not know where to go.'

'Good that she's getting a last taste of freedom, then, given as how the Duke'll be keeping her close by,' the older man muttered, not quite under his breath.

'She's a hostage, Duncan, nothing more,'

Hugh snapped. 'He'll keep her until he negotiates trade concessions or land, then send her home.'

Duncan snorted. 'Do you really believe that? Even if that's true he's not going to keep a pretty thing like her around without taking the opportunity to amuse himself, is he?'

Hugh clenched his fists as the fears he had been harbouring were voiced so starkly. 'He wouldn't dare try anything so foolish once she's in the citadel—and why do you think I insisted it was me who brought her here rather than some of Stephen's brutes?' Hugh replied.

'Hugh,' Duncan said, wielding the name like a whip, 'I've known you for over twenty years. I know why you owe him your loyalty. But listen to an older and wiser friend for once. In just two years Stephen has nearly ruined the province with his reckless decisions. How much longer will you let him act this way?' Duncan asked the question quietly.

'I guard the interests of the province as best as I can—you know that. I am bound by my vows and I'll do what I always have: try to counsel him wisely and temper his impulses.'

Duncan looked at him for what seemed like eternity before he spoke. 'He's getting worse, isn't he? Stephen may be Duke, but the people would follow you willingly and you know it.'

'Are you suggesting treason?' Hugh glared at the old soldier.

Duncan pursed his lips and shrugged. He shook the reins and the carthorse redoubled its efforts.

Moodily Hugh wondered what his life would be when he was no longer of use to the Duke. Would he share the fate of many of Rufus's old advisors and find his end with a knife in the back? He sat hunched over, brooding on Duncan's words, his mood worsening by the minute.

They rounded a bend to discover the horses standing patiently, where a knot of trees began to thicken into forest. Aline stood on a low bough, throwing down greengages to Jack, who caught them in his saddlebag.

'I thought you might like some fruit, sir,' he called to Hugh.

He reached up to Aline, who was now standing on the lower branch. She jumped down into his waiting arms and the boy caught her round the waist to steady her. The sight of her in Jack's arms hit Hugh like a punch to the stomach.

'We'll stop for ten minutes. Water the horses,' he instructed Jack curtly.

He climbed down from the seat and held out his good arm to Aline. She hesitated briefly before accepting, and together they walked into the forest. Hugh bit his lip, racking his brains as to how to warn Aline of the threats she might face. He rejected his words four or five times before he began to speak.

'Lady Aline, I want you to understand how sorry I am for my part in this business. You saved my life; I don't believe I have thanked you properly for that. I am in your debt.'

Aline said nothing but continued walking, her pace steady. When she spoke her voice was so low Hugh had to strain to hear.

'Then set me free. Say I escaped, or that you never found me.'

That scenario had crossed Hugh's mind so many times that to hear it from Aline brought home the treachery it implied. He dropped her arm and rounded on her crossly. 'Do I seem so dishonourable a man that you think I would break my oath just on a whim? Would you be so quick to betray *your* province, my lady?'

Aline recoiled as though he had slapped her. She broke away from him and stumbled back towards the cart.

'Aline! Stop—please!'

She leaned against the trunk of a tree as though to steady her legs. Hugh desperately fought the urge to pull her into his arms. Instead he took her hands in his, resisting her attempts to pull free.

'Please,' he repeated.

Aline stopped struggling but Hugh kept hold of her hands. He brushed his thumb lightly across her knuckles.

'You know I cannot do that,' he explained, his voice softer now. 'I have made promises I am honour-bound to keep, and for ill or good I must do my duty. I swear, though, I will protect you as much as I am able. I offer you...'

Aline looked up at him with such an intense expression in her grey eyes that Hugh's heart began to race. For one moment he thought she might kiss him. If she did he would be lost.

He looked away. 'I offer you my friendship,' he finished.

Aline's eyes clouded. Wordlessly she twisted free and pushed past him. She stalked back to the cart, ignoring the mug of ale Duncan held out, and climbed inside, pulling the curtains closed behind her. The guards looked at Hugh, but he held his hand up to forestall their questions.

'Jack, tether Bayliss to the cart. We need to move out. We have a delivery to make and we're late.'

The sun was setting when they met the escort. Half a dozen men sat around a low brazier; a carriage hitched with four horses stood nearby. The Sergeant leaped to his feet and saluted smartly, though his eyes widened as he noticed Hugh's bandages.

'Wolf. I'm fine,' Hugh explained curtly. 'I'll fetch Lady Aline.'

He climbed into the cart and offered his hand. Aline turned her head away. She climbed out, paying no attention to the new guards, instead brushing her skirts down with infinite care.

The Sergeant's forehead wrinkled. 'Sir, forgive my impudence, but the Duke insisted the prisoner was to be brought in irons. Why is she not?'

'I've travelled with Lady Aline for days and I'm *not* putting her in chains,' Hugh answered curtly. 'What sort of threat do you think she will be with seven of us to guard her?'

The guard shuffled from foot to foot. 'My lord, I'm sorry, but those are my orders,' the unhappy looking man replied. 'I'm not going to put my own neck in a noose because she's convinced *you* she's not going to escape.'

Hugh's fists clenched impulsively. He took a step towards the man, his face like thunder, and then Aline's voice stopped him in his tracks.

'Thank you for your consideration, Captain, but you of all people should understand the need to follow orders.'

Her voice dripped with contempt and Hugh felt his forehead grow hot.

Aline allowed herself to be shackled, glancing at Duncan and Jack with a sad smile. Jack looked on the verge of tears. Aline refused to meet Hugh's eye as she climbed into the carriage. He did not blame her.

'I'll travel with the prisoner,' Hugh announced.

He climbed in before anyone could protest.

Aline had huddled in the furthest corner, her lips pressed so tightly together they were white. She pulled her legs away as Hugh seated himself opposite. Hugh cleared his throat, but the lump that threatened to choke him refused to go. Eventually he settled back into his seat and watched the passing of the countryside.

Chapter Eight

With fresh horses and a lighter vehicle the rest of the journey was much faster. The carriage raced along the rough path, rocking alarmingly. Aline's stomach lurched in response. As they came closer to Roxholm an ever-growing knot in the pit of her belly replaced the feeling of nausea: nervousness and loneliness. Duncan and Jack had been left behind to return with the slower cart and the horses. Aline would be arriving in her enemy's lands without the two companions she now almost considered friends.

After Aline had made it clear that she had no wish to talk to Sir Hugh he had pulled his cloak close around himself, huddling deep into the corner with a baleful look at Aline. Now he sprawled opposite her, soundly asleep, his long legs outstretched, almost touching her own, hair flopping across his face and arms folded across his chest. Aline scowled at the sleeping figure, envious of the easy way he had nodded off.

Aline's eyes kept closing, but as soon as she began to doze her mind flitted to what awaited her and she would wake with a start. Giving up the hope of sleep, she watched the soft rise and fall of Hugh's chest.

Since their encounter behind the cart that morning Aline could no longer deny his attractiveness. It seemed like a dream now, and she regretted the harsh words that had passed between them since. She did not want to examine her motives too closely, though she could not forget how her heart had sunk when he had offered her only friendship. Perhaps it was not too late. She leaned across and hesitantly touched his hand. He shifted, but carried on sleeping, and Aline's courage left her.

The sky was inky with dark clouds when they finally arrived at the imposing wall surrounding the Citadel of Roxholm. They travelled at a walking pace through the narrow winding streets leading to the centre. Familiar sounds and smells of daily life drifted through the shutters, causing Aline yet another stab of homesickness. They passed through a further heavily guarded gateway into the grounds of the stronghold itself. With a jerk the carriage came to a final stop in an enclosed courtyard outside an iron-studded wooden door.

In the darkness the keep looked foreboding. Torches blazed from iron hooks set into the stones and the walls loomed into the sky. Though Aline had sworn to herself not to show fear, she could not suppress the shiver that ran down her spine.

Sir Hugh woke as the carriage came to a halt. He stared out the window for a few moments, biting his lip thoughtfully. Unexpectedly he reached across and took hold of Aline's hands tightly. His fingers were warm in contrast to the chill of her skin and she was acutely aware of the tremor his touch sent through her. He watched her warily, as though he expected her to pull away, and when she did not the muscles around his eyes relaxed.

'Lady Aline, I will accompany you until you meet Duke Stephen, but I will not be permitted to stay, so please take my advice: he has a quick temper and is not accustomed to being opposed in any matter—' He broke off with a frown, before continuing in urgent tones, 'For your own wellbeing please guard your tongue and your actions.'

Before Aline could answer him the door to the carriage swung open. Hugh dropped her hand immediately and turned his face once again to the window. The Sergeant took Aline by the arm. A detachment of half a dozen guards had come to meet the carriage. The Duke could not possibly expect her to attempt an escape, so she reasoned it was simply designed to intimidate her. She lifted her head and tossed her hair back in a show of confidence she did not feel.

The guards led them through draughty corridors and up a wide staircase. Hugh walked close to Aline, his footsteps echoing loudly off the walls as he stamped along. He did not speak, and not for the first time she found herself exasperated by the man. He seemed reluctant to leave her side, but in front of his people was not prepared to reveal any of the kindness he had shown over their journey. She watched him from the corner of her eye, wondering what his position in the court truly was.

The Sergeant stopped in front of a door guarded by two sentries in plain uniforms of green. They waited while one of the sentries banged on the door. As the sound echoed along the corridor Aline's head swam. Every instinct screamed at her to run and she felt her body begin to sway.

A hand took hold of her elbow, gentle and reassuring. She glanced up, already knowing it would be Sir Hugh at her side.

'Thank you,' she managed, her voice a mere whisper.

His expression did not change, but the slight squeeze of his hand told her he had heard. He guided her inside a chamber furnished with ornate tapestries and oak furniture. An archway was set into one wall and hung with heavy velvet curtains, drawn back to reveal the glimpse of a high oak bed. These were clearly Duke Stephen's private rooms.

Duke Stephen sat in a low oak chair beside the fireplace. The fire was lit and the immense blaze sent shadows flickering across his face, giving him an otherworldly appearance. The remnants of a meal were scattered upon a low table at his side and a large jug of wine was close to his hand.

The Duke bristled visibly at seeing his cousin there. Hugh bowed and went to stand by the door. He leaned against the frame in what seemed at first glance to be a casual stance, though Aline was aware of his eyes taking in everything and the way his muscles were tensed, as if ready to spring at any moment.

Aline turned her attention to the Duke, the similarity between the two men striking her immediately; had she not known the connection they shared she would have guessed them as brothers. They had the same build and dark hair, though Stephen was younger, with a neatly trimmed beard and short hair combed back from his face. The Duke was a handsome man, more conventionally so than his cousin, but any advantage this might have given him was diminished by the way his mouth was twisted into a sneer.

His burgundy jerkin was decorated with abundant gold embroidery around the neck and sleeves. It was open to reveal a fine shirt unlaced at the neck, the whole ensemble giving the impression that he was halfway to undressing. The Duke lounged back in his chair with his legs splayed and permitted Aline to study him for a few minutes, staring back at her with ice-blue eyes.

Without breaking her gaze he poured two goblets of wine, picked one up and walked round the table to where she stood. He was taller than Aline, and she had to lift her head to look into his face.

'Welcome to Roxholm, Lady Aline.' He bowed deeply, a half smile playing on his full lips. 'I hope your journey wasn't too wearying and that your stay as my guest will not be unpleasant.' He held the wine out towards her.

Aline's scalp prickled at his words. A captive she might be, but she was still the Lady of Leavingham and his equal.

'Your guest!' she exclaimed. 'Are your guests

usually brought to you like this?' She raised her arms to show the shackles on her wrists.

At her tone Stephen's cheeks flushed. He banged the goblet down onto the table, close to where Aline stood. He seized hold of the chain between Aline's wrists and jerked her close. Aline gasped as she stumbled forwards.

'Stephen, be careful what you do.' Hugh's voice was a growl of warning.

The Duke glared at Hugh, though he released his hold on the chain. He brought his face close to Aline's, his lips almost touching her cheek. 'You can show me some courtesy and be treated as my guest in warm, comfortable rooms,' he whispered, 'or you can spend your time here in the cells in chains. The choice is entirely yours.'

Aline nodded.

Stephen walked to the door.

'Someone bring me the key to release the lady. She is our *guest* after all,' he said with a mocking bow. His eyes held Aline's as a guard unlocked the cuffs and retreated, bowing, from the room.

'You can go, too, cousin,' Stephen said, turning to Hugh. 'The lady will not need your protection. We are only going to talk.'

Hugh glanced at Aline, his brow lined with concern. She wanted to beg him to stay but instead drew herself up tall and gave him a smile she did not feel. Stephen's eyes narrowed and he motioned to Sir Hugh to leave the room with an abrupt wave of the hand.

Sir Hugh stood to attention and nodded his head briefly at his lord. He cast a final look at Aline that she could not interpret and left, leaving Aline and the Duke alone.

The Duke picked up his wine and carried it to the fire, where he stood facing Aline. She picked up her own goblet and drank deeply. The heady spices on an empty stomach made her head spin slightly.

'Tell me why you have brought me here,' she said. 'What is it you hope to achieve with such a rash act?'

The Duke raised his eyebrows as though he thought her slow-witted.

'Your family has held dominance for too long, and I grow tired of bowing to your grandfather's will. The other provinces may be happy to relinquish control while Leavingham dictates trade agreements, collects tax and becomes richer on the strength of your position. I am not.'

'Do you want independence?' Aline asked. A flutter of hope started in her chest that her abduction might be so simply explained.

'No. I want control of the Five Provinces,' the Duke stated simply, 'and unfortunately for you, Lady Aline, you are the key.'

The Duke drew out a chair and motioned her

to sit. She sank down as his words dashed her hopes to pieces.

'You will never have control. The other provinces will see this as a direct act of war. Release me now and I can assure you that Leavingham will show mercy to you.'

The Duke smiled at her, his face momentarily charming.

'Release you? Why would I do that? I want to be High Lord. I was going to ransom you in return for an assurance that I would be named successor when the High Lord finally stops clinging on to life. Of course there is a much simpler solution—I don't know why it didn't occur to me before. You need to marry. I shall write to your grandfather and inform him of my intentions: you will become my wife and our lands will be joined. You will sign the letter and give your assent.'

'I will do no such thing.' Aline spoke as calmly as she could, though she felt almost physically sick at the thought of this man bedding and controlling her.

The Duke moved to stand behind her seat. He put his hands on her shoulders and leaned in close. Aline flinched instinctively at his breath, warm and wine-scented, on her neck.

'Oh, come now,' he whispered in her ear. 'I won't be a bad husband, and you might even find

you grow to enjoy our time together. I can ensure
your needs will be met very, *very* thoroughly.'

Aline jerked out of his grasp and stood to face
him, her back to the table.

'The High Lord will never agree to your demands. And, as for your disgusting proposition,
I'd rather renounce my title and beg in the streets
than marry you!'

'Oh, Aline, you are wonderful!' The Duke
leered. 'Maybe I should introduce you to some
of the pleasures of marriage to me right now.'

With a cry of disgust Aline closed her hand
round the goblet and hurled it at the Duke. The
goblet bounced off his chest and landed on the
floor with a ringing that sounded ominously
loud.

Duke Stephen looked down at the wine stain
spreading across his shirt. Without warning he
struck Aline across the face with the back of
his hand. The blow sent her crashing against
the table and she dropped to the floor, stunned
and shaking.

Hugh paced back and forth along the corridor, his fingertips curling round the pommel of his knife. Through the heavy door he
could hear muffled voices but could make out
no words. The sound of something heavy and
metallic falling reverberated down the corridor,

shattering the silence. Every muscle in Hugh's body tensed. The two sentries marched into the chamber and Hugh followed before they could close the door.

His stomach knotted at the scene before him: Aline curled on the floor, shaking, one hand covering her face, and the Duke dripping with wine.

'Are you still here, cousin?' Stephen jeered. 'Don't you have anything better to do than skulk around outside my chambers? You don't appear to have taught Lady Aline any manners on your trip, so you can escort her to a cell and see if *that* will help.'

He kicked the goblet across the floor and stormed out of the room.

'You bloody fool. I warned you not to cross him,' Hugh muttered, bending over Aline.

He pulled her to her feet but her legs gave way as she tried to stand and she sank down again. Swearing under his breath, Hugh hoisted her up. He wrapped his good arm around her waist, then lifted her into his arms, wincing at the pain it caused in his shoulder and trying to ignore the sensations he felt at holding her so closely.

Motioning to the two sentries to follow, he carried her through the corridors of the castle and out across the courtyard until he came to a door set low into a wall. One of the guards hammered on the thick iron grille and after a few moments it was opened to reveal a steep torch-lit staircase leading downwards. Faint cries drifted up from the depths below and the air smelled foul and heavy.

The coarse-looking man who had opened the gate leered openly at Aline. 'Are you bringing your toys down here to play with now, Sir Hugh?' He smirked—until Hugh's look of undiluted venom made him draw back, muttering apologies.

'You'll have to walk now,' Hugh told Aline, setting her on her feet. She was still shaking so he gripped her firmly around the waist and led her down the stairs. The stench of human filth and blood increased as they reached the bottom. Hugh felt Aline's body stiffening in horror. He could not afford to be compassionate now or he would never carry out his orders. He stared straight ahead, angrily refusing to meet her eyes, and shushed her when she started to speak.

The jailer led them through the damp communal cells and down a narrow tunnel. They walked past chained and cowed figures who called out insults or pleas for mercy as they passed, or simply lay and moaned, lost deep in their own minds. They finally stopped in front of a door with a small grille set high. The jailer slid the bolt and motioned Aline inside. Hugh led her into the small windowless cell, bare apart from a low pallet in one corner. The door was closed behind them, leaving them in near darkness.

'Please don't do this, Hugh,' Aline implored, her voice faltering. 'Don't leave me here.'

It was the first time she had used his name and Hugh felt a fist of ice punch him in his heart. 'I tried to warn you to be cautious but you didn't heed me. What would you have me do now, Aline? Disobey Stephen and end up down here myself? What good would that do either of us?'

He turned and walked to the door. A wave of remorse crashed over him, stopping him in his tracks. He returned and stood in front of Aline, torn. A weaker man might have pulled her into his arms, kissed her with such passion that it would overwhelm them both. A stronger man would have carried her from the cell, damning the consequences of such disobedience. Hugh, however, simply took off his cloak and wrapped it around her shoulders, pulling the edges firmly together.

He looked into Aline's eyes and said earnestly, 'If he gives you a second opportunity don't be so foolish as to ignore it—otherwise there will be no way I can help you. He is not known for his fair temper.'

Before she could respond he turned and left the cell, slammed the door behind him and left

Aline in the darkness. Outside, he watched as the jailer slid the bolt across the door.

Hugh backed the man against the wall. 'Keep her safe or I won't be answerable for the consequences.'

The man nodded nervously. It wasn't enough to salve Hugh's conscience but it was all he could do for now. Moodily he stormed out into the night.

Chapter Nine

It was past midnight and Hugh was drunk.

He had gone from the cells to his rooms, where his manservant had exclaimed with a mixture of horror and curiosity at the sight of Hugh's injuries and the stitches, pressing his master for details of the procedure. Explaining Aline's unorthodox treatment had done nothing to salve his conscience at leaving her, serving only to remind him of the touch of her fingers upon his chest.

He'd ordered hot water and scrubbed viciously at his hair and skin. Perhaps by ridding himself of the stench from the dungeon he could erase the memories of the woman he had left there.

It had not worked.

He'd set himself to work, dealing with issues that had arisen in his absence. After reading the same document three times without seeing the content he had decided he neither knew nor cared which tenant should be given grazing rights. Irritably he'd pushed his chair from the desk, pacing back and forth for an hour. Finally he had stormed off into the narrow streets of the citadel, hoping that walking would bring a solution.

Now he sat in the corner of a grimy inn. An empty wine jug stood on the table in front of him. The noise and bustle were failing to raise his mood, but his wound was starting to ease, helped partly by the wine. It was becoming more of an irritation than a pain. He pulled at his collar to move the cloth, remembering the feeling of Aline's hands moving across his neck and shoulder.

For a brief moment he had felt a flash of attraction between them. His memory drifted to the sensation of her slender body above his as she treated his injuries, then further back to when he'd fought her into submission on the forest floor. He closed his eyes, daydreaming that she had not been fighting to escape, that she had not wanted or needed to, but had been returning his desire with her own.

But this was no good! None of the women he had bedded had managed to get inside his head to this extent, and Aline was so far beyond his reach. There was nothing to be gained in dwelling on her. He had delivered her to the Duke, as ordered, and his part in the matter was done. All he could do was protect her—though she would never know or care that he did.

He reached for his cup. It was empty, so he signalled across the room for another jug.

A serving girl brought it over. Dark-eyed and pretty, with hair too red to be natural, she put the wine on the table. When Hugh smiled his thanks the girl straddled his lap and leaned down to kiss his neck. Usually he would welcome this sort of distraction, but impatiently he brushed her hands away.

The memory of Aline lying asleep next to him—and how long ago the morning now seemed—brought an unexpected flush of heat to his neck. He remembered the way she'd stared at him as he'd washed, failing to hide her curiosity. The alarm in her eyes had been transformed to hungry interest, as though she'd never seen a man in that state of undress before. It struck him then that most likely she had not. Bewilderingly, he felt himself harden—which caused the girl on his lap to giggle and move in again to kiss him.

She whispered a suggestion in Hugh's ear.

Why not? he thought.

He shooed the girl off his lap and stood. Rummaging in the pouch at his belt to find payment for the wine, his fingers closed around something unfamiliar. Curiously he drew it out.

Aline's necklace! He had never returned it after taunting her.

The girl was watching him, hands on hips and head on one side. 'Are you coming or not?' she asked impatiently.

Hugh held Aline's gem tightly in his hand for a moment, before slipping it safely into his pouch. He flung some coins onto the table. With a nod of his head towards the girl he pushed his way through the crowd to the staircase leading to the upper floor.

In the dingy upstairs room he watched as the girl lit a lantern and fussed around the room. Impatiently he pulled her towards him and kissed her deeply, prising open her lips with his tongue. She returned the kiss with a deep moan of pleasure—*fake, naturally,* he thought. His hand found her breast and he traced the outline of her nipple with the tip of his thumb. At that she pushed her tongue deeper into his mouth.

Still kissing the girl, he manoeuvred his way to the low bed and lay back. The girl slid her hand down to pull the shirt from his breeches. Hugh sighed deeply as he felt her cool fingers at his waist. He closed his eyes, anticipating the release that was to come.

The girl straddled him and ran her fingers up his chest until her hand brushed the edge of his bandage. At this almost exact recreation of the night before Hugh froze, all desire gone. These dark eyes were not the ones he wanted to gaze into, the lips not those he yearned to kiss.

He reached out and gently took hold of her wrist. 'I'm sorry,' he said.

'What for?' the girl asked.

'I can't do this. You aren't the one I want.'

She climbed off the bed, the stream of abuse spewing from her lips casting aspersions on Hugh's anatomy, his capabilities, and every aspect of his being. Hugh stood up, and with her jibes echoing in his ears stormed out of the room and back to the dungeons.

Ignoring the protests of the jailer, he made his way back to Aline's cell. No sound came from the room. He lifted a torch and craned his neck to peer through the narrow grille in the door. Aline lay on her side, facing the door, Hugh's cloak wrapped tightly around her. The pale braid of hair fell coiled like a rope around her neck.

Hugh watched as she slept. He wanted to wake her, but her face was serene and untroubled and he knew it would only be for his sake. That she was peaceful now was enough—why disturb her rest? Satisfied with what he had seen, he returned to his room and fell into bed. Aline's face was the last thing he pictured before sleep claimed him, too.

* * *

Aline opened her eyes as she heard the door opening and was unsurprised to see Hugh enter. He was clean now, his beard trimmed close, his hair damp and curling about his jaw. Instead of the familiar leathers he wore a soft wool tunic.

Handsome in the candlelight, he smiled at her and crossed to where she lay. He gently peeled back the cloak from around her body and lowered himself onto the bed. His eyes remained fixed on hers as he undid the ribbon at the neck of her thin shift and pushed it down over her shoulders. He began to move his mouth over hers, gently at first, then firmer and faster. The scent of him was warm and musky and Aline closed her eyes, tilting her head back in pleasure at the sensation.

She gasped as his mouth started to work downwards, alternately planting soft kisses and nipping at her neck and shoulders. By the time his lips brushed her breast she could barely draw breath, and she arched her back to come up and meet his touch.

Unexpectedly he bit down hard, and the pain made her cry out. Her eyes flew open to find him looking down at her coldly. Before her eyes, his features changed into those of the Duke.

Stephen opened his mouth, revealing a wolf's

teeth. He snarled and ripped at Aline's throat, laughing as her blood spurted out in a stream...

Aline woke with a cry, her cheeks and neck flushed and hot to the touch. Her dream had been so vivid, and she blinked hard to rid her mind of Stephen's eyes coldly watching her die. Hugh's cloak had fallen from her as she slept and she shivered as she felt around with trembling fingers until she found it. She pulled it around her shoulders and buried her face in the warm softness, conscious of the scent on the wool of the man who had invaded her sleep in such an intimate manner.

The sound of the bolt being scraped back and the door opening made her jump. The jailer walked into the cell and pushed a bowl at her with a grunt, then stuck a bucket in the corner of the room and left again, leaving her in near blackness. She sniffed the contents of the bowl, then dipped in a cautious finger. It was pottage of some sort. The smell turned her stomach, but she hadn't eaten in so long she forced the greasy liquid down, then made grateful use of the bucket.

With the edge of her hunger blunted Aline closed her eyes, trying to conjure the comforting image of her rooms at home, her friends and grandfather—but this led her into dark thoughts. Try though she might, she could not stop berating herself. *This is all my fault. My folly with Dickon led me to being captured and now Leavingham will be lost!*

Time passed.

Aline paced from end to end of the small room, counting the number of steps it took. She practised all the sword movements she could remember. She stood on her tiptoes, craning her neck to peer through the grille in the door. Outside her cell the passageway was empty. In the flickering light of a brazier she made out the silhouette of the jailer, slumped on a low stool.

'I want to speak to the Duke!' she yelled. Then, 'Find me Sir Hugh!'

The man slept on. The only sound was screams coming from somewhere nearby. Aline's stomach heaved and a cold sweat pooled in the small of her back. Her throat tightened and she moved away from the door hastily. She wondered how long she would be able to remain there before she broke down and agreed to any condition the Duke cared to name.

More time passed.

Aline wasn't sure exactly how much, though her stomach was starting to ache from hunger again. Footsteps in the passageway broke the silence and she jumped. She moved towards the back wall as she heard the bolts drawn back.

The door swung open, revealing two guards, who walked in and gruffly ordered her to follow.

She was taken back through the dungeons and out across the courtyard. The sun was setting and Aline realised with a start that almost a day had passed since she had been taken to the cells. The two soldiers escorted her through the corridors before they pulled her to a stop outside the same state-room as the previous day. She had no time to compose herself before she was ushered inside.

The Duke was again waiting for her, standing by the fire with a heavy goblet in his hand. Two empty bottles on the table indicated he was probably not in a mood to be defied. The Duke gave an exaggerated bow as Aline entered and indicated a velvet-covered chair at the side of the table. Glad of some comfort for the first time that day, she sank into it, anxiously waiting to see what would happen.

'I hope a day in the dungeon has made you see some sense and fully appreciate my offer of remaining as a guest, Aline?' Stephen slurred.

Aline's body ached, she was cold and hungry and she needed sleep, but at that moment she would have denied it absolutely rather than admit it to this man. 'I have not given you permission to call me by my name,' she told him haughtily.

If Stephen was angered by her lack of emotion he did not show it. He lifted her hand to his lips and laughed again. He ignored her attempts to pull away. 'The consent is not yours to give or withhold, *my lady.*'

He indicated a piece of parchment and a quill on the table. 'This document contains my demands. I will return you to Leavingham unharmed when your grandfather surrenders to me the seal of the High Lord and abdicates in my favour. You will be freed in exchange for that. I want a guarantee that there will be no acts of vengeance or attempts to regain power. He shall continue to rule Leavingham until his death, whereupon it will become part of Roxholm's lands.'

He paused to let his words sink in, watching her expression closely.

'The High Lord won't agree to that!' Aline said, hoping her voice sounded more confident than she felt.

'Oh, I think he will,' Stephen said pleasantly. 'That is unless he wants to live with the knowledge that, having already lost his son and grandson, he condemned his granddaughter to life in my dungeon. Now, to the other matter I mentioned. I still mean to marry you, but I can see you need time to become accustomed to the idea. I am not an unfeeling man, so I shall not compel you now. However, when your grandfather dies

I will announce our betrothal.' He smiled at her and rested his hand on the back of Aline's chair. 'Of course if you were to choose before then to accept of your own volition it would make things much easier all round.'

Aline glared at the man. 'I'll *never* marry you!'

'You will,' Stephen assured her. 'You need to be married. Your grandfather understands that. Your future will be decided by the High Lord, as it should be. You must count yourself lucky you have had this many years of freedom. After all, you would have been wed many years ago if your father and brother had not died. I will need heirs, and how better to secure my position than marriage to the true heir? Besides, who else would have you now, after three days in the wilds with my soldiers and no chaperon? Your reputation is ruined. Now, sign the letter.'

Aline bowed her head to hide the tears that sprang to her eyes. She had refused so many marriages for what now seemed such insignificant reasons. Life as the consort of the new High Lord would be her penance. Still, she tried one final gesture of resistance.

'And if I refuse to sign it?' she asked.

'Oh, Aline, you are magnificent. So few of my court will dare to defy me in anything. Marriage to you will be a challenge I anticipate with pleasure.'

Stephen laughed, then leaned in close to her.

'It won't make the slightest difference. But until I receive a reply I'll throw you back into the dungeons—only this time into the condemned cell. I'm sure the inhabitants will appreciate a pretty plaything in the days before their necks are stretched. I estimate it will take at least six days for my messenger to travel to Leavingham and back. Imagine their hands on you…imagine their mouths. How long do you think you will last before you lose your mind?'

Bile rose in Aline's throat. Whatever she owed to her grandfather and Leavingham, no one could ask *that* of her. Reluctantly she picked up the quill and wrote her name with a trembling hand, then signed it 'your loyal granddaughter'—the code that would tell her grandfather that she was writing under duress.

'Thank you, my lady.' Stephen smiled. He scrutinised her signature before folding the letter and sealing it with wax. 'That was perfectly simple, wasn't it? Now I shall arrange for you to be moved to more appropriate accommodation for the remainder of your stay. I have a room already prepared for you.'

He moved to the wall and pulled a rope. A bell sounded in the corridor. The door opened and two servants appeared. The Duke instructed them to prepare a room, food and a bath and they left. He spoke briefly to the sentry standing outside the door and passed him the letter.

Stephen turned back to Aline and studied her in silence. She met his gaze steadily. The Duke's face darkened suddenly. He crossed the room and drew the cloak back from Aline's shoulders, ignoring the way she flinched at his touch. Aline's initial fears proved unfounded as Stephen appeared more interested in the cloak than the woman beneath it.

'This is an interesting addition to your wardrobe,' he remarked. 'I believe I recognise it from yesterday, and I find myself wondering what possessed my cousin to give it to you. What happened on your journey that would lead him to do that?'

So many images flickered through Aline's mind as she thought how best to respond. She hoped her face did not betray the way her chest tightened at the thought of Hugh.

'What happened?' she asked. 'I came to his aid when he was injured. I assume this must be his way of thanking me.'

'I would not blame you, given your situation, if you had tried to turn his head to your advantage. Many women would do that and more. You will have seen, though, that you failed.' Stephen laughed. 'No woman has managed to snare Sir Hugh yet. His loyalty to me is without equal.'

Aline said nothing but looked away quickly, which caused Stephen to laugh wildly. He was still laughing when a servant appeared and led Aline away.

Chapter Ten

A sentry was waiting outside the Duke's quarters. He led Aline and one of the maids across the grass courtyard to a square tower. It loomed dark in the moonlight, and even though the sky was now fully black Aline recognised the building as the one that held the entrance to the dungeon. A wave of panic swept over her at the thought that she was being taken there again. She found herself longing for Hugh to be there and hold her safe.

The Duke lied to me! she thought.

Her knees began to buckle under her. She forced herself upright, determined not to show weakness before her enemies. She had never been more relieved than when the servant gave directions to the guard and they carried on past the iron-grilled doorway leading down.

They entered the tower through a double doorway and climbed up three narrow, winding flights of stairs. Laughter and music floated along the corridors from one of the rooms they passed. The tune was familiar and Aline felt a stab of loneliness at the everyday sounds of castle life.

On the third floor the sounds faded away as the guard led the way to the end of the corridor and stopped in front of the only door. The servant unlocked it, leaving the key in the lock, then stepped back. The guard ushered Aline into the room.

The room was small and plainly decorated, but it was a room, not a cell, and for that Aline was grateful. A high bed with thick curtains around it stood against the back wall, while a table and a low basket chair sat in an alcove in front of a narrow window. Aline nearly wept with joy at the sight of the wooden bathtub standing in front of the fireplace, its sweet herb-scented water steaming. The fire had been lit, and torches burned in the sconces.

Aline heard the key turn in the lock, though scarcely noticed or cared. Her attention was drawn to the scent of food wafting from a tray on the table and her stomach growled. Pulling back the cloth with trembling fingers, she fell on the meal, devouring the chicken legs and bread where she stood. She bit into an apple with contentment. It was a simple meal, but rarely had food tasted so delicious.

When she had eaten she slipped off her clothes, stepped into the heavy wooden tub. She sank into the water, relishing the way the heat made her flesh smart. She rubbed her body and hair with a bundle of floating lavender until her skin turned pink, glad to rid herself of the dirt from the journey, the stench of the dungeon and the feeling of the Duke's hands upon her.

Once she finally felt clean she reclined against the side of the tub with a contented sigh and closed her eyes, letting the warmth of the water begin to ease her aching muscles.

Her encounter with Stephen shouted for attention, but she pushed the memories of the past day from her. She would think about the repercussions of the letter when she was not so exhausted. If she allowed those thoughts free rein now she knew she would have no peace at all.

When her head began to droop onto her chest she reluctantly climbed out and wrapped herself in the large linen sheet that lay folded next to the tub.

Aline poured a glass of wine. It was rich and smoky and made her head spin pleasantly, so she poured another cup, hoping it would ease her into sleep.

She was sitting on the fur in front of the fire

waiting for her hair to dry when it struck her that
there were no clothes in the room other than her
own—nothing to replace the ones she had taken
off. Her dress and undergarments were soiled
with dirt and blood, and the smell of the dungeon lingered too much for her to bear putting
them back on. Instead she snuffed the lamps and
climbed naked into the bed, drawing the curtains
closed behind her.

At home she never closed the drapes, prefer-
ring to be woken by the light entering the room,
but in this strange room she felt vulnerable. She
burrowed into the bed, drawing the thick feather-
filled coverlet close. The sheets were chilly, and
goosebumps broke out all over her flesh, but
Aline ignored the chill. Over the past few days
she had slept on bare wood, the forest floor and
the dirty straw of a cell, so the softness of the
mattress outweighed the mild discomfort.

The coolness of the sheets against her body
triggered the memory of her dream, and she felt
heat rising to her face.

Thinking of Hugh, and the role her unconscious mind had made him play, sent a ripple
through her body that she was not wholly at ease
with. Suddenly she found herself missing him—
missing his laughter and even his mockery. They
had not parted on good terms and a small worm
of regret burrowed into her. Slowly on their jour-

ney she had come to feel safe with him, to think of him not as a friend, exactly, but someone familiar. Certainly nothing more, she told herself. And as for those things she had dreamed about…

As she curled into a ball she wondered when she would see him again and what he was doing. Then, without even being aware it was happening, she fell into a dreamless sleep.

What Hugh was doing at that point was trying very hard to keep his temper. The battle between his urge to barge into the dungeon once more, in order to stand guard outside Aline's cell, and his sense of caution had been a hard one. He'd contented himself by making his presence felt around the citadel, dropping words into certain ears and ensuring all the guards knew what would happen if any harm befell the visitor.

By the time the sun had set his resolve had been weakening, and he had been in the process of fastening his dagger to his belt when he'd been summoned to Stephen's chambers. He had unbuckled the dagger and left it in his room, instructing himself to be calm.

On his arrival the Duke had listened calmly to his account of the journey—edited and selective—commiserated over his injury and then, just as Hugh had begun to relax, presented him with the cloak.

'What possessed you to give her this?' Stephen shouted, hurling the bundle onto the floor in a rage. 'I didn't put her down there to be comfortable. I wanted her broken. So why did you take it upon yourself to give the bitch the means to keep warm?'

'Do not speak of the lady in that way!' Hugh growled, the heat rising to his cheeks.

'Oh, *now* I see!' The Duke laughed. 'I know you find it hard to resist a pretty face, but this is glorious.'

Hugh cursed inwardly at his blunder. 'The lady means nothing to me—a passing fancy,' he said lightly. Even to his own ears the words sounded unconvincing. 'She saved my life. Giving her the cloak was a small kindness that cleared the debt I owed her, nothing more,' he explained, in what he hoped was a more casual voice. 'Where is she now?'

Stephen pursed his lips and walked slowly round to the fire. 'She's not where you left her, if you were thinking of looking,' he said serenely.

Methodically he prodded at the embers with a poker before turning back to his cousin. When he spoke his voice was full of spite.

'I asked Lady Aline why she thought you gave her the cloak. She said it had not even occurred to her to wonder—that she had no interest in finding out. Any passion you might have is not returned. What *could* she feel for someone who left her chained in a cart for days other than hate?'

Hugh brought himself up level with Stephen. Evenly matched in height, the two men stared at each other, their faces grim, until Stephen shrugged and turned away with a sneer.

'If I think your loyalty is in doubt I might well rid myself of you once and for all. Tell me I can trust you, cousin. Swear it!'

'You know well that I am bound to you by the oaths I swore to your father. My allegiance to you is as it ever was,' Hugh replied.

Stephen nodded, satisfied. 'The men you took with you returned with the cart and your horse this morning. Go back to your own estate, Hugh. There is nothing to keep you here.'

Hugh ignored the jibe. He bowed deeply, gathered up his cloak and left the room, thinking intently. He walked purposefully through the citadel until he came to a small house above a bakery and banged on the door until he heard footsteps coming down the stairs. A dark-haired young woman, who gaped in surprise at seeing the nobleman standing there, opened the door.

'I'm here to see your grandfather,' Hugh explained.

The girl took Hugh's arm and pulled him

through the door, and led him upstairs to where the old man sat by the fire.

Duncan took one look at the expression on Hugh's face and gave a rueful smile. 'You had better tell me what happened,' he said, pushing a stool towards his guest.

Hugh poured out the tale of the past two days, answering the questions Duncan interrupted with, his voice cracking with anger as he spoke of his own deeds.

'Well, it was obvious to anyone with eyes that you were falling for her. But what did you think would happen?' Duncan asked when Hugh had finished. 'Did you honestly think the Duke would just send her home again and she would accept you as a husband on the journey back?'

'I didn't think I would care what he did,' Hugh answered with a frustrated sigh. 'Now I'm as good as banished from the citadel. I promised to protect Lady Aline, but I can do nothing for her—not visibly, at any rate. If Stephen suspects I have an interest he'll put every obstacle in my path.'

He smiled at Duncan's granddaughter. 'Kate, I have a request. You work in the castle. Please contrive to watch over Lady Aline in my stead and keep her as safe as you can. If you believe her to be in any danger send word and I will return.'

Kate nodded her agreement with a smile.

Hugh stood up to depart, satisfied that Aline was in the best hands he could leave her in. As he reached the door he paused and pulled the necklace from his pouch. He held it tightly for a moment, lost in his memories, before pressing it into Kate's hand.

'This belongs to Lady Aline. Please will you give it to her if you can. Tell her… Tell her I am sorry I was unable to return it myself,' he said. He shook hands with Duncan, then walked back to his rooms with a lighter step than when he had set out.

The sound of singing woke Aline the next morning. Her sleep had been one of complete exhaustion, and for the few moments she fancied herself in her own bed. Smiling, she rolled onto her back and opened her eyes before reality crashed back in on her. The sounds were the same, though, and the scent of freshly baked bread wafted invitingly through the air.

Wrapping one of the soft blankets about her body for modesty, Aline stuck her head between the curtains. A maid was sweeping the embers from the fireplace. She jumped, putting her hand to her heart, at the sight of Aline's disembodied head.

'Oh, my lady, you startled me! I didn't mean to wake you,' the servant exclaimed. She stood up and brushed the ash from her apron with a smile. 'My name is Kate. You travelled here with my grandfather, Duncan. I brought you some breakfast,' the girl said with a wave of her hand to the table. 'Please, come and eat while it is hot.'

Aline blushed. 'I have no clothes. The ones I was wearing were too filthy to put back on,' she explained, indicating the bundle by the bathtub.

Kate rolled her eyes. 'Well, isn't that just like a man to make no such preparations? My lady, you stay there—I'll bring the tray over to you. Once I've finished here I'll see about finding you something to wear.'

Aline sat back in the bed and Kate placed the tray on her lap. There was a hunk of bread, still hot, with a piece of honeycomb melting in the centre, a plate with fish in a buttery sauce and a mug of milk. Aline ate hungrily while the maid busied herself around the room, her mood lifting as she watched.

Footsteps echoed unexpectedly in the corridor. Kate hurried to the door and spoke quietly to someone outside. At the sound of the answering voice Aline felt faint with disbelief. It was a voice she had never thought to hear again.

She leaped from the bed, barely aware that she was only wearing a sheet, and lurched to the door, her heart in her mouth.

Chapter Eleven

Aline rounded the door in time to see Hugh pat Kate on the shoulder and begin to walk away.

'Sir Hugh, wait!' she called, her voice urgent.

Hugh paused at her voice. He looked over his shoulder, his eyes burning into her. *'Sir?'* He frowned. 'The last time we spoke you called me by name.'

'The last time we spoke you left me in a dungeon!' Aline retorted.

Hugh strode back down the passageway. He towered over her, so close Aline could almost feel the heat of his body.

'A place you would not have ended up in if you had taken my advice and been more cautious!' Hugh said forcefully. 'You make it very hard for me to guard your wellbeing, my lady.'

Aline looked away, not wanting to admit the truth of his words. 'Why did you come here?' she asked.

'I am leaving the citadel,' Hugh said. 'I wanted to see for myself that you were safe before I departed.'

'To see for yourself, but not to see me?' Aline blurted out accusingly, her heart twisting. She moved towards him but Hugh stepped backwards and she faltered.

She tried not to think what she must look like to him, unclothed as she was. Hugh's eyes ranged over her body and his eyes widened as though he was noticing for the first time how she was clad. Aline's dream came back to her in a rush and she felt heat rising in her belly. A low sigh of longing escaped her lips, and at the sound Hugh brought his head up sharply, his body tensing. His jaw tightened and he looked away.

Aline's blood ran cold. Had she misjudged his feelings all along? She bunched her fists by her sides, fighting the urge to throw herself against his broad chest and plead with him to stay.

'You weren't going to say goodbye?' she asked, her voice a whisper.

Hugh's lips were tight, his expression unreadable. 'No, I was not. It would have been better that way. Nothing good can come of my staying here,' he said darkly. 'To think about the time we spent together can only cause sorrow or harm.'

He reached a hand to Aline's face, briefly brushing his thumb across her cheek. His touch burned into her skin and she closed her eyes, overcome with a longing she could barely contain.

'Farewell, Aline.'

He turned and walked away before Aline could reply.

Kate had been watching the exchange. She took Aline's hand and pressed something into it. Aline looked down at her necklace. She closed her hand around the jewel and bowed her head so Kate would not see the tears that sprang to her eyes. She had been foolish enough to believe that Hugh cared about her existence, but she had been wrong. The realisation was like a knife through Aline's heart.

She heard Kate give a small sigh of pity, then leave the room. When she heard the door shut and the key turn Aline lay down on the bed, curled her knees up to her chest and sobbed until she could cry no more.

Kate was true to her word and returned before noon, waking Aline, who had fallen asleep again, fretfully curled in the tangle of sheets. The maid had brought an old woman she introduced as Goodwife Themper, the castle's chief seamstress.

The goodwife stared at Aline through half-narrowed eyes. She handed Aline a cream linen shift and a grey wool dress. Kate helped Aline into the dress, then laced it as tightly as it would go, though it still hung from Aline's slim frame. It was too large, but the goodwife explained that she had nothing else to spare.

'We did not expect to have such a guest as you, my lady,' she explained as she measured Aline.

She departed with the promise of instructing the seamstresses to create dresses more suited to a noblewoman's taste as quickly as possible.

Aline's necklace was lying in the bed, where it had dropped from her hand as she slept. Kate scooped it up and fastened it round Aline's neck. Aline touched her hand to the jewel, wondering if Kate knew the significance of what she had delivered.

'My grandfather told me about your journey here,' Kate said, as if she had read Aline's thoughts. 'He said you were very courageous when Sir Hugh was injured, and he isn't one to waste his compliments!'

'I don't feel very brave now,' Aline whispered, her voice shaking.

The mention of Hugh threatened to tip her back into misery. How could she bear to speak of him, knowing he had left her here?

Aline expected Kate to say that everything would be all right, or that the Duke was a kinder man than Aline thought or some such platitude, but the girl said nothing, only patted Aline's hand. Somehow this was worse.

Aline had little need for fine clothes in the first days of her captivity. Her body finally succumbed to the fatigue she had been denying and she felt weak and feverish. For three days she did little but sleep or sit at the window, wrapped in furs to keep her from shivering.

Invitations from the Duke arrived daily, requesting that she join him to dine—and they *were* invitations, not commands or threats. Each one was accompanied by a gift: an embroidered veil one day, a pair of caged wrens the next. She refused them all and released the wrens, having little taste to see creatures in cages, wondering briefly whether the Duke had intended the irony of his gift.

From the tower she could see into the courtyard outside the castle, where people went busily about their lives, unaware of the prisoner watching from above. If she stood in the window arch she could see further into the citadel itself, with its narrow streets winding down to the heavy walls and the hills purple and hazy in the distance.

She pictured the rider speeding from Leavingham, bearing the message that would decide her destiny. In her wilder moments she made rash plans to escape, somehow finding her way out of the castle and down into the city. But then what? Even if she could slip free she had no one to turn to and nowhere to go. The one man who might have aided her had made his allegiances clear.

She thought for hours at a time on Hugh's departure, running their conversations over and over in her mind and picking at the words he had spoken at their last meeting. If she had heeded his words would he have left? His face haunted her nights: sometimes bloody and lifeless as the wolf tore at his throat, other times smiling, his blue eyes sparkling with promise. She was unable to decide which disturbed her more.

Her face grew hot as she remembered his arms around her. She did not love him—she knew too little about him for that—but her stomach turned somersaults at the thought that she might have in time. She would try to forget the tremor that had passed through her when he caught her eye and the feel of his body as they had ridden together.

Aline came to the conclusion that the protection he had offered had been nothing more than a fiction. He had been kind enough to try to soothe her as he led her into captivity but nothing more.

Gradually her feelings changed from sorrow at his leaving to anger at his deception and he no longer visited her dreams.

Maybe it was this that made her decide, on

the morning of her fourth day in the tower, to accept Stephen's invitation. It was delivered as usual, in the middle of the morning, and sent this time with a glazed dish containing ripe fruits in honey: pears, apricots, and the first of autumn's blackberries.

Aline read the note expressing the Duke's hope that she was recovering from her illness and requesting her company that evening. She crumpled it in her fist and was about to throw it in the fire when she hesitated.

Her two encounters with the Duke had been frightening, but in these letters his manner seemed gentler and more courteous. She was lonely, too; it would be at least another two days before an answer arrived from Leavingham and she was unused to such solitude and inactivity.

She smiled at the pageboy, who was waiting patiently for the customary refusal.

'Tell the Duke that I will join him today.'

Mid-afternoon a heavy wooden box was delivered to the room. Aline opened it curiously. Her exclamation of surprise caused Kate to rush from the fire to her side. Nestling inside the box was a circlet of silver, the threads twisted into spirals and flowers. Rubies glittered in the centre of each twist and caught the sunlight as she lifted it from the case.

'You should read what the Duke says,' Kate prompted.

Aline picked up the letter with shaking hands. This gift was so much more extravagant than any he had sent previously. She feared what he expected in exchange.

Lady Aline,
You would do me a great honour if you were to wear this tonight, along with your finest gown.
Your servant, Stephen

'I think I had better speak to the goodwife!' Kate remarked.

From then until evening the day passed in a blur of activity. Kate supervised the delivery of pails of hot water and helped Aline bathe and wash her hair in water infused with rosemary. From the chest of dresses that had been delivered Aline chose a sleeveless blue gown embroidered with silver roses over a white chemise with full, billowing sleeves.

She slipped the velvet dress over her head, the cloth falling in heavy folds before gathering in a belt of brocade that emphasised her small waist. The neckline plunged low, hinting at the mounds of her breasts. Kate dressed her hair in thick curls that cascaded down her back. She topped them with the circlet.

Staring at her reflection in the polished brass mirror, Aline felt doubts begin to gnaw. 'This is too formal. I can't wear this,' she protested.

'Duke Stephen requested that you wear your finest gown, and he sent the jewellery himself,' Kate reminded her. 'My lady, you look beautiful,' she said.

Aline shook her head and looked away. 'I should have refused his invitation,' she whispered.

'Now, my lady!' Kate exclaimed. 'It will do you no good to stay in this room dwelling on matters you cannot control.'

'I know, but I dread what lies ahead of me. How can I spend time with the Duke knowing how he brought me here and what he plans for me?'

'Well, many a marriage has started on bad terms. Mayhap the more time you spend with him the happier you'll be?' Kate suggested, though Aline saw uncertainty in her eyes.

Aline's mind flew back to Stephen's words regarding marriage. He was right; it was not for a woman to decide her own fate, however much she wished it. She had been more fortunate than many women who had been given to husbands who cared for nothing but the wealth and power they brought. If she had not been brought here under such circumstances—if her grandfather had arranged a match in the conventional manner—would she have found it an acceptable union?

But as she stared at her reflection another face rose in her memory and her heart lurched painfully. Marriage to someone she did not love might be bearable, but marriage to a man who looked so similar to Hugh would be unendurable. She was glad now that he had left the citadel; he had been wise to do so. She found her resentment melting away.

A knock at the door caused both women to jump. Kate opened it to admit a man, plump, with a straggly beard, dressed in velvet robes. He bowed to Aline with a flourish.

'Lady Aline, it is indeed an honour. I am Lorrimer, Chamberlain to Duke Stephen. His Lordship bids me to escort you to his chambers,' he said. He held out an arm and Aline took it with a sideways glance at Kate, who gave a small smile of encouragement.

Together Aline and Lorrimer walked through the castle, with Lorrimer pointing out what he considered interesting features of its architecture. Aline was glad of the distraction and the friendly arm to hold, as both went someway to calm her nerves. She turned to walk towards the

Duke's chambers but Lorrimer held out an arm across her path.

'Not that way, my lady, His Lordship wishes you join him in the Great Hall,' he explained as he guided her across the courtyard.

Heralds stood before a pair of large double-height doors and threw them open as Aline approached. As soon as she stepped through them she was overwhelmed by heat and noise. She froze in shock. This was no private supper but a public banquet! She whipped round to run from the hall, her heart racing, but the door had been closed behind her. She had no choice but to stay.

The guests were occupied watching a troupe of jugglers, performing in the middle of the room, so Aline's arrival went largely unnoticed. Thankful for this small mercy, she moved her eyes around the room as she tried to regain her composure. Stephen sat at the centre of a long table. His face looked grim as an old man standing behind him whispered in his ear.

Then Aline's heart stopped as blue eyes bored into her from a face she had never expected to see again. Her head swam and she clutched Lorrimer's arm tightly, fearing she might faint at any moment and longing to run from the room.

Hugh was there, and he looked furious!

Chapter Twelve

Hugh had not wanted to attend a banquet. He could think of fifty places he would rather be. But since he had returned to the citadel he'd had no choice but to attend. He had placed himself as far from Stephen as his status would allow without questions being asked and tongues wagging. He ignored the laughter around him while he reflected that he would have stayed away another day if he had known this was planned.

He could not truly say that he'd sensed Aline's arrival. There had been a slight shift in the atmosphere, a whisper of curiosity that rippled round the room. He'd glanced up from his plate, wondering what this new source of interest was, and she'd been there on the arm of the chamberlain.

Since their first meeting Hugh had seen Aline asleep, unconscious, wet and half dressed. He could have described every contour of her face, the precise colour of the hair at the nape of her neck, the arch of her back as she stretched awake. Now a stranger stood before him. She stood poised and elegant in the light of the braziers. By torchlight her pale hair shone golden. Shadows from the great fireplace moved across her body, enticingly highlighting the curves of her slender figure.

Hugh paused, goblet halfway raised to his mouth. With disbelief he recognised the circlet of silver she wore in her hair. Disgust washed over him at the implication of what he saw. It had been less than a week and Aline was already wearing the coronet of the Duchess and parading in front of the court. No messenger could have travelled to Leavingham and back in that time. How many days had passed before she had accepted Stephen's proposition? Jealousy fought with contempt to stab his heart.

He reached for the flagon to refill his goblet but his hand stilled as he saw Aline looking straight at him. In an instant he saw the surprise on her face change to wretchedness. Aline looked away as a herald dressed in the red and gold livery of Roxholm appeared at her side, seeming to shrink into herself at his approach. Hugh looked closer at her, now she was not watching him, and saw with distress that she was trembling. She held herself steady through strength of will alone; her eyes were shadowed with dark circles and her hands were knotted into fists at her sides.

Hugh had been mistaken: she was no willing participant in this!

His anger dissolved in an all-consuming urge to protect her. He opened his mouth to call to her, knowing as he did that she would never hear him over the music and noise. He watched as Lorrimer led her towards Stephen and she moved out of his sight. He was too late to tell her he had misunderstood, and too late to tell her he was sorry.

'…is she?'

'No one I've ever…'

'…the Duke did not inform the guests…'

Scraps of conversation drifted to Aline's ears as she allowed herself to be escorted to where Stephen sat as though in a dream. She had no interest in the talk her presence was provoking. She had seen the way Hugh had looked at her and was bewildered by his hostility. Her heart had leaped at seeing him there, so why had he looked at her with such an expression? Was it— and this thought made her head reel—that he believed she *welcomed* the Duke's attentions?

She took her place next to Stephen at the table, inclining her head in greeting as faces blurred into one. Automatically she smiled as Stephen explained that she had arrived recently as his guest but been too fatigued to leave her chambers, his eyes steely and daring her to contradict him.

The jugglers finished and were replaced by a trio of musicians. The doors were flung open again and a procession of servants appeared. Aline shook her head at the two servants who stopped in front of her, their tray laden with roast meats. The smell and sight of the pig's head glistening with fat surrounded by pheasants made her nauseous in the overbearing heat of the hall. She stared down at the trencher of bread in front of her, afraid that if she did not leave soon she was in danger of passing out.

'Lady Aline, you are not eating!' Stephen breathed in her ear.

A shiver ran down her spine. Gone was the charming man she had spent the evening with and here again was the Duke who had ordered her to be incarcerated in the dungeon.

'I was not prepared for such company. Why did you not tell me of this before?' she asked him in a whisper.

'Why? Because I thought you might refuse to be present.'

'I feel ill. I wish to return to my room,' Aline said, pushing her chair back.

Stephen took hold of her wrist and lifted it from the table, his fingers digging into her flesh painfully. He spoke in an undertone, giving his most charming smile. 'You will not leave. I will not be defied or humiliated in front of my subjects.'

'You're hurting me,' Aline gasped. She tried to pull away but the Duke tightened his grip.

'This is nothing to what I *could* do. You will sit here and you will smile and be as charming as you have been reared to be. After all, these men and women will be your subjects when you are High Lady. If you make me the subject of any scandal I will hurt you more than you can imagine. Do you understand me?'

Aline nodded and Stephen released his hold. The blood rushed back and she cradled her sore wrist in misery.

Somehow Aline forced herself to get through the evening. The training Stephen had so rightly assumed she had received came into play as never before. She nibbled at a bowl of leeks and smiled as the grey-haired man to her right refilled her wine goblet. She laughed and applauded along with the other guests as a flock of birds circled the room when the crust was lifted from a dish.

Stephen showed his approval of her behaviour by graciously passing her dainty pastries filled with honeyed nuts. She was the perfect lady. But all the while her eyes searched the room for the one person she wished to speak to but could not.

She caught a glimpse of Hugh once, deep in conversation. His hair had been cut to jaw-length since she had last seen him, and his beard had been neatly trimmed, making him look younger. His companion nodded in Aline's direction and she looked away quickly, before Hugh turned, unwilling to see hatred in his eyes as before.

The meal ended and the musicians ceased to play.

Stephen slammed his goblet onto the table. 'We should dance!' he shouted, and applause filled the room.

He reached out his hand to Aline, his jaw set and his eyes narrowed. Reluctantly she took his hand and walked to the centre of the room, her eyes cast down. A hush descended over the hall.

'A quadrille for Lady Aline,' Stephen announced.

The musicians took up their instruments once more and began to play a simple melody. Stephen took Aline's hands and together they began to circle the room, the familiar steps of the dance coming back to her as they moved together. She caught a glimpse of Hugh again, deep in conversation with a young woman dressed in scarlet. The woman put her hand to his arm and dipped her head coyly. Hugh smiled. Aline frowned, then caught herself in the act. What was it to her who he talked to?

Hugh gave no indication of noticing her, though she thought she saw him glance in her direction as Stephen lifted and spun her. Stephen didn't look away from her face, however, and she dared not stare too obviously.

The musicians increased their tempo and other couples joined Aline and Stephen on the floor. The dance became more intricate now: the pairs were weaving between each other, now in one circle, now in two, now in lines, the men lifting the women in sweeping arcs before moving speedily on to a new partner. After her long confinement Aline leaped high and swung wildly, laughing and lost in the dance—until she looked into the face of her newest partner.

A half smile played upon Hugh's lips as he bowed to her. His blue eyes met her own. Familiar arms encircled her waist and lifted her off her feet, spun her. They passed shoulder to shoulder, their hands brushing fleetingly as they circled round, their eyes never breaking away. Then he was gone. He passed on to the next in the line so quickly she could not quite believe he had been there.

Her new partner took her hand, but she was distracted and fumbled the steps. Only because the dance was so familiar did she manage to regain her balance and complete the movement. Eventually the dancers were reunited with their original partners and the music came to a stop. Aline curtseyed to Stephen, who bowed in return, then clapped his hands together to signal another dance to begin.

The dancers formed a large circle and began to move around the room, whirling faster and faster before pairing off. Aline searched in vain for Hugh as she wove her way through the lines but he was no longer there.

The music went on longer and became more involved. The enthusiasm of the dancers began to diminish but still Stephen demanded faster and faster pieces, dancing more and more wildly.

Finally, as Aline felt she was close to collapse, Stephen threw back his head, his eyes wild, and roared, 'Enough!'

The musicians stopped abruptly and Stephen swept from the hall, leaving the dancers in confusion. Steadily people began to disperse, until the hall was almost empty save for the kitchen skivvies wearily clearing the tables. Aline stood alone in the centre of the room, uncertain where to go until a guard appeared at her side. She turned to follow him, but as she reached the door a shadow fell across the doorway and a voice stopped her in her tracks.

'Soldier, you can stand down from your duty

tonight. I will see to it that the lady is delivered safely to her quarters.'

The guard wavered uncertainly. 'My orders were very clear. I don't think...'

'If anyone questions you I will see to it that you are not punished, but take this for your trouble.'

Aline had barely moments to compose herself before a coin changed hands and the figure waved the soldier away with a nod of his head.

Alone with the man she had never expected to see again, Aline lifted her head to greet the speaker warily. 'Good evening, Sir Hugh,' she said, 'Can I help you?'

Hugh's scalp prickled as he heard the chill in Aline's tone. 'I understand why you're angry with me,' he said.

'You left,' Aline said, her voice low and controlled. 'You promised to protect me and you left.'

'As I told you, I thought it prudent to obey the Duke. How would it have helped you if I were also imprisoned, or worse?' Hugh asked. 'You have seen what kind of man Duke Stephen is—though maybe it is another side of his character you are more familiar with.'

'What are you implying, Sir Hugh?' Aline asked sharply.

Some self-destructive part of him took over and he ranted more at himself than at Aline. 'When I left you were a prisoner. I return to find you dining with him in front of the assembled court and dancing in his arms! And will you please stop calling me sir?'

He spun on his heels and slammed his palms in frustration against the heavy doors. The servants paused their work in alarm. A hand touched his shoulder gently and he turned. Aline was standing closer than he'd expected and jumped back slightly as he faced her. She was close enough still that he could feel her breath on his cheek.

Hugh looked around at the servants, who were staring openly at them. With a glare he sent them back to work and, taking Aline's arm, led her into the moonlit courtyard.

Aline's face remained rigid. 'Why did you return?' she asked.

Because I love you. The thought rose unbidden and passed unsaid.

'Because I have my duties as Captain.' He gave a wry smile. 'And because whatever decision you make I wish to be here.'

At his side Aline gave a strangled sob and pulled her arm from his.

'What decision *I* make? I have no control over my future. I had no wish to be present tonight!'

She paused and her eyes narrowed. 'Did you think I had given him my hand? Or my heart?'

Hugh put his hand to Aline's hair and touched the coronet gently, ignoring the sensations that this gesture of intimacy sent through him.

'Do you realise the significance of what you wear?' he asked.

Aline shook her head, confusion clouding her eyes.

'This was worn by Stephen's mother, and every duchess before her,' he explained. 'I saw you tonight and I believed…' His voice died away as Aline gave a moan and covered her face with her hands.

Her distress was too much to endure and Hugh's resistance crumpled. He reached out, as he had wanted to for so long, and pulled Aline to his chest. She struggled half-heartedly, turning her head away from him. He wrapped his arms around her, holding her close against his chest until the sobs racking her frame subsided. Her hair smelled of rosemary and he closed his eyes and bowed his head, the better to catch the sharp scent of the herb. Clouds passed in front of the moon, granting them some privacy, and they stood motionless in the night.

Chapter Thirteen

Aline could not tell how much time passed, only that there was nowhere else she wanted to be. The sky cleared and moonlight fell once more on the courtyard, breaking the spell. Hugh's arms tightened and pulled her closer fleetingly before he released her from his embrace. She shivered in the night air after the warmth of his body.

'And now I must fulfil my obligation and return you to your room.' Hugh sighed. 'Do you know where he has housed you?' he asked, sudden anger changing his voice.

Aline shook her head, not understanding. Hugh pointed to the window beneath her own. 'Those are *my* chambers,' he fumed. 'That bastard has housed you almost within my reach! No doubt he derives pleasure from the knowledge.'

The venom in his voice made Aline jump. 'Duncan told me you grew up as brothers. Why does your cousin hate you so much?' she asked when she could trust her voice to be steady. 'Tell me why you remain loyal to someone who bears you such malice?'

Hugh pursed his lips. 'There are many things in my life I am ashamed of. Please do not ask this of me.'

Aline stepped back and folded her arms, fixing Hugh with a stern gaze. 'I *do* ask it of you! I do not understand the Duke, and he scares me, yet I am in all likelihood to be married to him. If you have it in your power to make sense of him, then please,' she begged, 'tell me.'

Hugh ran his fingers through his hair, then rubbed his eyes. 'Very well—but not here. We should go inside the tower, where you can be warmer. Oh, don't fear,' he said with a smile, 'not my room or yours. I would not make you a part of such an indiscretion. But there are public rooms where we can sit in comfort before you take a chill.'

He offered her his arm and she took it, ignoring the flutter in her stomach that his touch caused her. Aline dreaded what revelation she was about to hear, but she couldn't help but be amused that Hugh would not risk her reputation by sitting with her behind closed doors when not minutes before he had held her so closely where anyone might see.

* * *

Hugh led Aline to the first floor and through the small dining hall, where a handful of late revellers sat drinking. He escorted her to a deep window seat and summoned an attendant to bring wine. He stared out of the window unspeaking. Knowing he could put it off no longer, he drank deeply from his cup then turned to face Aline, his expression grim.

'The reasons for my hatred and loyalty are inextricably connected,' Hugh said reluctantly.

He paused and balanced his goblet precariously on the arm of his chair. He surreptitiously watched Aline from the corner of his eye. She sat perched on the edge of her seat, as though she was about to flee, her wine cup clutched tightly between her hands. Her cheeks were hollow and dark smudges ringed her eyes, but there were no signs of the imagined maltreatments that had woken Hugh nightly in a cold sweat.

She had felt so enticing in his arms, her frame hinting at such wonderful possibilities that he ached to hold her again. The thought of Stephen touching her was almost too much to bear. She was right: he owed her this explanation, though he had hoped his past would remain a secret from her. Now that it seemed her future lay with Stephen it would make no difference what she thought of him. Even so, he found that he desperately wanted her good opinion.

He took another deep drink and began again. 'You have no doubt seen how changeable in temperament Stephen can be?'

Aline nodded. A shadow crossed her face, enhancing the fragility of her looks. Hugh could not begin to understand the torment she had endured. She began to speak, but Hugh held up his hand to silence her, knowing that unless he poured his tale out soon the courage would leave him.

'He is subject to great variation of temper and sudden outbursts,' Hugh continued. 'I believe—and the physicians believe—it is due to my actions when I was young…'

Aline listened as Hugh told her of the events she had partly heard about from Duncan. Despite the hopes of all around them, Hugh and Stephen had grown apart as they grew older. Stephen had displayed a cruel streak, and his favourite pastime had been to taunt Hugh for the low rank of his father and for his position at court. Hugh, for his part, had countered by parading his superior wit and the advantage five years gave him in combat.

To Aline, the tale of childhood rivalry was familiar, but unremarkable.

'I know something of your past,' she broke in. 'Duncan explained to me how you lost your position. But I don't understand why you feel so beholden to him.'

Hugh stood and paced restlessly about the small room, his lithe body and the suggestion of tensed muscles reminding Aline of an animal, caged against its will. Moving to the window, he rested his back against the stone ledge and continued his tale.

'I was sixteen when the rivalry between us came to a head. Winter was almost over, and after long months of enforced closeness everyone had become intolerant of company. When the first clear day came my uncle suggested a hunt. There was a young lady I had developed an infatuation for and I was eager to impress her.'

Hugh's face softened at the memory. Discomforted to feel a ripple of envy run through her, Aline found she could not meet his eyes.

'I hoped to win her favour, and Stephen noticed my ambitions. He was determined to outride and outhunt me at every opportunity that day,' Hugh continued. 'When he found he could not, he resorted to goading me, pointing out that a nobleman would never let his daughter marry the son of a servant. In a moment of rage I set my hawk on him.'

He took a deep breath and closed his eyes as he relived the moment.

'What happened?' Aline prompted softly.

'Stephen tried to shield his face. He slipped from his horse and was struck on the head by its hooves. He lay close to death for six days, then in a stupor for more than a full turn of the moon. No one knew if he would survive. When he eventually recovered he was…changed. He'd fly into sudden fits of laughter and became quick to anger at the slightest provocation. The physicians said the blows had altered his mind.'

'But you didn't mean to cause such harm!' Aline exclaimed.

Hugh gave her a smile so sad she felt her heart might break.

'So my uncle said. Rufus knew Stephen would never be the Duke he should be. He understood our rivalry and laid the means of recompense at my feet. When I reached manhood he elected me Captain of the Guard. On his deathbed I vowed that I would serve Roxholm and protect Stephen from himself as best I can. So I am bound to him and must do my best to moderate his excesses. Stephen knows, and he hates me for it.'

Aline hugged her chest, overwhelmed with pity for the man in front of her. It seemed characteristic of Hugh's nature that he would allow himself to carry this guilt for so long.

'But Stephen was cruel even before that day! How do you know this would not have been his way whatever happened?' she said. 'You cannot live your life atoning for one act, and Stephen has other advisors. You are not the only one who can curb his actions.'

Hugh shook his head. 'That might have been the case once, but now his inconstant side is growing stronger. He refused to listen to caution about bringing you here, though it could set us at war with every other province.'

'And now I must become his bride,' Aline said bitterly, 'and the responsibility to try and temper his desires will fall on *my* shoulders.'

Hugh's head jerked sharply, Aline's words striking him more deeply than a knife to his heart. He reached for Aline's hand and pressed it tightly. 'There has been no answer from Leavingham yet,' he said. 'You may yet be spared.'

'Maybe…' Aline shrugged, sounding doubtful. 'My grandfather might see this as the easiest way to solve the issue of my marriage. I have refused so many proposals already.'

Hugh could not help but ask the question that tugged at his stomach. 'Has anyone…? Did none of the petitioners manage to capture your heart?'

'My heart? No,' Aline said bitterly, drawing her hand away. 'None of them even tried. Once

I became heir my chance of marrying for love vanished. I've always known that I have to do what is right for the good of my province.' A wistful look came into her eyes. 'I kept hoping that if I continued to refuse suitors then the next one might be someone I could care for, but love is for ballads and tales for children. I was foolish to ever dream of more.'

She walked to the window and stood beside Hugh, staring out at the sea beyond the castle walls. He wondered what she would do if he drew her into his arms as he so longed to do. An insipid purple tinge was beginning to break the blackness of the horizon. Hugh realised with surprise that they had talked almost until dawn. He could not keep her to himself any longer.

He drew a dozen slow breaths until, feeling calmer, he turned and offered his arm to Aline.

'Come, Lady Aline. Let me return you to your chamber. This conversation has been hard for both of us and I would not see you any more fatigued or distressed.'

Aline hesitated, then took his arm formally. Hugh was desperate to draw her closer to his side. They climbed the stairs of the tower in silence, both lost in their own thoughts. Outside Aline's chamber a guard sat slumped on a stool, snoring gently. Hugh put his foot out and knocked the stool from underneath the sleeping guard.

'Wake up and let the lady into her chamber,' he commanded.

The soldier rubbed his eyes blearily, then jerked upright and gave a salute. He pulled a large iron key down from a nail stuck high into the doorframe and fumbled with the lock.

Aline dropped Hugh's arm and fixed him with a serious look. 'Rufus is dead. How long will you live your life for Roxholm?' she asked. 'Do you not have your own dreams to follow?'

Hugh smiled and laughed quietly, more to himself than Aline. 'Ah, Aline. Such dreams as I have do not hold up a good mirror to my sense of honour. How many of us can truly say we are ever free to follow our hearts?'

'Who, indeed?' Aline murmured.

To his great surprise she leaned towards him and brushed her lips lightly across his cheek.

'Good night, Hugh,' she said, and slipped inside her chamber before he could respond.

Hugh watched while the door was locked, then walked back to his own rooms, grinning madly, his hand to his face as Aline's kiss burrowed into his memory and his heart.

Aline awoke late the next day. The fire was unlit and the room was shadowy and cold. She shivered as a chill ran across her shoulders and, slipping a fur-trimmed mantle over her thin chemise, walked to the window. The sky was heavy, with ominous-looking clouds hiding all trace of the sun, as though the weather had decided to sympathise with her mood.

She was determined to confront Stephen about his deception. Her eyes fell on the coronet and her indignation flooded back. Hugh had believed that her wearing it signalled degree of intimacy with the Duke that simply did not exist. The rest of the court must have assumed the same. Her dignity would not allow her to be the subject of such scandal.

If what Hugh said were true then angering Stephen would almost certainly hold risks, but she had to return it to him, whatever the chance of his displeasure. She climbed from the bed and hammered loudly on the door, bouncing impatiently from foot to foot as she waited for it to be unlocked. The door swung open to reveal an unexpected figure.

'Jack!' Aline exclaimed with pleasure. 'Oh, it's good to see a familiar face!'

The boy reddened at her welcome. 'Lady Aline, I'm pleased to see you again. Duncan and I were so worried when we heard what had happened when you arrived at the citadel. I've been trying to get put on duty here but somehow it never happened. Then this morning the duty lists were changed and here I am.'

Aline smiled inwardly, wondering how much the reappearance of Hugh in the citadel had to do with that. She explained to Jack that she wanted an audience with the Duke, ignoring the look of panic that crossed his face.

'I'll go now, my lady,' Jack said, then, glancing down at her attire, he added, 'Um, should I find a maid to help you dress?'

Aline nodded her agreement and Jack left. Moments later there was a knock at the door. Jack stood there again, a small leather-bound book in his hand.

'I almost forgot—somebody asked me to give you this,' he said, and held it out. He pushed the slim book into her hands with a twitch of the eye that might have been an attempted wink.

Aline turned the slim volume over curiously, then opened it. It was a book of poetry, well-thumbed and dog-eared. She flipped through the pages with a lump in her throat.

Knight Harald
The Maid of Kempe
The Heart's Honour

All well-known verses she recognised from her youth.

Love is for ballads and tales for children. Aline's cheeks flamed as she remembered the impulsive kiss she had given Hugh. No letter needed to accompany this gift for her to guess who had sent it.

'Thank you, Jack,' she said. 'If you should see that somebody please will you thank him from me, and tell him I accept it with pleasure.'

The boy bowed and left. Aline waited until she heard the key turn in the lock, then walked to the window seat and started to read. Today would bring a reckoning, she felt sure of it, and even Hugh's gift could not prevent Aline's stomach from twisting into knots.

She tried to focus on the words, but the tales of courtship and thwarted love sent her thoughts down paths she would rather ignore. She stared out of the window at the darkening clouds until Kate appeared, bearing a fresh tray of food. A fire soon warmed the room and Aline's spirits lifted slightly.

She chose her warmest dress of blue wool, adding her own necklace to the outfit, and as Kate braided Aline's hair, Aline patiently answered the maid's questions about the night before.

Kate was entranced by the account, going into raptures of excitement about Aline dancing with the Duke. Aline wanted to scream at the maid's foolishness. How could she think being forced to perform like a puppet in a mummers' show was anything less than torture? She bit her tongue, however; Kate was young enough to believe any man as handsome as Stephen must be an agreeable partner.

Aline closed her eyes, remembering the too brief moment when she had danced in Hugh's arms. Lost in her thoughts, she did not notice Kate pick up the book from the table until the girl's voice broke her reverie.

'Oh, a book. Is this from His Lordship? You must be disappointed after the beautiful gift he sent you yesterday.'

Aline reached out and gently took the book. 'No, it isn't from the Duke—and, no, I am not disappointed,' she answered with a faint smile.

'Oh, my lady, do you have an admirer?' Kate grinned, tossing her dark curls back over her shoulders.

'Not every gift signals love,' Aline said, realising as the words left her lips how much she hoped this one did.

'What is it about?' Kate asked.

'Love. Despair. Hope.' Aline sighed with a smile. 'Shall I read you some?'

Jack returned from his errand to discover both women sitting by the fire, their faces contorted with joyful anguish as Aline read aloud.

She closed the book. 'Did Duke Stephen agree to my request?' she asked anxiously.

'I'm sorry, my lady, but I was unsuccessful. Duke Stephen is out hunting,' Jack reported. 'He will not be back until dusk.'

'And did you see...? Were you able to pass on my other message?' Aline asked as indifferently as she could.

'I'm afraid not. He is with Duke Stephen's party,' Jack replied, a sympathetic look crossing his face and telling Aline he had not been fooled by her uninterest.

Aline began to pace the room in agitation, suddenly feeling the walls closing in upon her. She knew she was in danger of losing her mind if she stayed there all day.

'Jack, the Duke says I am permitted to walk in the grounds of the castle with an escort. Will you accompany me, please?'

'I am yours to command, my lady,' Jack answered.

Aline noted with amusement Jack's eyes sliding to Kate, who was looking more demure than Aline had yet seen her.

'I believe I should also take a chaperon, for the sake of propriety.' Aline smiled, raising her eyebrows at the young man.

He grinned back at her.

'Very well, then.' Aline smiled again. 'Kate, bring my cloak—I would like to see your city.'

Chapter Fourteen

The doe leaped out of the gorse bushes, flanks foamy with sweat, running with the last of her strength to escape the baying hounds. An outrider caught sight and spurred his horse on, closely followed by the rest of the company.

Hugh rode at the rear of the group. He had scarcely crawled into his bed when a hammering at the door had roused him with news of the hunt. Though a day in the saddle usually served to rid him of all worries, today he felt his tiredness keenly. His chest ached where his wound had not completely healed and he mentally added a visit to the physician to his list of tasks.

Bayliss tossed his head impatiently and whinnied as the rest of the horses galloped away. Hugh dug his heels sharply into the stallion's flanks to urge him on.

By the time he arrived the dogs had cornered the doe and were circling her, snapping whenever she made a move. Stephen wheeled his horse around and dismounted. He held out a hand to an attendant, who passed him a lance. Moving with care, he took aim and thrust his weapon at the cornered animal, piercing her chest. She gave a rasping cry and fell to the ground.

Hugh watched with revulsion as life died in the doe's golden eyes, their eloquence reminding him of another pair of long-lashed orbs he had stared into so recently. Bile rose in his throat and he looked away.

The knights offered Stephen their praise for the kill, while squires lifted the carcass across a horse and the dogs moved in to lick the gore from the ground. Wanting no part of the celebration, Hugh had turned his horse to head for home when Stephen caught his eye and stalked towards him.

'There was a time when you would have been at the front of the pack and competing for the kill, Sir Hugh. Are you feeling your age upon you today?' Stephen asked with a cold smile.

'Today I have no enthusiasm for destroying the life of an innocent creature,' Hugh replied darkly.

A murmur went round the assembled men at his open animosity and Stephen stiffened, his hand moving to the sword at his side. Out of the corner of his eye Hugh saw Lorrimer give an almost imperceptible shake of head, the meaning of which was clear: *Now is not the time*.

'Or it may be as you say, my lord,' he amended, 'I am feeling a lack of sleep and my mood is too dark to benefit from the enjoyment a chase brings.'

'Perhaps your recent mission overtaxed you. If you feel you are no longer capable of command I will accept your retirement and withdrawal from court life,' Stephen replied, his voice like oiled silk.

A sudden shout broke the tension that was almost tangible between the two men. Both looked in the direction the page was pointing. A figure on horseback was galloping along the road to Roxholm.

Stephen leaped astride his horse and set off at full speed with the aim of intercepting the rider. The company followed behind and arrived as the rider knelt before Stephen and handed him a thick fold of parchment.

A sense of dread curled about Hugh's stomach as Stephen studied the messages in silence before tucking them into his coat. With a triumphant yell he circled his horse and galloped in the direction of Roxholm, the rest of the court close behind.

When she looked back on her time in Roxholm, Aline would remember that afternoon as one rare time when she was content. With delight she watched the seeds of courtship grow between her two companions. Jack was tongue-tied at first, and Kate shy, but over the course of the afternoon their bashful smiles turned to open smiles and then animated laughter that warmed Aline's heart.

When the sky turned black and heavy with rain-laden clouds they climbed the steps onto the ramparts, and higher up to the signal tower, pulling their cloaks around them tightly to ward off the cold wind that whipped up from the sea. Aline gazed out over the sweeping shoreline, captivated by the beauty of the churning water, half listening to Jack as he thrilled Kate with the tale of the wolf: an account in which the lad featured much more courageously than Aline remembered.

Life would be simple for Kate and Jack. There were no ties, no responsibilities and no one to stop them declaring their love. Aline remembered the warmth of Hugh's body as she had woken curled against him the morning after the wolf attack, and again the previous night as they had stood in the moonlight. A knot in her throat threatened to choke her as she thought of her own future without any hope of happiness or love.

She turned away so her companions would

not see her expression and out of the corner of her eye caught movement along the road. Figures on horses were galloping towards the citadel, one ahead by some distance and the rest speeding behind. The hunting party were returning, and in haste.

The fury and apprehension she had suppressed all afternoon surged up unbidden and instinctively she turned to run. She was halfway to the steps before Jack caught her up, calling out in concern.

'Jack—look!' she gasped, clutching at his sleeve.

He followed where she pointed, seeing the riders, closer now and sounding horns to announce their imminent arrival.

'Take me to the main gate,' Aline ordered. 'I must speak to the Duke without delay.'

Jack's face creased with panic, 'My lady, I can't do that. It isn't proper for—'

'Jack,' Aline interrupted, 'no part of my being here is "proper." I *must* speak with him today.' She held his gaze until he sighed and agreed to escort her.

They arrived at a run, just as the gatekeepers shouted their orders and the imposing doors swung wide. Stephen was the first person to pass through the gate. He steered his horse slowly, in a relaxed walk. His fur-trimmed cloak was thrown back to reveal a leather surcoat underneath and flecks of blood spattered his boots. He looked hearty and confident.

Aline stepped forwards as he drew close, breathing deeply to steady her nerves.

'I must speak with you, my lord,' she said firmly.

'Lady Aline, what an unexpected pleasure.' Stephen smirked. 'You do me great honour with such a warm reception.'

He leaned over and beckoned her towards him with a leather-gloved finger. Aline moved to his side as though her legs were obeying against her will.

'I have something you desire,' he breathed. 'I have what you have been waiting for.'

He reached into his coat and pulled out a sheaf of papers. Aline's heart quickened: an answer from Leavingham! She reached out her hand for the documents but Stephen whipped them away.

'Ask me *nicely*,' he murmured, licking his lips.

A clatter of hooves on the stone path made him turn his head and Aline stepped back, her heart pounding in her throat. The other horsemen had arrived and were now assembling behind Stephen. Aline searched the group, recognising faces from the ball, including Lorrimer, sweating profusely on his mount, searching for the one she feared to see.

After a moment she spotted the lithe figure of Hugh on Bayliss. He sat rigid in his saddle, hair dishevelled and coat open to reveal a glimpse of his tanned throat. His eyes widened as they met Aline's, burning into her. Indecision tore through her. Last night she had allowed herself to admit that he held feelings for her. The memory of his arms around her made her draw a breath even now. She would give almost anything not to have this confrontation in his presence, however much she wished him to see that she wanted no part of Stephen's plans.

Stephen leaned closer to Aline until she could feel his breath on her face. Hugh said nothing but, possibly unconsciously, raised his hand to his cheek, where Aline's lips had brushed. His face was a mask of anxiety and Aline looked away in distress.

Stephen manoeuvred his horse around to face the company and when he spoke his voice was heavy with triumph.

'Gentlemen, this is the second time today I ask for your congratulations. I have not one hour ago received news of great importance. On the night of the next new moon I will be crowned High Lord. And,' he said, fixing his gaze on Aline, 'I'm going to be married!'

Gasps of surprise and congratulation echoed distantly in Aline's ears. Very slowly she felt her head spin. Very gently her knees buckled from under her and her vision blurred. The world slipped away.

The last thing she heard was Hugh's cry of warning. The last thing she felt was the arms of Jack and Kate as they caught her and lowered her to the ground.

Hugh's fists clenched involuntarily and blood pounded in his ears. He became aware that he had half risen from his saddle and forced himself to sit back. To draw attention to himself now would be unwise.

Stephen stared dispassionately at Aline. 'It appears the happy news is too much for my bride to take in!' He addressed Kate. 'When she is revived bring her to my chamber. I would speak with her.' He turned again to the courtiers, though his eyes were fixed on Hugh. 'In the meantime, sirs, we will convene in the Great Hall. There is much to discuss and many plans to make.' He galloped towards the stables, followed by the procession of nobles.

With difficulty Hugh tore his eyes from Aline. He wheeled his horse around to follow Stephen, then cursed under his breath. He couldn't leave her like that. He pulled the reins sharply and dismounted. He strode to where the unconscious woman lay cradled in Jack's arms, her face ashen. Suppressing the urge to take her from the boy, he instead knelt beside her.

'My lord, I'm sorry—she commanded me to bring her here,' Jack began. 'I tried to stop her, but…'

Hugh shook his head. 'She wouldn't listen? Not your fault, lad, when would she ever?'

Hugh was unsure whether to admire her resolve or despair of it. Tendrils of hair had come loose from Aline's braid and he smoothed them from her face. Her eyelids fluttered but she did not wake and Hugh thanked his stars, knowing that if she did he would never leave.

'Do as the Duke says, but stay with her,' he commanded. 'I must attend our lord and find out what he intends.' He swung himself back into the saddle and followed in the direction of the party, his stomach leaden with jealousy and hatred.

'If you will excuse my impertinence, I don't believe that announcement came as a surprise to you, Sir Hugh.'

The voice pulled Hugh out of his well of misery. Lorrimer had lingered under the archway and now drew alongside Hugh.

'To my shame, I am the one who brought Lady Aline here,' Hugh answered quietly.

The chamberlain sucked at his teeth and fixed Hugh with a penetrating look. 'I did wonder where you had gone, but I never thought you would lower yourself to play kidnapper!' He paused and pulled at a stray thread on his sleeve. 'What do you say, Sir Hugh? Do you think this marriage might transform our lord into something approximating a human being?'

'The sacrifice would be too great to make!' Hugh replied, rage boiling inside him.

When Lorrimer spoke next his voice was thoughtful. 'From what I have seen of Lady Aline she would not have been a compliant captive, yet last night you danced with her. I find that interesting.'

'Do you? Why so?' As so often when talking to Lorrimer, Hugh was reminded that, although the man played the part of the genial old bore, he was one of the few who had survived Stephen's ascent.

'Well...' Lorrimer smiled. 'You never willingly dance unless there is someone you want to dance with, so that tells me one thing. Also, cruelty is not in your nature. You would never subject a lady who has a very good reason to hate you to public discomfort. Which tells me another.'

Hugh gave a snort and cracked the reins to move off, unnerved at the man's insight.

As they neared the stable yard Lorrimer drew level again, speaking in a low voice. 'Take care, my friend. I don't have to warn you of the penalty for adultery; you've seen enough poor bastards deprived of their *coillons* and their eyes in the town square!'

Hugh's anger flared and he drew himself up in the saddle. 'I could call you out for what you are insinuating!'

'You've enough sense not to draw attention to yourself at this point.' Lorrimer shrugged. 'Now, let us hasten to the Great Hall to discover what our lord and master has to say. Remember: guard your tongue, man—for her sake if not for your own.'

The atmosphere in the Great Hall was one of hushed anticipation. Stephen had not yet arrived and the occupants stood in groups, knights and councillors speaking together in low whispers. Hugh stood alone, noting who was standing with whom. The petty factions and intrigues of court never held much interest for him, but now he found himself wondering how many were his enemies and, after Lorrimer's unexpected revelation, how many had arrived at the same conclusion.

He wondered if Aline was recovered from her shock. The urge to find her and hold her until she felt safe was almost too much to stand. But that was not his place, he thought bitterly, and it never would be. Shuddering, he remembered the chamberlain's warning: blinding and castration—a fate no man would care to suffer. Of course Aline would not escape unharmed either. The fate of a woman caught in adultery was for her shame to be burned into her face for all to see. Hugh's stomach heaved. He vowed he would leave the citadel for ever rather than risk subjecting Aline to any such danger.

A herald appeared at the door, beating the stone floor with his heavy staff, and the conversations died. Stephen entered and the men took their places at the large table.

'Thank you for your attendance. Let us begin,' Stephen said with a smile.

Triumphantly he told the assembled men of his plan, Hugh's role as abductor, and his own success in acquiring the title of High Lord. With a flourish he produced a parchment and laid it on the table.

'This is from the High Lord, signed by his own hand,' he said. 'He agrees to all my terms. Five days from tonight we begin the journey to Tegge's Eyot. The High Lord will personally hand me the Great Seal and proclaim me his successor.'

There were nods of approval at this detail.

Tegge's Eyot had long been the crowning place of the High Lords, and before them the kings of old. The rocky island sat at the point of the River Arlen where four of the provinces met.

Stephen fielded questions of logistics; how many men would he take? Where would they strike camp beforehand? How could he be sure there would be no ambush?

'There will be no ambush because I have possession of Lady Aline. Should anything unexpected happen I will slit her throat myself,' he said smugly. 'Leavingham knows this, and will not risk her coming to harm.'

'As you speak of her, what of Lady Aline? When will your marriage take place?'

The speaker was Lorrimer. Hugh shot him a grateful glance and received a twitch of the lips in return.

'I admit I may have been a little misleading in telling the lady that joyful news,' Stephen said smoothly. 'The marriage will take place in twelve months' time, or when the High Lord dies—whichever is sooner. Until then Lady Aline will be returned to Leavingham Keep. A unit of soldiers will be stationed there to ensure nothing occurs to prevent that part of the agreement from taking place.'

Hugh could have cheerfully slit Stephen's

own throat, but he controlled his fury. Stephen's announcement to Aline had been deliberately malicious, he thought, adding it to his ever-increasing list of resentments against his cousin. A meaningful cough caught his attention and he opened his eyes to discover that all present were watching him, including Stephen, whose face was openly hostile.

'I *said*, Captain, that you will not be part of the detachment to travel to Tegge's Eyot or Leavingham,' Stephen said contemptuously. 'However, I expect you to spend the coming days ensuring my troops are ready.'

'Naturally, my lord,' Hugh answered coolly. 'With your permission, I will begin preparations immediately.' He pushed his chair back and stood, holding Stephen's gaze with a challenge.

The Duke broke eye contact first and with a casual wave Hugh was dismissed.

Leaving the hall, Hugh broke into a run and headed straight to the tower.

One last time, he told himself, *just to say farewell.*

He climbed the stairs two at a time, arriving at Aline's chamber out of breath and dishevelled, a dull ache in his injured chest. No guard was there to see his lack of composure, however. He hammered on the door but there was no response. The key was hanging on the nail so he lifted it down and unlocked the door.

Cautiously he pushed the door open, but the room was deserted. Aline was not there.

Chapter Fifteen

Aline waited in the Duke's chambers, sick to her stomach. She had awoken from her faint, bewildered to find herself lying on the ground. Brushing aside Jack's and Kate's pleas for her to return to her own room to recover, she had insisted on going straight to Stephen's quarters to wait. Seeing her determination, the pair had escorted her there before Jack had reluctantly left the two women together and returned to his duties.

The late-afternoon sky had turned a murky purple-grey before the door was slammed open and Stephen marched in. Aline rose from her seat, disconcerted to feel her legs shaking. She willed herself not to faint again, not entirely sure that Stephen would not leave her unconscious on the floor.

The Duke shrugged off his cloak, draping it over a chair. With a mocking look in his eye he

bowed in an exaggerated flourish, then tugged
Aline's unwilling hand to his lips in a parody
of chivalry. Aline could smell the wine on his
breath and her apprehension increased.

Kate moved to stand at Aline's shoulder and
Stephen's eyes turned to the girl.

'Leave us,' he ordered.

Kate looked to Aline for confirmation. Stephen walked around Aline to where she stood.
Aline watched with revulsion as he took the girl
by the hand. He led her to the doorway and took
her chin in his hand, tilting her face upwards to
gaze into her wary eyes.

'Your concern for your mistress does you
credit, my dear, but we need no chaperon. Farewell.' He pushed her gently out of the room and
closed the door firmly behind her, then turned
to Aline, running his tongue around his lips with
a leer.

'You disgust me!' she said.

His response was a scornful laugh. Aline
found her palms itching to slap him and fought
to control her anger.

'I think you should start treating me with
more deference now you are to be my loving
and dutiful wife,' Stephen said mockingly.

'I will *never* love you,' Aline shot at him.

'I don't need your love.' He laughed. 'I don't
want it.'

He crossed the room and stood in front of Aline. Taller by a head, he towered over her, a tight smile transforming his handsome face into something grotesque.

'I want your obedience and somewhere to spill my seed until you give me an heir.'

With a gasp of horror Aline stumbled away from him and backed against the table.

'Tell me when!' she cried out, her voice cracking, no longer caring to hide her torment.

A look of triumph crossed Stephen's face and she feared he would not answer—that he would force her to beg, or worse, for the information—but to her surprise he drew a fold of parchment from his jerkin and passed it to her.

Aline sank onto a chair and scanned the message rapidly. 'And you agree to this?' she asked warily. 'I am to return to Leavingham for a year?'

'Or until your grandfather dies.' Stephen nodded. 'So long, I know, but I'm sure it will barely feel like days.'

It was late before the Duke allowed Aline to return to her chamber. In a daze she barely registered the fact that the door was unguarded and unlocked. Walking into the room, she stopped in shock. Seated in her chair, silhouetted in the light of the dying fire, was a figure. Her hands flew to her mouth to stifle her cry of alarm and at the sound the intruder looked up.

'I'm sorry,' Hugh said gently. 'I did not mean to startle you.'

'What are you doing here?' Aline demanded.

Her heart thumped in her chest. Her eyes slipped to the curtained bed and she felt heat rising to her cheeks and throat as images crossed her mind that she knew were utterly inappropriate.

Hugh rose from the chair. At some point he had removed his coat. The flickering light of the fire caused interesting shadows to move across his chest, where his shirt lay open.

'Waiting for you, of course.' He smiled.

'But *why* are you here?' Aline asked.

Hugh's eyebrows shot up in surprise. 'After this afternoon, where else could I be? I needed to see how you fared.' He brushed back a stray lock of hair that had fallen across his eyes and fixed Aline with a look that sent shivers through her. 'I had come to bid you goodbye,' he whispered gruffly.

'*Had* come?' Aline asked, her heart missing a beat at his words.

'I was going to leave Roxholm,' Hugh admitted. 'For ever. The thought of seeing you every day, knowing you belonged to Stephen, was too much to bear. But that would be the

coward's way. I will not let you face him alone
and friendless.'

He took her hands, pulling her closer, and
Aline felt the enticing warmth of his body.

'Say the word, Aline, and I will be your champion, your defender. Whatever you wish of me
I will do.'

Aline's mind flashed back to Stephen's parting words: *'Your conduct will be impeccable. If
I hear the mere hint of you casting your eyes at
another man I will have him executed and brand
you as an adulteress. As much as it would pain
me to see your beautiful face disfigured, I will
do it.'*

'No!' she shook her head. 'I don't want
a champion.' She pulled her hands free and
stepped back. 'I wish I had never met you—
never laid eyes on you!'

At the bitterness in her voice Hugh recoiled
as though he had been stabbed. He balled his
fists and lifted his chin sharply. 'Then, if it is
your wish, I shall leave Roxholm immediately.'

He stalked past her to the door. She caught him
within three paces, the sound of her light step
causing him to pause in his exit. 'Don't leave!'

'What do you want of me, Aline?' he asked,
flinging his arms wide in exasperation.

She recoiled at the anger in his voice and
shook her head, momentarily lost for words.

'How else do you want to wound me?' Hugh asked, his voice gentler now but full of pain.

'I...I'm sorry... I didn't mean... I only meant...' Aline stopped, her eyes brimming with tears.

Hugh reached his hand to her face but stopped short of touching her.

Aline raised her face and closed her eyes. 'Because marriage to *him* might have been bearable if I had never known you,' Aline whispered, her voice trembling.

At her words a hot burst of passion raced through Hugh and he could restrain himself no longer. With a fervour that took him by surprise he pulled Aline close, his strong arms imprisoning her, one hand encircling her slender waist, the other across her back as he buried his face deep in her hair.

Aline leaned her head against Hugh's chest with a soft sigh. Her arms found their way around his waist, pulling him closer as her breaths came deep and fast. He pulled her tighter until he could feel every contour of her body. She melted against him as if she was wax, her fingers sliding up to his jaw, brushing against his beard, and he gave an involuntary moan of desire, his lips parting in anticipation.

At the sound Aline froze, her arms dropping to her sides. Hugh opened his eyes in surprise.

Aline's eyes were closed and tears glinted on her long lashes, coursed down her pale cheeks.

'Aline—' Hugh began, but Aline cut his words off with a strangled sob. He wrapped his arms about her again but she broke away from him, her shoulders shaking. 'I just want to protect you,' he said gruffly. 'Let me look after you.'

'I don't need your help—it's too late for that now. I asked you to release me before, but you refused. I can't blame you for all my ills, but *you* brought me here on his orders.'

Aline looked deep into Hugh's eyes and he saw the anguish mirroring her own.

'I cannot do this, Hugh. I cannot let myself get close to you. If you feel anything for me at all, go now. Please don't make me ask again.'

Hugh nodded. He turned on his heel and left, closing the door softly. Through the heavy wood he could hear Aline's sobs as they grew thicker and faster. He stood there, for how long he could not say, his forehead and hands pressed against the door, sharing in her grief until no further sounds came from the room. Then, with strength of will he had not known he possessed, he walked away.

Loud knocks on the door jarred Aline from her sleep the next morning. In her distress she had simply collapsed onto the bed, crying until exhausted. As she untangled the sheets—the night spent tossing and turning had twisted them into a knot around her legs—she realised she was still fully dressed.

Kate's worried voice came through the door. 'What are you doing? You'll wake Lady Aline.'

'I have a message for your mistress. I'll bang as I like, girl,' came the haughty reply.

There followed a stream of high-pitched insults, the result of which was that when Kate entered, bearing a covered tray, she was followed into the room by a crimson-faced page.

'My master instructs you to join him,' the youth said, nervously eyeing Kate. 'He will be waiting in the council room and bids you not to delay.'

So hers was now a life of summonses and demands? Aline thought angrily. 'Tell Duke Stephen I will join him when I have eaten and bathed,' she replied firmly. 'I shall be with him before the hour is up.'

Stephen was sitting with his back to the roaring fire when Aline eventually entered the room. The surly expression on his face warned Aline that this would not be a friendly encounter, and she began to wish she had not kept him waiting so long.

'You took your time arriving,' he remarked.

'I'll expect more compliance once you're my wife.'

Ignoring the jibe, Aline folded her arms and looked him in the eye. 'What do you want of me?'

'There is something I want to show you.'

Stephen led her through the castle until they came to a balcony directly over the combat yard, where guards were practising swordplay. A tall figure in a loose black tunic strode between the men. Though she could not make out his features, Aline could picture the concentration on Hugh's face as he spun and parried with his opponents.

Though powerful, his movements held a grace that sent her thoughts tumbling back to their dance together, and the sensation of his muscular arms holding her tightly rose far too easily in her memory. She recalled the way she had responded so eagerly to his touch the previous night and her breath caught in her throat. It would have been so easy to kiss him, but where would that have led? She had been right last night to refuse her desires—right to insist he leave.

She felt Stephen's eyes upon her and tore her gaze away. 'Why have you brought me here?' she asked coldly.

'To meet your honour guard, my lady,' Stephen breathed into her ear, his lips curling back. 'And to confirm something I have long suspected. I noticed how you danced with my cousin at the ball. I saw, too, how you looked at him just now. I would take great pleasure in causing him pain. I wonder how long I could keep him alive for? Certainly until our wedding, I imagine. Think on *that*, Aline.'

Aline felt the colour drain from her face. She gripped the stone ledge to steady herself. Stephen laughed softly, watching her, then with a snap of his fingers summoned a herald to announce their arrival.

Since dawn Hugh had pushed himself through the motions of life, though anyone who knew him well would have seen that he held the shape of a man through determination alone. He'd pushed the men hard and himself harder, working out his frustration with his sword. The morning had passed in a whirl of swords and lances, formations and drill. Tirelessly he'd moved among the soldiers, stripping down to his shirt as he took on man after man in mock combat.

An abrupt fanfare sounded. Panting heavily, Hugh turned in the direction of the sound to see Stephen on the balcony. Standing beside him, her face devoid of emotion, was Aline. Hugh's surroundings faded to grey, the mere sight of her nearly threatening to unman him.

He wiped his brow with the back of one arm and barked rapid orders to the men, conscious of how unkempt he must look after hours on the field. Sheathing his sword, he marched to Stephen and saluted, keeping his eyes fixed on the Duke, not daring to let them slide to Aline's.

Stephen acknowledged Hugh with a curt nod. 'Thank you, Captain. Soldiers of Roxholm, I bring you news. This beautiful lady—' he inclined his head to Aline '—has consented to become my wife.'

Consented! Hugh's hand moved unconsciously to the sword at his waist as cheers broke out around the yard and Stephen waved his hand graciously. Aline's eyes remained steadfastly focused on the ground, but her mouth twisted with disgust at his words.

Hugh bit down on his lip, relishing the taste of blood in his mouth. Last night she had admitted she blamed him for her misery. The words had been said in anger, and had cut him to the quick, but he could not hold them against her.

'I shall be crowned High Lord before the month is out,' Stephen continued. 'And Lady Aline will return to Leavingham, where she shall remain until our wedding day. You will travel there as her escort. You will guard Lady Aline night and day until such time as I summon you back to Roxholm.'

If I killed him now, Hugh wondered, *if I struck him down in front of everyone, how many of these men would rise up to avenge him and how many would turn away or offer me their swords?*

He looked back to the balcony and with a start discovered that Aline was staring at him. He'd expected coldness or hate but she merely looked sad. She raised her hand briefly to him, then was gone, borne away on Stephen's arm. Hugh felt a lump in his throat; her gesture had been one of resignation and of farewell.

He ordered the troops back to their exercises and threw himself into the drill until his body cried out for respite and Aline's grey eyes no longer filled his mind.

The guards were beginning to flag visibly before Hugh released them from their drill. He was halfway across the courtyard, returning to his chambers, when he caught sight of Aline returning to the tower. He almost turned away, remembering how their last encounter had ended and telling himself there was no hope of anything different today.

He would only check that she was well, he promised as he broke into a run. He caught up with Aline at the bottom of the stairs. Her eyes were ringed with dark circles and her face pale. Hugh swore under his breath as the urge to protect her engulfed him again. He dismissed the guard and stepped in front of Aline, blocking her passage up the stairs.

'Lady Aline, we need to speak.'

Chapter Sixteen

Hugh's hair was tangled from his exertions and fell about his collarbone, where the neck of his loose shirt was open, hinting at the contours of his chest. Aline's stomach flipped slowly with desire as he gazed down at her, his eyes searching for something she could not give. She fought down the urge to reach out and touch him, knowing that if she did her resolve to avoid him would melt.

'Let me pass, Hugh,' she said, her voice catching in her throat.

'Not until I know you are unharmed. Have you been with Stephen all this time?'

Aline nodded. 'Yes, I have—and, no, he did not harm me. Why do you persist in seeking me out, Hugh? Did I not make myself clear enough last night? I want you to stay away from me.'

'You told me one thing, my lady,' Hugh said

passionately, 'but your body told me another. Don't try to hide what you felt.'

Hugh put a hand cautiously to her cheek, rubbing a callused thumb across her cheekbone.

Aline closed her eyes and inclined her head, covering his hand with her own. Hugh sighed and Aline felt his arms slide round her as he caught her up into an embrace. Though every instinct in Aline's body told her to cling to him, she forced her muscles to freeze and stood rigid in his arms. Hugh pulled away and stared at her, his brow wrinkled in concern.

'What I might have felt is immaterial. What we did last night can never happen again,' Aline said as firmly as she could manage. 'Stephen claims me, and though he has not yet taken what is his I am bound to him.'

'You are free until the year is up,' Hugh said earnestly.

'Would you make a cuckold of your lord and an adulteress of me?' Aline asked gently. 'I think you have more honour than that, Hugh.'

He gave a mirthless laugh and released her from his embrace. 'Do you really?'

Aline stared at the floor, digging her nails into her palms to stop herself weeping. 'Last night I was harsh, and I apologise. I have no right to expect you to forswear your loyalty to Stephen.

Not after everything I know of your history. I know the value you place on your honour.'

'Then I must leave you,' Hugh said in a voice thick with emotion, 'for my honour is stretched to breaking point.'

'We should both be thankful it is so long before I return,' Aline said with a faint smile. 'A year is long enough for any man to forget a woman.'

'A lifetime would not be long enough for that,' Hugh insisted.

Hearing the passion in his voice, Aline felt her knees go weak. For both their sakes this had to end now.

She set her shoulders and raised her chin, her eyes boring into Hugh. 'Last night you promised to do anything I wish,' Aline said. 'Well, do this: learn to forget.'

She pushed past him and fled up the stairs, leaving Hugh lingering below.

For the next few days Aline spent her time wandering listlessly through the grounds of the castle. Her door was no longer locked or guarded and she was free to come and go as she pleased. More than once she found her feet leading her towards the parade ground, though she stopped herself stepping through the gate. Her determination to forget Hugh was as strong as ever.

On the occasions when they came face to face they avoided speaking more than the required formalities, and one or the other contrived to depart as soon as possible. Though each encounter left Aline with a longing she had never experienced before, she had almost convinced herself that she would survive her remaining days unscathed.

On the final day everything changed. Preparing for a morning walk, Aline was about to leave her chamber when a messenger arrived. He handed over a thin roll of parchment. Puzzled, Aline broke the seal. She recognised the handwriting as her own chamberlain's elegant script. Quinter! Why would he write to her here? With trembling hands she unfurled the letter.

My lady,
I am most grieved to be the bearer of devastating news. The day after the High Lord agreed to Duke Stephen's terms he became ill. Suspecting foul dealings, his men fed his meat to some dogs. They all died within the hour. It is my saddest duty to inform you that the two days later your grandfather suffered the same fate.

Duke Stephen has been informed of this turn of events, though doubtless he was already aware of this act of murder. As your grandfather died before he could forfeit the Great Seal to Duke Stephen you are now High Lady. Even now we are preparing to march to Tegge's Eyot. We have no reason to believe the Duke will do anything other than continue with his plans to control the provinces.

Be on your guard, Lady Aline. Trust no one.

Your most constant friend,

Thos Quinter

Aline could hear a scream, high-pitched and unending. She knew it was coming from her own lips, but was unable to halt the sound as it rose and fell, rose and fell, over and over and over. The heavy thumping of blood in her ears drowned out all thoughts except one: vengeance.

Full of rage, she let her eyes fall on the heavy candlestick on the table. Picking it up, she hurled it across the room. A half-full wine jug followed. Something glinted on the tray on the table and her eyes fell on a knife. Not sharp enough to kill, but she could steal an eye. She could etch her hatred on his face!

She pushed it inside her sleeve and, clutching the parchment in her hand, staggered to the door.

Head bowed to hide the heat in her face, Aline made her way through the castle, oblivious to everyone she passed. The page standing to attention outside Stephen's room swallowed nervously at the sight of her.

'Let me in. I must see the Duke urgently,' Aline demanded, waving the parchment in front of her.

'I can't, my lady,' the page said, his eyes fearful. 'I apologise, but Duke Stephen has expressly insisted that—'

'Move, if you value your position!' Aline cried. The man hurried away with an anxious glance. Aline tore the heavy door open.

Stephen was leaned over the table, upon which a girl was bent backwards. One of Stephen's fists was tangled in her curly black hair. Her dress had been pulled from her shoulders, leaving her breasts almost entirely bare. With disgust, Aline recognised Kate's tear-stained face.

Stephen rose to face Aline. 'Who let you through?' he bellowed, his face twisting with fury.

Kate slid to the floor with a sob, pulling her torn dress around her shoulders. Aline slid the knife into her hand. 'Run—now!' she yelled, and Kate staggered from the room.

Stephen's eyes fell on the knife. 'What do you plan to do with that?' He laughed, then folded his arms and planted his feet apart.

'You were never going to wait a year,' Aline snarled. She took a step towards Stephen, thrusting the parchment at him. Her eyes were blurred with tears. 'You planned this all along!'

'You begin to test my tolerance, Aline,' Stephen warned her, his brow creasing. He took a step back against the table.

Distantly Aline could hear the sound of voices. Someone was coming. It was now or never. With a scream of rage she hurled herself at Stephen, the knife held high and death in her eyes.

Cold metal pierced Hugh's skin. He winced, shifting into a more comfortable position on the edge of his bed as the physician prodded the stitches on his chest.

'The wound is healing smoothly. A remarkable technique,' the physician commented.

He smeared a foul-smelling unguent on the area. A pitcher of water stood on the windowsill and Hugh sluiced his face and hair, wrinkling his nose as the scent of the salve reached his nostrils.

A piercing scream from above broke his reverie, followed by banging and the sound of metal on stone. Hugh's blood turned to ice in his veins. He fumbled a tunic over his head and dashed to the door, pausing only to find his dagger. He ran along the corridor and took the stone steps two at a time, arriving at Aline's room with his heart pounding. The room was silent now, and the door swung open ominously.

Hugh drew the dagger from its sheath and grasped the handle firmly in his palm, the blade resting along his forearm. His precautions were unnecessary however: the room was empty.

He stared in disbelief at the destruction. Where was Aline? He must have narrowly missed her on the stairs. He raced to the window and caught the flash of a blue skirt disappearing into the main wing of the castle. Panic flowed over him and he raced out of the room in pursuit, his heart thumping wildly. There was only one place she could be going.

He almost collided with the physician on the stairs as he leaped down them three at a time. 'Follow me,' he ordered.

He arrived at the corridor where Stephen's chamber was, but pulled up short at the sight of Aline's maid, leaning against the wall, her dress in disarray. Words tumbled from her tearfully as she explained what Aline had rescued her from.

'Lady Aline's in there. She stopped the Duke. She has a knife…'

Hugh's blood ran cold. He hurled himself through the open door in time to see Aline throw herself at Stephen and swing her arm out wildly, the knife glinting in her hand. Stephen sidestepped towards the fireplace, moving out of her reach with ease, his feet dancing. Aline advanced again, oblivious to the sword leaning against the wall that Stephen was moving ever closer to.

'Aline! Stop!' Hugh commanded.

She either did not hear, or ignored his cry.

In three strides Hugh crossed the room and seized her around the waist. He twisted her round, out of Stephen's reach, and stood between them, arms outstretched towards Aline. Her eyes burned into him with a fury he could hardly bear to see.

'Don't you *dare* try to stop me, Hugh!' she warned him, her voice laden with menace.

'I have to, Aline,' he replied. 'You know I can't let you do this. Whatever he has done, this is not the answer.'

Out of the corner of his eye Hugh saw Stephen was shaking with anger, his eyes glinting dangerously.

'It's fortunate you arrived, Captain. She's lost her mind,' he hissed.

A cold sweat curled down Hugh's spine at the expression on Stephen's face. Whatever had led to this was unimportant now. All that mattered was to defuse the situation and get Aline safely out of the room before any further damage could be done.

'Aline, whatever has happened, it's finished,' Hugh said quietly. 'Give me the knife.'

Aline made a sudden feint and tried to slip past Hugh. The knife brushed his sleeve. Quickly he seized hold of her wrist. He twisted her arm downwards, holding it in a fierce grip, until she dropped the knife to the floor with a rasping cry of rage.

Hugh pulled Aline towards him, her back to his chest, his arms crossed about her body, pinning her arms to her sides. Still she fought against him, writhing and kicking, her eyes swimming with tears. He wrapped his arms tightly about Aline's struggling frame, doing his best to ignore the feelings that holding her so close against his chest aroused within him.

'I won't let you harm him,' he repeated firmly.

'Let me go!' she screamed, 'Why did you stop me?' She twisted wildly, aimed a blow at Hugh's face.

'Will somebody help me?' Hugh roared. 'Where is the physician?'

The physician sidled nervously through the door, his bag clutched in front of him as though it were a shield. He peered into Aline's red-rimmed eyes, then brusquely reached for her wrist and pressed his fingers into the soft flesh.

'Her heart spasms are too strong. I must act now before the hysteria becomes permanent,' the physician announced. 'Take her to my infirmary.' He dropped her wrist, which flopped like the limb of a broken doll.

'Get the bitch out of here, Hugh,' Stephen barked, 'or I'll see her back in the dungeons.'

Aline's body sagged at Stephen's words.

Hugh lifted her into his arms and carried her from the room. He strode after the physician along dimly lit corridors until they arrived at the infirmary. He laid Aline on the narrow bed. She curled into a ball, arms wrapped around her head protectively, still sobbing wildly. For the first time Hugh noticed she held a crumpled piece of parchment bunched tightly in her other hand. He tugged it from her grip, stuffing it into his pocket.

The physician rummaged in a chest and produced a vial of crimson powder. Working quickly, he measured a dose and tipped it into a beaker of wine. A pungent aroma filled the room.

'What do you think you are doing?' Hugh demanded, stepping protectively in front of Aline.

The physician stared at him and gestured to Aline, who was lying motionless, knees still curled to her chest and her pale hair a tangled mask across her face. 'Look at her. She has taken leave of her senses. Sedating her is the safest way to restore her equilibrium. Who can say what further injury she might inflict upon herself or to another?'

* * *

On the bed, Aline twisted at his words and gave a moan. 'I trusted you… How could I…? I should never have…never believed…' Her voice came out in great, gulping sobs.

Hugh knelt and took her hands. She flinched at his touch and his heart jerked. 'What? Aline, tell me what has happened?'

She looked at him as if for the first time seeing him clearly. She jerked upright and snarled accusingly, '*You!* How much did you know?'

'Know about what?' Hugh cried in frustration, still at a loss to understand what had occurred. 'Tell me!'

At the ferocity in his voice Aline's hand shot towards his face, fingers splayed in a twisted claw. Hugh dodged the blow and pulled her close. He buried his face in her rosemary-scented hair, murmuring endearments he knew she did not hear. He could have gladly stayed that way for eternity.

'Sir Hugh, you are delaying my treatment and endangering Her Ladyship,' the physician cautioned. 'If you are not prepared to assist me while I treat Lady Aline, then leave this room!'

He carried the cup across the room and Hugh laid Aline back against the pillow. As soon as he released his hold Aline slid from the bed, knocking the cup from the physician's hand. She pushed past him, running on shaky legs towards the open door. She made it halfway across the room before Hugh intercepted her, seizing her round the waist. She fought him off with blows and curses as he enveloped her in his arms.

'Aline, you're not thinking,' Hugh insisted. 'I would never let you come to harm. You have to believe me. What he proposes will help you.'

'Sir Hugh, her senses are too disturbed for her to understand,' the physician said, his brow furrowing with worry. 'She needs to be restrained while I administer the draught.'

Hugh looked down at Aline, her hair loose and wild and her face twisted with misery. As gently as he could Hugh held her close while the surgeon mixed another cup and brought it over. Aline turned her head away, twisting in vain against Hugh's grip.

'Trust me now, Aline. Let us help you,' Hugh said, his voice husky with emotion.

Aline stared at him, her eyes full of betrayal.

Hugh carried her back to the bed and knelt, pulling Aline against his chest, pinning her arms to her sides. The physician gripped Aline's chin and with a practised hand forced her lips open. She gagged and cried out as the liquid slipped down her throat.

Hugh stroked the tangled hair back from her brow as her eyes began to close.

'Get out,' Aline whispered, her voice bitter. 'Run back to your master, lapdog, and tell him he is safe.'

Every word was a knife in Hugh's heart. 'Sleep now. I'll return soon,' he promised, though he doubted she heard.

'You're *his* man,' Aline mumbled, her voice starting to slur. 'You've always been his.'

Hugh opened his mouth to protest but Aline had turned her face to the wall. He held her in his arms and watched as the rise and fall of her chest became shallower. Her body became limp as she slid fitfully into sleep.

As the physician drew a blanket over the motionless woman Hugh suddenly recalled the parchment Aline had been clutching and pulled it from his pocket. The brief communication gave him all the explanation he needed. He had been wrong about the cause of Aline's attack on Stephen.

'When Lady Aline awakes keep her here,' he instructed the physician. 'Whatever it takes, make her well again.'

He crumpled the letter in his fist, feeling sick to the stomach. Aline was out of time. *He* was out of time. Setting his jaw, he hastened his pace, vowing that Stephen would answer for this.

Chapter Seventeen

Stephen was sitting by the fire, drinking wine, when Hugh marched in. He offered the bottle to Hugh, who shook his head.

Stephen burst out laughing. 'It isn't poisoned,' he said, drinking deeply. 'If I ever have you killed it will be a proper death. I want to look into your eyes and see the light leave them. Perhaps I will make my wife give the signal for the axe to drop.'

'And it would amuse you to involve her?' Hugh asked, flames of anger igniting at the mention of Aline. He slammed the parchment down on the table in front of Stephen. 'You planned this all along,' he spat. 'There was never an intention to return Aline to Leavingham.'

Stephen's disdainful smile was his answer.

'Aline believes me complicit in this,' Hugh raged. 'I have supported you for years, and followed your orders, however foolhardy, but no more.'

'So you play the chivalrous knight, come here to defend your lady love?' Stephen mocked. 'Are you going to challenge me publicly? Or strike me down now?'

Despite the tone of his voice Hugh saw fear briefly slide across Stephen's face as he spoke. It was enough to allow him to pull his temper back under control. 'Neither—for now. Stephen, what were you thinking?' he asked contemptuously. 'Why could you not be content with what you had already won? You could destroy Roxholm altogether with this thoughtless act!'

'I was thinking that a year is a long time and loyalties change,' Stephen replied. 'Promises can be broken. Mostly I was thinking it was a long time to wait to bed Aline.'

Hugh could not prevent his angry intake of breath at the Duke's words, nor hide the shadow that crossed his face.

'I wonder how many more things you desire and I will take possession of?' Stephen sneered. 'I've seen the way you look at her. At first I thought it was merely hunger in your eyes, but I think you love her. I wonder if she returns your love? What do you think, cousin? Will it be you she thinks of as I bed her? Not for long—I promise you that!'

Stephen's words were cut off mid-sentence as Hugh grabbed him by the throat and slammed him onto the table, squeezing tightly. Stephen reached out an arm, fingers clawing desperately towards the discarded goblet. He snatched the heavy vessel and smashed it against the side of Hugh's head. Lights burst behind Hugh's eyes and, dazed, he loosened his grip.

Stephen pulled himself to his feet and staggered to the door. 'Guards!' he bellowed.

Hugh scrambled to his feet, panting heavily, and drew his dagger with a shaking hand. He could feel a sticky wetness on his cheek. Reaching his fingers up, he discovered blood trickling from the cut on his head. Four guards rushed into the room, their swords drawn, but stopped in confusion at the sight before them.

'Sir Hugh is under arrest,' Stephen announced. 'Seize him.'

The men looked from their lord to their captain, worry and uncertainty on their faces.

'Do it!' Stephen shrieked, his face contorted with fury. 'You have become too much of an inconvenience, Hugh.'

Hugh's mind whirled as he searched for a way out of the situation. 'Well, this is interesting. What are you going to do with me now?' He laughed with a confidence he did not feel. 'Part my head from my body in the courtyard? Stretch my neck on the gallows?'

Stephen's eyes bulged and Hugh felt calm descending over him.

'Give me one reason why I shouldn't kill you today,' Stephen said, though he looked suddenly wary.

'If you execute me now what signal will it send to all the knights and nobles who have gathered to support you? Who can say how many might rise against you to avenge me? What a good way to start your campaign tomorrow!'

Stephen stood silently for what felt like minutes. An unbearable knot grew in Hugh's stomach as he watched the Duke contemplating his words.

'Take him to the armoury and keep him under close watch,' Stephen announced.

To Hugh's satisfaction the guards' eyes slid briefly to him for confirmation. With a nod of his head Hugh threw his dagger to the ground and raised his arms in a gesture of surrender. The guards moved to surround Hugh, their swords pointing at his chest and throat.

Stephen stepped closer to Hugh, his voice low. 'Don't think your argument has persuaded me. At first light you will be escorted from the citadel to your estate. Here and now I strip you of your title and your lands. You are no longer Captain of the Guard.'

He snapped his fingers and two of the guards took hold of Hugh's arms, the others walking in front and behind. As they escorted him from the room they, at least, had the grace to avoid his eyes.

The sight of Hugh being led through the castle, with his clothing in disarray and a blood-streaked face, drew whispers and stares from everyone they passed. The sentry outside the cells turned an incredulous face to Hugh, then rapidly dragged a drunken soldier out of the cooling-off cell. The man's jaw dropped as he recognised his former captain. Doubtless word of Hugh's fall from grace would spread around the citadel immediately.

'In there please, Captain,' the guard requested.

Hugh stepped into the low room. The guard ordered Hugh to raise his arms, then patted him down, searching for weapons.

'Do you know nothing?' Hugh admonished sternly. 'If I had a knife you would be dead by now. Never search a prisoner alone in an enclosed room.'

The man mumbled apologies and completed his search, then retreated.

Self-recrimination gripped Hugh as he heard

the key turn. He should have killed Stephen the moment he entered the room, without preamble or explanation, and dealt with the consequences afterwards. He paced the room, beating his fists in anger and frustration against the thick stone walls until eventually he wore himself out.

Night fell. Hugh lay on the low bed, staring at the shadows as they moved slowly across the wall. The moon was almost full: a matter of days and Stephen's triumph would be complete. And yet a spark of optimism refused to die. He had his life, if not his freedom. While he lived he could not give up. He would find his way to Aline if it meant slaughtering every man Stephen sent to hold him back.

He hoped the news would reach Aline and that she would discover why he was gone. The thought that she might believe he had abandoned her again brought him closer to despair than he had ever been. But she believed him complicit in Stephen's deceit, so why would she even care?

Lapdog, she had called him. Somehow he had to see her again, to explain—if she would ever speak to him again after his deeds today. It mattered more than he'd thought possible that she thought him untrustworthy. He closed his eyes and conjured her face—not pale and contorted with pain, as he had last seen her, but radiant as it had been on the night of the banquet, her expression soft and loving. Concentrating on the memory of her arms around him and her lips on his, he gradually slipped into sleep.

Shouts of anxiety woke him some time later. Immediately alert, he sprang from the bed and hammered on the door.

'What's happening?' he demanded.

A worried face appeared. 'There's someone causing a disturbance.'

'I can tell that!' Hugh remarked. 'Let me out. I want to see what's going on.'

The guards were standing with crossbows trained on him, but as Hugh raised a scornful eyebrow the weapons were lowered. He strode down the familiar passageway until he came to the room where the sounds were coming from. The cause of the disturbance lurched around the room.

'Jack, what do you think you're doing?'

The youth reeled around, knocking helmets and lances to the floor before selecting a short, wide sword and buckling it to his waist with trembling fingers.

'I'll kill him!' Jack raged.

He rounded on Hugh with a ferocity that took the older man by surprise.

'He's a monster. It was Kate this time—my Kate, but what will happen when it is Aline? Will you let him take her and do nothing to—?'

Hugh spun and grasped Jack on either side of

his head, his fingers digging into the boy's hair. The sane part of his brain was shouting that this boy was not his target, but the rage he felt threatened to consume him.

'She. Owns. My. Heart,' he hissed. 'When I think of him near her it is agony! You *dare* to suggest I would stand by and do nothing?'

The youth's eyes widened and he gave a whimper. At the sound Hugh dropped his shoulders. He released his grip and slumped next to Jack against the wall.

'Ah, lad,' Hugh said gently. 'This isn't the way. You should take your girl and leave this rotten place while you can. Go and start afresh somewhere else before it is too late. I tried to kill the Duke. I tried and I failed. And now—'

He broke off, suddenly overwhelmed by emotion, but as he studied the young soldier the beginnings of a plan started to form inside him.

'I need to reach Tegge's Eyot before Stephen is crowned. I have to find Aline. Will you aid me?'

Jack was silent, his fingers gripping his arms, clenching and unclenching. Finally he turned to Hugh and wiped the streaks of tears from his face.

'What must I do?' he asked.

Aline awoke from her drugged sleep disorientated but with fury in her heart. She had no idea how long she had been there, but the room was dark and a solitary candle burned on the table. She climbed from the bed and stumbled towards the door.

The physician had been sitting in a chair and now stepped in front of her, his hands out-held. 'My lady, you cannot leave,' he said forcefully. 'Sir Hugh expressly forbade it.'

Aline's lip curled with contempt at the mention of Hugh. She stepped round the man, determined to leave, but he grabbed her by the arm, pulling her back towards the bed. She twisted around and slapped him across the face. To Aline's relief he let go of her arm and left the room. She raced to the door but heard the key turn in the lock and sagged against the wall.

A short while later the physician returned with two men, a sour-faced woman and a box bearing the gore-spattered evidence of previous surgical procedures. Aline felt the colour drain from her face as she stared at the stained wood. She bolted to the door once more, but the men were too quick. Together the assistants held Aline to the bed while the woman wrapped cuffs of leather around her wrists and ankles, securing them to the sides and foot of the bed with wide straps.

Muttering under his breath, the physician rummaged in the box and produced a copper bowl and a slender-bladed knife, rolling the delicate wooden handle between his finger and thumb. Aline blanched at the sight of the blade. Terror coursed through her body and she screamed, pleading with them to let her free.

'When Sir Hugh finds out what you have done he will kill you,' she threatened.

The physician shook his head, though his eyes were kind. 'Sir Hugh instructed me to keep you here,' he explained. 'He has sanctioned any treatment that will help you.'

Aline shook her head in disbelief. She felt the last of her strength leave her as the true extent of her abandonment struck her.

The physician drew back Aline's sleeve and applied a tight leather thong around her upper arm. She cried weakly as the blade punctured her vein and a stab of pain shot through her arm. Her vision blurred as she tried to focus on the face floating above her, but the loss of blood was making her head spin. It hurt her throat and chest to draw breath.

I don't want to die, she thought. *Please don't let me die.* Her eyes began to close and her final thought before she slipped into unconsciousness once more was a curse against Hugh for his betrayal.

Some time later the physician returned and this time Aline offered no resistance. She stared at him through heavy-lidded eyes as he unwound the bandage from her arm, not even attempting to pull against her restraints. She barely cried out as the blade reopened her vein.

From the bed she could just about see the murky sky, though it seemed as though she was staring at the reflection in a dull mirror. Was it dusk or dawn? She had lost all sense of time, and knew this should worry her, but she was so tired…

Someone entered the room. Through her delirium she could make out dark hair and a slim frame. Hugh? Had he come to free her at last? How could she have doubted he would return to her? A sob burst from her as she hoped he would explain it had all been an error, that her ordeal was finally over.

She looked closer. The hair was too short, the posture all wrong. Not Hugh but Stephen. The Duke stood at the foot of the bed, his eyes travelling over the contours of her body beneath the thin coverlet.

'I can see why he desires you,' Stephen mused, 'but love? I don't know…'

Fear coursed through Aline's veins. The sense of her complete vulnerability hit her like a blow to the stomach. If he touched her now, if he violated her while she was so completely unable to defend herself, she knew she truly would die.

Stephen walked round the bed and stood by her side. 'I came to tell you that I pardon you for your actions yesterday. You were distressed, which is understandable, and fortunately my cousin was on hand to protect me—as he always is. I do not intend to mention the matter again.'

I hate you!

She must have spoken aloud because his face clouded. Aline shrank back against the mattress as he shook his head sadly.

'I am not going to hurt you,' he said, a touch of reproach entering his voice. 'Whatever lies *he* has told you, I am not inhuman.' He turned to the physician, who had been listening silently in the corner. 'Release Lady Aline from these bonds and ensure she is fit enough to travel. In a few hours we travel to Tegge's Eyot. My bride must be well.'

He bowed to Aline and left the room.

The physician pressed his thumb over the wound to stem the bleeding and wadded a hank of wool onto to the cut before wrapping the bandage back around Aline's arm.

'Please...' Aline rasped, her throat painfully dry. 'Please, no more bleeding.'

The physician smiled kindly and nodded. He unwound the straps at her wrists, gently massaging the skin where they had rubbed. With a groan of relief Aline rolled over, her limbs objecting to the unaccustomed movements after so long in the same position.

Bewildered, she considered what had just happened. Stephen—her enemy and the cause of all her troubles—had freed her from her suffering, whereas Hugh had brought her here and sentenced her to agony. She fought back anger as she remembered how he had leaped to Stephen's defence. He had stopped her doing what she needed to do and had imprisoned her here. With her mind reeling, she mercifully slipped into oblivion.

The pale sun had just begun to creep across the dismal sky when four men leading two horses apiece made their way to the castle gates. Heavily wrapped in oiled leather cloaks, they grumbled their way through the drizzle that hung in the air. They checked their weapons, inspecting the crossbows that adorned seven of the eight steeds. Four more men appeared.

From the way he carried himself, it would seem that the man in front was in command, though a keen-eyed observer would notice his hands were chained and he was unarmed, while the others held short swords pointed at him.

Hugh walked across the rough ground, head held high and shoulders set. He nodded to his escort, regarding them thoughtfully. He recognised them all—had trained them, faced them in mock combat, and was determined that he would show no weakness in front of them. Their responses varied from curt nods to sad smiles, and in one case a salute and a wink that caused him to glare at the youth in question.

His spirits lifted at the sight of Jack. At least the lad had managed to talk—or bribe—his way onto the escort. He wondered how many of the others were truly loyal to their Duke, hoping he would find the moment when that could be put to the test.

With a swagger in his step Stephen crossed the green to the waiting band of men. 'Good morning, cousin. I trust you slept well last night? You have such a long journey today to your estate.'

Hugh glared at him.

'I have just been visiting Lady Aline,' Stephen remarked. 'I'm pleased to say she seemed much calmer. There should be no obstacle to our wedding, as far as I can tell!'

Hugh breathed in and out deeply and slowly. Stephen would not get the satisfaction of seeing him lose his temper again. If he thought to taunt him with Aline's name it would not work any longer. He pictured her grey eyes, the mention of her name only making his resolve stronger.

'Do you have anything else to say or have you come merely to goad me?' he asked coldly.

'Only this: today I leave as planned for Tegge's Eyot with Lady Aline,' Stephen said. 'I want you to live knowing that every day she wakes next to me. I want your last thought at night to be that as you sleep alone, she sleeps in my arms and you can do nothing to prevent it. If I ever see you again your sentence will be death. Now, get out of my sight!'

He lowered his sword and the cousins stared at each other, the air between them heavy with animosity.

'Be kind to her,' Hugh said, his voice low.

He expected a further taunt, but to his surprise Stephen simply nodded. With a lump in his throat Hugh mounted Bayliss, then wheeled around. He cracked the reins and spurred the horse towards the gate, his heart tugging him backwards but his mind on the task ahead.

Chapter Eighteen

With the air of a condemned prisoner climbing the scaffold, Aline walked to the courtyard. She pulled her new fur-lined cloak around her shoulders whilst stifling a yawn. Since escaping the physician's knife she had drifted in and out of consciousness for most of the night. She no longer felt the dizziness she had before, but every move emphasised how weary she still felt.

Throughout the past week nobles from all over Roxholm had been arriving with troops to swear allegiance to Stephen, and now they stood assembled in long lines. Were there similar scenes in Leavingham? Aline wondered. Had her own nobles sent armies to help defend the province against Stephen? Was Sir Godfrey riding to Tegge's Eyot even now? Her spirits lifted slightly at the possibility that Stephen might yet be defeated.

There was one man missing, of course. In vain her eyes searched for Hugh.

Stephen rode up on his horse. 'If you're looking for Sir Hugh you won't find him. He left the citadel this morning,' Stephen informed her, his eyes sparkling with malice.

'He left?' Aline's voice cracked, the last of her hopes dying. She did not even care that Stephen saw the grief it caused her.

'He has returned to his own estate,' Stephen said.

He dismounted and took Aline by the arm. Aline walked with him compliantly. He handed her into a waiting coach and bowed.

'Haven't his actions convinced you of what I told you before? Do you think you are the first woman he has made empty promises to, Aline? Yours is not the first pretty face his head has been turned by, and it won't be the last, but whatever he may have implied Sir Hugh's loyalty lies with me.'

He mounted his horse, leaving his cruel words echoing in Aline's ears as she slumped back in her seat.

By evening the rain had set in. It beat down upon the roof of the carriage, an insistent drumming that lulled Aline to sleep, her head resting on the shuttered window frame. She awoke with a yawn as the carriage drew to a halt and looked around, slightly disorientated. She was halfway risen from her seat when Stephen climbed in.

'Good evening, Aline, I trust your journey has been pleasant?'

Unconsciously Aline pulled her cloak closer round herself.

Stephen frowned. 'I wish you would not look at me like that,' he said petulantly. 'I know you think badly of me, but I can be kind. I stopped the physician from bleeding you further, did I not? That fool would have drained your life away if I had not intervened.'

Aline could not deny it. He had been her saviour then, when no one else had come. Hugh had not even enquired if she was alive or dead before he'd abandoned her to her fate. 'Thank you,' she said, taking care to keep her voice neutral. 'I am grateful to you for that. I cannot blame the physician, though. He believed he was helping.'

'I blamed him.' Stephen's voice was suddenly hard. 'I had him executed this morning. His head adorns a spike on the citadel wall. He would have loved all that blood, if only he could have seen it.'

He drew her unresisting hand to his lips, then left the carriage.

Aline squeezed her eyes shut, picturing the fate of the innocent man. Just when she had started to think the Duke was not the monster she'd thought he was, he proved it to her beyond all doubt.

Hugh's jailers rode for half a day with no respite, pushing the horses to their limits. Every mile underfoot took Hugh further from Aline and he began to give up hope of ever breaking free, anxiety twisting his guts. Once he was back in his manor he would be under lock and key, with no chance of escape. He needed to make his move soon, but how?

The chance did not come until they were nearing the boundary of Hugh's estate. At the river they dismounted to allow the horses to drink. Knowing it would be his only chance, Hugh nodded to Jack. The youth drew his sword and threw it to Hugh before the nearest guard had realised what happened. Back to back, Hugh and Jack faced their opponents.

'Release me or die,' Hugh growled.

He gritted his teeth, prepared to fight to the death if necessary, but luck was with him. Two of the remaining guards proved loyal to their former captain. Evenly matched, they overpowered Stephen's men with ease. A guard produced keys and unlocked the shackles that bound Hugh's wrists.

'Well done, lad,' Hugh said grimly, patting

Jack on the back. 'Keep them here tonight—that should give me enough of a start.'

He stripped the surcoat from one of the men who lay bound on the grass and swiftly changed. He did not know what he would do when he reached Aline, but he had a day's journey in which to plan. He mounted his horse and set off in pursuit of Stephen, far behind but with hope blossoming for the first time in days.

The journey became harder and slower as the travellers moved higher into the heavily wooded hills. Aline spent the time devising plans to escape or to kill Stephen. All seemed destined to fail, but as they travelled closer to their destination they were all that kept her sane. What else could she do but try? she asked herself. There was no one else she could rely on.

She thought again of Stephen's words regarding Hugh. Had everything he had said and done been a lie? His words had seemed so sincere and his kisses had left her reeling. So fierce and impassioned had they been that she did not want to believe it.

Yours is not the first pretty face his head has been turned by, Stephen had told her. Had he ever truly cared, or was it merely desire that drove him towards her? Or, worse, was he just another man, like so many others, hoping to gain power by using her? It didn't matter now, she told herself. He was gone and she was alone.

By late afternoon they'd reached the River Arlen. The banks had burst as the result of the unexpectedly heavy rainfall. The soldiers were forced to heave the supply carts and carriages across the ford, tempers fraying. They made camp for the final time at the top of a windswept ridge. Tomorrow they would begin the final leg of the journey, down the steep gorge to the river and finally to Tegge's Eyot.

Aline lay on a low cot, her eyes drifting to the dress hanging on a peg, rippling in the draught that blew under the tent's sides. It had been waiting when she'd entered, accompanied by a letter from Stephen instructing her to wear it the next day. The cloth was deep velvet, the dark ruby of old wine. It was full in skirt, and the neckline and billowing sleeves were embroidered with gold thread and tiny pearls. It was exquisite.

If she'd had a knife she would have slashed it to ribbons; a torch and she would have burned it to a cinder.

Her bridal gown.

Her wedding day.

In the early hours she was lost so deeply in a restless sleep that she was completely unaware that someone had slipped into the tent until a figure loomed above her, his deep-hooded riding cloak covering the livery of Roxholm.

Panic coursed through Aline and she opened her mouth to scream. Like lightning the intruder knelt and clasped a hand to her mouth. She struggled, eyes wide with fear. The intruder spoke her name and her heart lurched in disbelief. She jerked upright as the man released her and lowered the hood of his riding cloak. Aline's mouth dropped open, her hands flying to her face.

When he saw her reaction a weary smile lit up Hugh's face. He swept Aline into his arms with an intensity that almost drove the breath from her body.

Aline pulled away from Hugh's embrace, her initial astonishment at seeing him replaced by all the fury and resentment she had allowed to grow since their last meeting. She drew her hand back and delivered a slap to Hugh's cheek that rang out loudly in the silence. Hugh jerked back, his eyes full of surprise. He gave a growl of rage and seized her outstretched wrist before she could land another blow.

'Explain that, please, my lady!' he demanded, his eyes narrowing.

'You left me at Stephen's mercy,' Aline ranted, hot tears of fury springing to her eyes. 'You defended him from me after everything you said and then simply returned to your home without a second thought for me. Now you appear, when I thought you miles away, and feign amazement that I am not pleased to see you.'

'Is that what Stephen told you? That I went of my own accord?' Hugh asked furiously. 'And you believed him so willingly?' He gave a snort of derision. 'Such confidence you have in my fidelity, my lady!'

Exhaustion was writ large on Hugh's face and his clothing bore the stains of a long, hard ride. A worm of doubt crept into Aline's mind.

'It was not for the first time,' Aline reminded him icily, her lip trembling. 'Why would I have believed it otherwise?'

She met Hugh's eyes: intense blue depths she could lose herself in if she was not careful. They were currently full of indignation.

Hugh swore under his breath and balled his fists. 'Stephen lied!' he shouted, his voice heavy with exasperation.

Aline's eyes darted to the doorway anxiously.

Hugh lowered his voice. 'He has no conscience. He'll say anything to get what he wants.'

'He said that about you, too,' Aline retorted, her voice rising in fury. 'Why are you here, anyway?'

Hugh held out his hands towards her. 'Come with me. Let me look after you. We'll cross the

river downstream and make our way to Leavingham.'

His intensity was overwhelming, but as he
spoke of protection Aline bristled. 'No, I won't
run. Some day you will have to choose where
your loyalties lie, but until that day tell me how
I can ever trust you again after—'

She stopped abruptly as shadows moved
across the canvas wall and the sound of voices
came close. She exchanged a glance with Hugh,
their quarrel forgotten, suddenly allies. Hugh
stood ready, every muscle tensed, his sword now
drawn.

'I swear I heard voices in her tent.'

'Check she is safe. *Our* necks will be stretched
if anyone has hurt her!'

Aline turned back to Hugh, her face stricken.
'Go!' she whispered urgently, pushing Hugh towards the back of the tent.

He stole a last glance at her, then raised his
hood, dropped to his knees and slipped underneath the gap between wall and floor.

Aline heard the sound of metal scraping.
Sick to her stomach, she ran to the tent door
and peered through the folds. Two soldiers
were standing outside with swords drawn. She
counted to five, then gave a piercing scream. The
soldiers jumped as though they had been stung
and ran into her tent.

'Someone was in my tent!' she cried, clutching at their arms, her eyes wide with fear.

The men stared around the empty room in confusion.

'He ran off that way,' she panted, running to the door and pointing in the opposite direction from the one Hugh had gone in. 'Quickly—I don't know what he might do!'

The men ran off in pursuit of their quarry. In the shadows Aline saw a figure slip between two tents and slowly move away. She let out a breath she hadn't known she had been holding.

By now more men had arrived, bringing flaming torches. Stephen pushed his way through the throng.

He stalked into Aline's tent. 'What happened here?'

Aline repeated her tale, adding a few sobs that came all too easily, hoping that the half-truths would satisfy him.

Stephen faced her, his arms folded, his eyes suspicious. 'Describe him to me.'

'I didn't see him clearly,' Aline wept. 'He was tall and wore a green hood, pulled deep over his face. He had black gloves on. I woke to find him standing over me and when I shouted for help he ran. Then I screamed.'

'You're lying,' Stephen said, walking round her.

Aline felt her head swim with desperation,

wondering what else she could say to convince him. Stephen stopped behind her. He grasped her by the hair and twisted her to her knees. Aline cried out in pain.

'I don't think there was anyone here. What was your plan, Aline? To run while my men were distracted, hunting for no one? Did you really think that would work?' Stephen snarled.

Aline shook her head, another sob bursting from her lips even as her heart soared in relief.

Stephen let go of her hair with a shake. 'I will be crowned High Lord tomorrow, and you will be my wife by the time the sun sets,' he murmured. He pushed back the curtain over the doorway. 'Sleep well, my dear. Or don't. It is all the same to me.'

Aline could feel her body shaking violently. Fingers of ice wound themselves around her throat. She bit her knuckles to stop from screaming aloud. The whole incident, from Hugh's arrival to Stephen's departure, seemed like a nightmare. She could scarcely believe Stephen had been fooled, but the camp was quiet now.

It struck her that she had been so busy fighting with Hugh she had never asked why there had been such a need for secrecy. There were so many things she should have said to him, but she had wasted her chance on recriminations.

Wearily Aline climbed back into bed and stared at the ceiling, waiting for the dawn.

Chapter Nineteen

Aline greeted the arrival of morning with a head that ached. If she had slept at all it had been by drifting in and out of troubled unconsciousness. She had witnessed the torches burn to nothing outside her tent and seen the watery sun crawl above the horizon.

With a heavy heart she dressed in the wedding gown. To her red-rimmed eyes it was no longer the colour of wine but the foreboding hue of congealed blood. Yesterday Aline would have wept at the thought of her marriage, but today she was beyond that. Deep within her she determined that she would not be wed today.

This day would bring freedom or her death, though she could not say which, and she no longer cared.

As Aline was led through the rows of tents to the edge of the camp she could feel tension hanging in the air as real as the mist curling about the flag-tops. The soldiers eyed her as she passed, with expressions of curiosity, desire and pity. Though she had commanded them not to, her eyes roamed for Hugh, a tumult of emotions churning inside her. But he was nowhere to be seen, and her heart sank even as relief coursed through her. He would be miles away by now, safe from any danger.

Stephen was waiting on horseback at the edge of the camp. With a look of undisguised malice he galloped forwards, bringing the horse to a standstill barely inches from where Aline stood. 'You took long enough to arrive! You will do nothing to jeopardise today or I promise your future will be more wretched than you can possibly imagine.'

Aline held her ground, determined not to let this petty attempt at intimidation work. She wondered again why Hugh continued to be loyal to such a man.

Stephen snapped his fingers and a soldier came forwards, leading a white mare. He stopped by Aline and linked his hands for her to mount. She stepped into his waiting palms and swung up into the saddle, settling into position as the steed whinnied and shifted.

The man produced a rope and, taking Aline's hands, deftly bound her wrists together. He tied the free end of the rope around the pommel of the saddle, smiling up at Aline with a boldness that made her blood boil. Stephen laughed and she turned her head away haughtily. The man took hold of the bridle and led the animal to the centre of a rank of men. He mounted his own steed and, with a yell from the Duke, they left camp.

Hugh had spent the night lying in the damp, muddy undergrowth a mile or two from the camp. At some point in the night he had ended up lying on his side on the dew-soaked ground and his arm was stiff and numb. He shuffled and twisted his limbs to bring the feeling back.

He had tried not to think of Aline as he'd crept from the camp last night, knowing that if he dwelt on her he would return and damn the consequences. He had heard her scream and had had to hope it was the diversion he suspected it to be.

His pulse quickened and he smiled as he thought of her quick wit. Whatever she had said had worked, as no one had followed him from the camp.

Aline had appeared to him unbidden in his dreams. She'd smiled and pulled him close, her warm hands gently stroking the hair from his brow, telling him that she loved him, that she would always be his.

He had woken from his slumber with black

claws ripping at his guts as he remembered her accusations. From the moment he had arrived in her tent he had blundered everything. It stung him deeply that she believed Stephen's lies. More than anything else, he needed to have the chance to convince her she had been wrong about that.

Last night he had been rash, and could have caused tragedy for them both by bursting into the camp. Today he would be more cautious. He would watch and wait for his moment.

Stiffly he stood and led his horse towards the river. He was cold and hungry, the last of the food he had brought with him a distant memory. He pushed those complaints from his mind and pressed on.

As they reached the path above the water's edge the ground underfoot became more treacherous and Aline clung on to the saddle tightly. With her hands tied she had little control over the animal, and her legs ached from trying to grip the horse's flanks. Days of rain had created a quagmire and the animals slid about, losing their footing. Even the most experienced riders struggled to stay upright.

Eventually Stephen called a halt and summoned the three accompanying nobles to the front. After a brief and from what Aline could gather heated conference it was decided to abandon the horses and continue on foot.

The trek was difficult, doubly so for Aline, wearing soft boots and with her hands still bound. She stumbled over the rough ground, the men struggling to prevent her from slipping to her knees on a number of occasions.

They made their way slowly along the undulating path, where a steep slope on the left bank led to the river below. Tiny in the distance, Aline could see the high defence tower of Tegge's Eyot. She had abandoned any hope of killing Stephen—he was too far in front and too well protected—but could she break free and try to swim to freedom?

The path had risen high once more when Aline saw a flash of movement on the other bank. The purple and silver colours of Leavingham's army were moving between the trees! Her countrymen were close by, tracking Stephen's progress. Her heart sang as she started to believe for the first time that she might succeed. Now she just needed the opportunity.

Her moment came not long after. A tree had grown out over the path, meaning that the troops had to stoop and go in single file. The first soldier let go of her arm to duck under the branch. The second bent Aline's head to guide her, then let go to steady himself. When he rose up again

Aline spun and delivered a sharp kick to his groin. As he doubled over with a grunt Aline hurled herself outwards. She slid down the side of the bank, rolled once, and managed to stop just before she reached the edge of the overhang.

She heard furious shouts from the bank. There was no turning back now. She pushed herself to her feet and threw herself out wide over the water, her legs running on nothing. She hit the rushing water and sank below the surface. The force smacked her head backwards and the cold snatched the breath from her lungs. She was weightless for a moment, spinning, until with a kick she rose and broke the surface, gasping for air before she sank down again.

Nothing had prepared her for the chill shock of the water as it closed over her. But the current was carrying her downstream, in the direction they had come from, moving faster than the men on the bank could retrace their steps along the treacherous path. Euphoria washed over her. She had done it!

Suddenly she was in trouble. The churning water caught her and spun her below the surface. Her mouth filled with acrid water. She tried to kick her way upwards but her skirt was too heavy, tangling around her legs. With her hands tied she was helpless to direct herself. She broke the surface again and managed to grab a shallow breath before the current dragged her under. Her chest and throat were agony and spots of black burst painfully behind her eyes.

A vision of Hugh's face swam before her eyes and she was glad of the comfort it brought as she once more sank below the surface. Something brushed past her, knocked her arms and jerked her head back sharply. The pain almost caught her attention, but she was too weary to care as she lost consciousness completely.

Hugh had the procession in his sight when Aline made her attempt to escape. He had ridden fiercely, abandoning his horse when he saw the others tethered and waiting, then running with all the strength he possessed. He stopped, bent almost double with exertion, on hearing the shouts of alarm. Helplessly he observed Aline fling herself into the river. He heard Stephen's cries, saw him instruct the soldiers, watched as too slowly they began to shrug off their shirts and chainmail. He knew they would never reach her in time.

But by some stroke of fortune the current was carrying her in his direction. He darted down the crag, ripping the cloak and sword from his body as he ran. He dived into the water, kicking powerfully as he plunged under the surface of the ice-cold depths.

The current was powerful, but Hugh was a strong swimmer. He surfaced and looked in desperation for Aline. A flash of red swirled to the surface, then vanished below the swirling waves. *There!* He struck out again and reached Aline as she went under for the third time. He dived down and reached about in the churning depths. His fingers brushed against floating strands of hair and he bunched his fist and pulled.

She was unresponsive, and her weight threatened to drag them both under. The current tried to pull her from his grasp and he forced himself to hold tighter. He somehow twisted his arm around her slender body and struck out for the shore, hoping he could reach the far bank before his strength gave out or the coldness of the water froze his limbs beyond the ability to swim. Fighting against the current, he was only half aware of the shouts coming from both sides of the river getting fainter as they were swept away.

After what seemed to be miles Hugh made it to the bank. Exhausted and retching, he dragged the limp woman out of the water, his boots sliding in the mud. Aline slipped from his grip to the ground and lay unmoving, her limbs contorted at impossible angles. Her skin was drained of colour; her lips held an unnatural blue streak. Hugh let out a moan of distress and fell to his knees, refusing to believe he had failed her.

Redoubling his efforts, he wrapped his arms around Aline's chest and heaved upwards. As he wrenched the limp woman upright a gush of water surged from her mouth. He pulled again and another jet of filthy liquid spurted out. He lay her down and straddled her, driving his hands fiercely against her chest. More water gushed out but she still did not move. He worked until nothing more appeared, and still he continued.

Tears of anguish filled his eyes as he shouted rhythmically, 'Don't leave me. Come back to me,' over and over.

A small voice told him it was impossible, that she had passed beyond his help, but he ignored it. He was nearing the point of exhaustion when he saw the slightest flicker of Aline's eyelids. The movement was so small he might have imagined it, but then her throat tightened and she coughed. She drew a deep ragged breath, then retched before collapsing back, her eyes still closed.

Relief flooded over Hugh and he threw his head back, half laughing, half screaming in elation. He buried his face in her bodice, relishing the softness of her flesh, clinging on to her, his body racked with sobs of relief.

Aline's hands were still bound. Fumbling at his waist for his dagger, Hugh was unprepared for the sudden kick to the ribs that came from nowhere, sending him reeling.

'Get your filthy hands off her!'

Three men had appeared, wearing the purple-and-silver crest of Leavingham. One of them, a tall blond man, had already jumped from his horse, and it was he who had delivered the kick. He lashed out again, striking Hugh across the face. Hugh doubled over as the second horseman rained blows down, delivering a kick to his kidneys that left Hugh writhing in pain on the ground. He found himself seized, his arms twisted up behind his back and a knife at his throat.

The blond giant knelt by Aline, gently cradling her head in his arms. He moved his head close to her mouth and listened to the faint breaths. Having confirmed Aline was alive, the man spoke. 'Tie this dog up and bring him back to the camp. I'll ride ahead with the High Lady.'

While the two soldiers set about binding Hugh's arms tightly the man bent beside Aline, who was starting to stir. Deftly he cut the ropes binding her wrists.

'Aline, you're safe now,' he said gently.

Aline gave a weak cry of disbelief. 'Godfrey? Oh, Godfrey. I thought I'd never see you again!' She flung her arms about his neck and clung to him as she cried huge, gulping sobs of pure release.

To Hugh, the joy in her voice was a knife in

his chest. He had never even suspected she might have already given her heart to someone. Powerless to attract her attention, he watched as the knight lifted Aline onto his horse, then climbed behind her. He wheeled around, Aline held tenderly in front of him, and galloped off.

She was lost to him in every way possible.

The two soldiers finished securing Hugh and pulled him to his feet. One of them tied a further rope around Hugh's neck and removed his dagger. Then, mounting up, he jerked on the rope, forcing Hugh to hobble after him or choke.

Chapter Twenty

'How did you find me?' The question burst from Aline's lips almost as soon as they'd left the clearing.

'We had men stationed along the length of the river between our camp and Tegge's Eyot, following your progress.' Godfrey regarded her sternly. 'What were you thinking of, Aline? You could have died!'

At the sharpness in his tone cold and shock finally began to take their effect on Aline. She shivered uncontrollably, her face crumpling. Her chest hurt, as though a heavy load had been smashed into it. She did not understand why and the missing knowledge gnawed at her mind.

She remembered leaping into the water, the icy current tugging her under, but nothing more until Godfrey's voice had pulled her back to the world.

Godfrey brought the horse to a standstill,

shrugged off his coat and wound it around the shaking woman's shoulders. 'Did you think I would do nothing and let any man hurt you, Aline, my dear friend?'

Warmth began to penetrate Aline's chilled bones. She yawned. If only she could lie down for just a few minutes...

'We can't stop here,' Godfrey cautioned. 'I need to get you somewhere warm and dry. And I must send a message to the other parties that you're safe and they can stop the search.' He spurred the horse on to a canter.

Drowsily Aline huddled close to the man behind her. She closed her eyes, feeling the rhythm of the horse as it moved along, aware only of being held in strong arms and being cared for. As she slipped into a doze against the broad chest her muddled memories collided.

Her thoughts drifted back to the last time they had ridden together, his body indecently close to hers, every muscle taut and controlled. It seemed so long ago, and it seemed ridiculous now how much she had hated him. She had been so angry, scared of his presence, yet at the same time acutely aware of the lightning that shot through her at his touch.

Foolish of her to have ever feared those cool blue eyes. She smiled and twisted in the saddle to tell Hugh of her thoughts.

Blond hair and brown eyes in a different face greeted her. She wrinkled her forehead in confusion. Godfrey, her friend—not Hugh, her…her what? What could he ever be to her now?

It struck her that she would never know his fate, but to think about Hugh now would open her up to emotions she was not yet prepared to confront.

'Godfrey, we must stop the Duke,' she said firmly.

'Of course we will. We'll slaughter him, and every man of his, for the dishonour he has served you. But what has happened, Aline? What are you not telling me?'

Would Godfrey understand? she wondered. They had known each other for years, had shared so many secrets. 'Later…' was all she could manage to whisper. She sought around for something to distract him. 'Tell me, how is Matilda? Has she had the baby?'

She watched Godfrey's handsome face glow at the mention of his wife and new child. Would anyone ever speak of *her* with such adoration? Where was the man whose touch made her heart stop? Was he safe? Was he even alive?

Aline and Godfrey arrived at the encampment shortly before the sun sank. Aline was amazed at the scale of the site: whereas Stephen's had contained no more than thirty tents, this was at least three times the size.

'Half the nobles of Leavingham wanted to mount an assault on Roxholm itself to rescue you,' Godfrey explained to the overwhelmed woman.

Aline bit hard on her lip to hold back the emotions that threatened to overwhelm her. To witness this demonstration of loyalty was almost more than she could bear.

Evidently the soldiers of Leavingham had been confident of their success, as a chest of clothes had been brought along for her. In the comfortable tent that had been set aside for her she peeled off the hated red gown and changed into a dress of soft blue wool. Exhaustion caught up with her and she lay on the bed, curled into a tight ball. She knew she should be overjoyed at being safe. All she felt was hollow.

She declined the invitation to eat with her noblemen, and instead sat long into the evening talking with Godfrey, describing her time in the citadel. She made no mention of Hugh, afraid that if she spoke of him her voice would betray too much.

Towards the end of the evening a messenger slipped into the tent. He spoke briefly to Godfrey, who excused himself abruptly. At Aline's raised eyebrow he explained about the man who had been found with her.

'I intend to find out who he is and what he can tell us,' Godfrey said.

A small flicker of hope stirred inside Aline which she hardly dared give name to. 'Certainly,' she replied, 'and I should come with you and thank the man you tell me saved my life.'

'I don't think that is wise.' Godfrey frowned. 'From his manner when we found you I don't imagine this will be a friendly conversation.'

Shivering with cold, wet, and hungry almost to the point of collapse, Hugh had been led stumbling to the outskirts of the camp. With the jeers of the two soldiers echoing in his ears he'd been forced to his knees, their kicks keeping him down when he'd tried to rise.

Through a veil of pain he glared up at the blond knight, who now introduced himself as Sir Godfrey.

The man was of equal height to Hugh, but younger. Handsome and confident, this was the man Aline had called by name with such warmth. For that reason alone Hugh was damned if he would tell him anything. He imagined the two of them lying entwined in the throes of lovemaking and his stomach rolled over with jealousy. Did she know he was here? The thought that she had so easily forgotten him struck him suddenly.

'You have one chance to speak before I start to hurt you,' Sir Godfrey said harshly.

'You can rot,' Hugh spat. 'I'll speak to Aline and no one else.'

Sir Godfrey snapped his fingers. Two soldiers seized Hugh. A rope was looped over the branch of a tree and tied around his wrists. He felt himself hoisted violently upwards, his arms pulled taut, shoulders and chest screaming. Sir Godfrey nodded and one of the soldiers delivered a punch to Hugh's stomach. He struggled for breath as nausea washed over him.

'Lady Aline is recovering from her ordeal. I speak on her behalf. You will not speak *of* her or *to* her,' Godfrey said harshly, his face close to Hugh's. 'After the treatment your master subjected her to, I'm not going to let any damned enemy soldier near her.'

So Aline did know, and had sent her lover in her place. Hugh felt sick.

'My master? Not anymore!' Hugh muttered, knowing it was unwise to provoke the man but in his delirium unable to stop himself. 'I have no master. I have nothing.'

Godfrey brought his face level with Hugh's and grabbed him by the throat, fingers gripping tightly. 'Are you going to tell me what the Duke has planned?' Godfrey asked him. 'What do you know?'

'I know nothing of what he intends now. Nor do I care. You have Aline.'

'How do you want to die? You know it will happen—and I'm going to be the one to kill you. Tell me what I want to know and I'll ensure it is quick.'

Godfrey's fingers squeezed tighter. His face swam before Hugh's eyes; the pain was now intense.

Hugh dragged himself back through the haze of agony and cold to focus on the man. 'What do I have to live for?' he choked out. 'Why should I care how I die when my wolf-killer prefers a fool in her bed?'

'Who *are* you? You're clearly high-born—I can tell that from your voice.'

Hugh locked eyes with Godfrey and said nothing. Godfrey delivered a kick to the back of Hugh's knee. His legs gave out and he swung by the wrists.

'Watch him closely. If he says anything useful tell me immediately,' Godfrey ordered. 'I will be with Lady Aline. We'll talk again in the morning,' he said to Hugh, his eyes travelling down Hugh's body. 'If you last that long.'

'I do have something to say,' Hugh wheezed, with a laugh that was verging on the hysterical.

'Tell Aline that if she wanted to rip my heart out the wolf would have been a more merciful fate.'

Godfrey brought his fist back and punched Hugh across the jaw. After everything else this was finally too much. Hugh's knees buckled. As welcome unconsciousness closed over him he heard Godfrey's final words to the guards.

'Get what you can out of him when he wakes. I don't care how.'

As soon as Godfrey entered the tent Aline rushed to him, questions pouring from her lips. 'What did he look like? How was he dressed?' she asked.

Godfrey shook his head and shrugged. 'Dark hair, like most of them. He wore a soldier's uniform—a common one—though he sounded well-born. I think his mind is feeble,' he said in puzzlement. 'He kept rambling about wolves.'

'Wolves?' Aline's stomach flipped, a horrific suspicion creeping over her. 'What did he say? Tell me *exactly*,' she demanded.

'Just that death by wolf would have been kinder. They aren't so barbaric in Roxholm, surely?' Godfrey asked in wonderment.

'Tell me where he is!' Aline choked out.

'Aline, I don't think you should see him,' Godfrey protested. 'He isn't a pretty sight. It isn't suitable for a woman.'

Aline rounded on him furiously, his words chilling her to the bone. *What had they done to him?* 'I have seen and done things over the past weeks that would make your heart blanch— and I am not *just* a woman,' she stormed. 'I am your ruler, and I *will* see this man. Now, tell me where he is!'

The knight pointed a finger, confusion visible on his face at her urgency. Aline tore off into the night, running as though it was her life that depended on it. She pushed her way past the guards to where a figure hung limply from a tree. His head was slumped onto his chest and he was unmoving.

Her heart skipped a beat as an overwhelming sense of loss enveloped her. She had come too late to save him.

Barely conscious, and with a body that was more pain than flesh, Hugh hung from the tree. Despite the agony and the cold enveloping him he sensed the change in atmosphere. The background sounds of the camp seemed to still and he became aware of somebody coming close.

So this is it, he thought numbly, expecting the sharp kiss of a knife across his throat. His final regret was that he had never got to see Aline before he died. She would never know he loved her.

Instead of the sound of steel being drawn, he

heard a woman's voice. Hardly daring to believe, he forced his aching eyes open and looked at the figure standing before him.

Aline. She was standing pale and radiant in the torchlight, her face twisted in misery.

'I didn't know it was you. I'm sorry,' she sobbed.

She brushed blood-matted hair from his eyes, her hands caressing the bruises on his face.

The sensation of her touch almost unmanned him. His legs gave out and his body slumped down. The ropes cut into his wrist agonisingly, sending bolts of lightning through his body. He no longer cared about the pain. This wonderful, unpredictable woman had come for him after all.

Aline cried an order and a soldier stepped forwards and cut the ropes binding Hugh's wrists. He collapsed, but instead of landing painfully on the hard earth he found himself enveloped in Aline's waiting arms. Two of the soldiers came at her sharp command and between them carried him into a tent and laid him on a bed. A lamp was lit, and before long matters were firmly out of Hugh's control.

Servants bustled around, stripping off his soiled, filthy clothing. Firm hands washed the dirt and blood from his body and face. Ordinarily he would have rebuffed such an intrusion, but on this night he was content to lie still with his eyes closed and let them carry out their ministrations. Someone threw a light coverlet over his lower half to hide his nakedness. Voices muttered softly, then there was silence and he knew he was alone.

By now the feeling was starting to return to Hugh's arms and legs and the pain was excruciating. His groan of agony was met with a soothing, *'Shh....'* He had been mistaken in thinking he was alone. Moreover, he knew the voice as well as he knew his own.

Aline's soft hands drew the cover over him further. He whispered her name, finding that his voice would barely come. In response she slid her arm around his back to sit him upright and cradled his body against hers. Weakened as he was, her touch still set his skin on fire with desire.

She lifted a cup to his lips. He drank thirstily, recognising the taste of herbs in the warm liquid that would mean welcome oblivion. Aline placed the cup on the floor and began to rub his wrists and arms slowly and firmly, massaging the feeling back into them. Her tenderness was almost too much for him to endure.

'You came for me,' he murmured.

Her reply was a smile and she twined her fingers into his. 'Sleep now,' she murmured. 'Tomorrow we'll talk.'

Her words sounded ominous in his muddled head, filling him with apprehension. She could never be his to keep—he knew that—but for now he could not bear to let go his hold.

'Stay. Please,' he whispered, and closed his eyes.

Aline sat on the edge of the bed, watching the rise and fall of Hugh's chest become shallower as the herbs took effect. She held his hand tightly as sleep stole him away and his grip loosened. Signs of the ill treatment he had suffered were apparent on all the parts of his flesh she could see. Bruises covered his face and chest, over-lapping earlier scars, and red weals ringed his wrists. She tried not to stare at his body but was intensely aware of his nakedness, the contours of his form barely masked by the light coverlet.

The rush of craving she had tried to deny for so long overwhelmed her anger and mistrust. She would deal with that tomorrow, but now the only thing that consumed her attention was his injuries and how close to death he had come. She broke out in a cold sweat at the thought that his chance words to Godfrey had been all that saved him.

A realisation struck her and she smiled to her-self. His words had not been chance at all. He had known exactly what he was saying. Impul-sively she traced her finger across the scar the

wolf had given him, silently thanking the animal for providing the means by which she had
found him. He murmured and shifted, swaddled
in the blanket of sleep.

He would never know she had done it, so
she leaned over and kissed him gently on the
lips. She was startled to find his mouth answering hers, his lips beckoning her on. She started
to pull away, only to find his arms coming
around her body and drawing her back down.
He reached up with a trembling hand and ran a
smooth thumb along her cheekbone. She kissed
him again, with more passion than she had
thought herself capable of, and found him responding just as forcefully.

His mouth was sweet with the taste of gin-
ger and wine. She told herself it was the trace
of sleeping draught she had taken from his lips
that made her light-headed. She knew it was not.

Hugh opened his eyes and met her gaze,
studying her with such intensity she almost lost
control of her self-possession. Aline ran her fingers through his hair and leaned closer. Their
lips met again. He began to kiss her slowly, his
tongue gently parting her lips to dive between,
hungrily moving with a slow, sensuous rhythm.

She could feel every curve and hollow of
Hugh's frame through the thin fabric that sepa-

rated them, conscious of the hardness of his muscles and…and other parts of his body!

She pulled away, alarmed at the flames of exhilaration that rose deep within her at the implication.

Hugh smiled, sweeter and warmer than she had seen before, and laughed softly at the pink flush spreading from her neck to her cheeks. His eyes flickered downwards and she realised that he knew. His eyes closed, opened again, and became unfocused as his head began to cloud and the sleeping draught took full effect.

'I fear I may be…may not…Aline…' Hugh's voice trailed off, his arms went limp and he drifted into a dreamless sleep.

Chapter Twenty-One

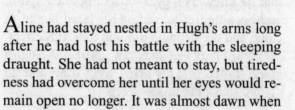

Aline had stayed nestled in Hugh's arms long after he had lost his battle with the sleeping draught. She had not meant to stay, but tiredness had overcome her until her eyes would remain open no longer. It was almost dawn when she awoke and crept through the silent camp to her own tent. She burrowed into the furs covering her bed until the sky grew light.

She summoned servants and by the warmth of an iron brazier she bathed, yet still she imagined she could smell Hugh's scent on her skin. Her fingers brushed the scab on her arm where the physician's knife had cut her and fury coursed through her anew.

She still had so many unanswered questions. There was too much Hugh needed to explain before she could decide what course of action to take. As she smoothed a tendril of hair behind her ears the gesture spun her back to Hugh's fingers, curling and tangling in her locks as he overpowered her with his kiss, and a new worry struck her. How could she face him after last night?

Aline rummaged through the chest until she found a dress of green wool, remembering Hugh's casual aside in the forest so long ago. Halfway to slipping it on, she shook her head and exchanged it for one of grey. She summoned a messenger and issued instructions, then sat on the bed combing the tangles from her hair and waited.

Hugh woke alone. He knew that when he stretched out his arm there would be a cold empty space instead of Aline's warm, yielding body. He wondered if it had all been the desperate fantasy of a man pushed beyond all endurance, or was it the result of the sleeping draught? If so he would gladly drink himself to death on it, if only he could spend his last moments with such delusions.

But it had been no dream, he knew. She really had been there, soft and eager in his arms, and…and he had passed out. He cursed the sleeping draught for cheating him of what they might have done and felt himself hardening at the thought.

At the foot of the bed his clothes lay dried and

folded. Hugh dressed in the rough breeches and tunic and walked out of the tent. To his astonishment four hulking guards stood to attention outside, weapons drawn. His eyes narrowed warily.

'Good morning,' he said pleasantly. 'I need to speak to Lady Aline.'

The largest soldier looked him up and down. 'I have instructions to take you to her. Follow me.'

The men led Hugh through the camp until they stopped outside an imposing tent. Hugh had expected them to leave, but instead they surrounded him. He took a deep breath and walked inside.

Aline stood as Hugh entered, her stomach twisting into knots at the sight of his injuries. Half his face was a livid purple bruise, disappearing under the shaggy growth of unkempt beard. He looked dangerous, and if she had not known him to be gentle she would have shrunk from him.

He bowed to her formally, then glanced pointedly at the guards around him and raised an eyebrow questioningly. Embarrassment washed over Aline and she dismissed the men.

'Sir Hugh,' she began cautiously, once they were alone, 'I must apologise for your treatment yesterday. If I had known you were the man Sir

Godfrey had brought I would have come instantly. I trust you are beginning to recover?'

'I believe I will live. I received exceptional
care.' Hugh smiled at her, his eyes full of desire. 'Aline, when you came to me last night—'

'What I did last night was improper, and I
ask for your forgiveness,' Aline interrupted. She
stared at the ground, refusing to meet Hugh's
eyes. 'I have no excuse for my actions. It was
relief at finding you alive, nothing more.'

'Relief!' Hugh's voice was incredulous. 'You
fell into my arms because of *relief*! You don't
expect me to believe that for a moment, surely?'

He crossed to her, his smile warm and invit-
ing.

'What you believe is entirely up to you. It matters not to me,' Aline said. 'Hugh, you saved my
life yesterday, and I will always be indebted to
you, but we have nothing further to say to each
other. When I needed you most your allegiance
was with Stephen. I cannot forget what you did.'

'Is that the reason for the guards, Aline?' Hugh
asked, folding his arms and staring at her. 'Do
you think you have anything to fear from me?
Am I a prisoner still?'

His voice was not unfriendly, but nonetheless
Aline felt a pang of shame at the directness of
his questions. Then she remembered the way he
had restrained her as the physician had forced

274 Falling for Her Captor

bitter drugs down her throat, and what had happened afterwards.

'In truth, I don't know what you are, Sir Hugh,' she said coldly. 'Only that you are an enemy soldier among my people. I have seen where your loyalties lie. You stopped me killing Stephen once. How do I know I can trust you not to flee straight back to him with reports of our numbers?'

'How can you *trust* me?' Hugh's mouth dropped open in astonishment. 'You can accuse me of such treachery, Aline? Don't you understand I am devoted to you?'

With trembling fingers Aline drew up her sleeve to reveal the knife-wounds on her arm. 'I bear the scars of your *devotion*,' she said scornfully.

The colour drained from Hugh's face as his eyes fixed on the injury. 'What happened to you?' he asked, his eyes full of fury. 'Who sanctioned this?'

'*You* did! You left me at the mercy of the physician. He told me you had ordered him to keep me there by any means!' Aline shouted.

'But not that way!' Hugh insisted, his voice hoarse with shock. 'If I had known…'

He reached out a hand to touch her arm but Aline whipped it away.

'Have you any idea what it feels like to be

completely helpless? To think you might die at any moment?' she whispered, hugging herself tightly.

'Yes,' Hugh said quietly. He held his arms out to her, displaying the raw abrasions that ringed both wrists. 'Yes, I do.'

He pulled Aline's hands into his and looked deep into her eyes.

'Last night I came closer to giving up hope than ever before—until you came for me. When I think of how you must have suffered it almost kills me. I swear I will look after you. Nothing like that will ever happen again.'

'You will swear no such thing!' Aline said hotly. 'You waived any claim you may have had when you chose Stephen over me.'

'What I did had nothing to do with my loyalty to the Duke or to my country. Stephen was toying with you. You would never have succeeded in harming him,' Hugh said with exasperation.

'You should have let me try!' Aline raged.

'I should have let you put your head in the noose, you mean? Do you know what it is like to kill, Aline? You're no murderer. If you had succeeded, what do you think would have happened? Even if you were not executed you would never have been able to live with what you had done.'

Hugh's certainty in his actions shone through his voice and Aline found her temper flaring.

'You don't have the right to decide that for me! I am High Lady of the Five Provinces—not just some weak girl who can't look after herself. It isn't your place to protect me,' Aline said, pulling away from him. 'You relinquished any right you may have had when you chose to leave Roxholm.'

'I told you before—Stephen lied!' Hugh said, his jaw tight and a shadow of rage crossing his face. 'I did not leave willingly.'

His words sounded convincing, but Aline knew how much she wanted them to be true. 'Why didn't you tell me this before?' she asked cautiously.

'We were interrupted, if you recall,' Hugh remarked, arching an eyebrow. 'I thought you had confronted Stephen because of what he did to your maid. As soon as I discovered the true reason for your anger I challenged Stephen and we fought.'

He drew her to a low chair and helped her to sit, then stretched out at her feet as he told her of his escape. Aline sat silently, her mind in turmoil at his tale.

'I had already been banished from Roxholm before I came to you,' Hugh finished. He grimaced. 'Aline, I have lost my home, my wealth, my friends and my position. I have so little I can offer you. But please let me serve you,' he urged, reaching for Aline's hand.

He stared at her with an expression so intense Aline felt her knees go weak. When he looked at her with such desire plain on his face she knew it would be easy to forgive him almost anything.

'I don't know. I need time to consider your words.' She stood up and paced around the tent, hoping her own face had not betrayed her. 'Today, for the first time, I have to take my place as High Lady. My people will judge me worthy or unworthy based on what I decide to do regarding Stephen. I cannot think about this now. I must speak to my council. Please return to your tent. I will summon you later.'

Nodding her head in farewell, she swept from the tent before her composure crumpled completely.

The morning was a test of endurance for Aline. Tempers ran high as the councillors and nobles discussed the action to take against Stephen. She sat beside Godfrey, barely listening, her mind drifting back to her conversation with Hugh. A tumult of voices filled the tent, demanding vengeance and confrontation, planning assaults and assassination. Some suggested a siege; others preferred a quick assault.

Aline rapped on the table until there was

quiet, fighting to keep control of the situation. As silence descended a herald entered and spoke to Godfrey.

'The man you brought yesterday is outside, sir. He wishes to speak to the High Lady.'

Aline's breath caught in her throat. Her fingers squeezed Godfrey's arm involuntarily as shock and anger rippled through her. She had expressly told him to wait for her summons and he had disregarded everything she had said.

She realised all eyes were upon her.

'Send him in,' Godfrey instructed. 'I think now is an appropriate time to hear what he has to say.'

Aline sank into her seat, barely registering the words Godfrey whispered in her ear, and with no time to compose herself before Hugh stood before her.

Hugh's eye fell on Aline as soon as he entered. On her left sat a dignified-looking old man and on her right was Sir Godfrey. He had been leaning close to Aline, whispering into her ear, their blond heads almost touching. A twinge of jealousy twisted his guts.

He realised the room was silent and that he had been glaring openly at Sir Godfrey. He turned his attention to Aline, who met his gaze with an expression that looked far from welcoming. He stood stiffly, waiting for her to speak.

'Who are you, sir?' the old man sitting next to Aline asked.

Hugh stepped closer to the table, unaccustomed nervousness fluttering in his stomach, and wished he had a weapon. If these men decided to cut him down now he would never survive. 'I am Hugh of Eardham, cousin to Duke Stephen and, until lately, Captain of the Guard of Roxholm.'

At once there was the sound of swords being drawn and chairs scraping on wood as knights leaped to their feet. Every muscle in Hugh's body tensed in anticipation.

Aline was quicker. She rose and leaned on the table, arms spread wide. Surrounded by her men, she was a slight figure but when she spoke her voice rang out clear and Hugh's heart leaped with pride.

'Sheath your swords. This man saved my life yesterday. He is under my protection,' Aline said firmly.

'On what grounds?' a belligerent dark-haired man asked.

'On the grounds that I say so. That is enough,' Aline said sharply. 'Sir Hugh is not on trial. I vouch for him and that is enough. Moreover, he is my guest, and your question violates my hospitality!'

She walked round the table and stood before Hugh. In a voice so quiet he could barely hear it she muttered sharply, 'You treat me with no respect! I told you to wait for my summons, but you did not.'

'I beg your forgiveness for not waiting, but I wanted to be here,' Hugh said. 'You are not the only one with concerns about what must happen to Stephen.'

'Still you care about his wellbeing?' Aline snorted.

She faced Hugh, hands on her hips. A rose-coloured flush crept below the neck of her gown. She looked beautiful and fierce and Hugh had to force his eyes away from her.

She shook her head sadly. 'Very well, you may stay—but only as an observer. Don't think you have any part to play here.'

She motioned Hugh to be seated at the end of the table and returned to her own place. Sir Godfrey laid his hand on her arm protectively, his eyes fixed on Hugh. Hugh met the stare with challenge, though jealousy burned in his veins. He felt a small moment of triumph when Aline shook the knight's hand away with a gentle smile.

The leader of the scouting party returned,

delivering news that Stephen had established himself on Tegge's Eyot. 'We have the bridges on both banks of the river under observation,' the soldier reported. 'The Duke cannot leave the island without fighting across.'

'In that case we can wait until they are weak, then slaughter them like cattle at our leisure,' the dark-haired noble suggested.

'We are not so dishonourable, Sir Hennessey,' Aline insisted, glaring at him. 'We fight fairly, and we move tomorrow.'

Hugh's ears pricked up at Aline's words. He searched his memory, wondering why the knight's name was familiar.

'Weak!' Hennessey muttered. 'A High Lady with no taste for battle!' he sneered, showing a mouth full of broken teeth.

'It is *not* weakness,' Aline retorted, her cheeks flushing with indignation. 'Those men have as little choice in being there as our own have in being here. I would not see anyone die needlessly.'

'Perhaps we should reopen negotiations with the Duke regarding your marriage?' Hennessy suggested.

Aline flashed a look of disgust at him.

Hugh's fingers crept to where his dagger should have been; he cursed inwardly that it was not there.

Other voices took up the chorus.

'Your grandfather saw advantages to the match.'

'An alliance with Roxholm would have been beneficial for all involved.'

'You need to marry soon to secure your position.'

Aline pushed back her chair, glaring at the assembled men, her face white. 'Absolutely out of the question. I accept that I must marry, and it must be to Leavingham's advantage.' Her eyes met Hugh's and she faltered.

Hugh's heart began to race and he found he could barely swallow.

'I shall marry. But it will be when I choose— and never to that man!' Aline finished.

'Lady Aline is right.' Hugh spoke up. 'The decision should be hers alone. But that man has no claim and never will.'

'Why could you not just marry Stephen like you were supposed to, you wilful bitch?' Hennessey growled, lunging from his seat with a roar.

Hugh's memory clicked into place. He remembered why he knew the name.

With a cry of warning, he was moving towards Aline within a heartbeat.

Chapter Twenty-Two

Time seemed to slow as Aline watched Hennessey advancing. Her body felt like lead as she raised her arms to shield her face.

Hugh was already moving, his cry of warning ringing in her ears. He vaulted across the table, scattering cups and maps, and hurled himself between Aline and Hennessey. He pulled Aline to his chest, spinning his body away to protect her from the assailant and putting her head to his chest. Bringing his free arm round in an arc, he caught the nobleman square across the throat with a punch that felled him in one.

Hennessey sank to the floor, retching. Before he could rise Godfrey had his sword to the knight's chest.

Hugh tightened his grip on Aline, his chest rising and falling rapidly as he crushed her to him. 'Aline, my love, you're safe,' Hugh soothed.

His voice was calm. Only the force with

which he almost crushed her told Aline how
unsettled he was.

Wrapped in his arms, Aline knew there was
nothing else to fear. The words he had unconsciously said burned into her heart and she
wondered if Hugh could feel how fast her heart
pounded. She clutched on to him tightly as she
looked past him at the shocked faces of her subjects, their cries of alarm and amazement finally
registering.

'Traitor!' she muttered to Hennessey. 'What
part did you play in this matter?'

Hugh eased his hold on Aline. 'I know your
name, Hennessey. You were in collusion with
Stephen. It was you who brought the groom
Dickon into the High Lord's household, wasn't
it?' he said. His face changed, anger burning
in his eyes. 'Do you know the kind of man he
was? What he would have done to Lady Aline?'
he bellowed.

Aline squeezed Hugh's arm tightly, the intensity in his voice too stark a reminder of the emotions Aline wanted to deny existed.

'Not now,' she whispered. 'Please. The past
can't be changed but I want to forget that ordeal
ever happened.'

Hugh closed his eyes, as though reliving
it with her. When he opened them they were
hard. 'That man's death was at my hands—in

the name of defending *you*, my lady. Shall I add this one, too? Give me the word and I will run him through where he lies.'

A shiver ran down Aline's spine at his words. Since Hugh's gentle caresses and passionate kisses the night before she had all but forgotten the ferocious side of his nature. To be reminded in such a manner was unnerving.

'Did you murder my grandfather?' Aline asked Hennessey, her voice rising in anguish. 'You betrayed me to Stephen. What was your price?'

Hennessey laughed bitterly. 'Does it matter? I failed, did I not?'

Hugh swore under his breath and kicked Hennessey in the chest. Aline heard the crack of his ribs and was shocked at the satisfaction the sound gave her.

Guards arrived with chains and swords. They shackled Hennessey's arms behind his back.

'You'll never reign as High Lady,' he spat at Aline as the guards hauled him to his feet. 'You do not have the strength.'

'Take this worthless scum away,' Godfrey instructed the guards. 'The penalty for treason is to be hanged, drawn and quartered. Execute him accordingly.'

Aline closed her eyes, her stomach revolting at the thought of Hennessey's fate. She felt

Hugh's arm slide around her waist, holding her tight, and she leaned against him, feeling as though she would crumple to the ground without his vitality.

Upon hearing his sentence Hennessey's composure left him. His legs went limp and he fought as the guards dragged him through the tent. He passed Aline and twisted against his captors, hurling himself at her feet.

'Please, my lady, spare my life,' he snivelled.

'Would you have spared me *my* fate?' Aline asked, disgusted at his grovelling.

'Then grant me a quick death, I beg of you. Show me your compassion.'

Aline stared at the figure cowering before her. 'The compassion you derided as weakness?' she asked coldly.

Out of the corner of her eye she saw Hugh watching, his face impassive. Would he judge her for what she was about to do? She wished she could ask him, but here and now she was High Lady and she was alone.

'No mercy,' she said.

Hennessey's screams echoed in her ears as he was dragged away.

The execution took place within the hour. It seemed as though the entire camp had assembled to witness the demise of the traitor. Hugh stood beside Aline, his hand itching to slip around her waist and pull her to him, to take her away before the blood and screams started. They had not been alone since the incident had happened and the need to talk to her gnawed at him. He warned himself that such an intimate gesture would be inappropriate in front of her subjects, and with difficulty mastered his feelings.

Four soldiers appeared, dragging Hennessey's bound figure to the spot where a horse stood. It waited patiently, one end of a rope tied to its saddle, the other fashioned into a noose dangling over a high branch.

'Please, High Lady, forgive me. Show mercy,' Hennessey begged, throwing himself in her direction.

Every face turned to Aline. Hugh realised he had stopped breathing, even as he knew the man could do her no harm. Aline shook her head, the smallest of movements.

The executioner pulled the rope taut around Hennessey's neck. As the rope tightened Hennessey's pleas turned to threats and curses.

The executioner slapped the horse's rump. It lurched forwards and Hennessey's body was hoisted upwards, ending his abuse mid-sentence. His feet ran on air before he was cut down abruptly. The guards heaved him to the bench and a hush fell over the crowd as the executioner began his grisly task.

Hugh eyes slid to look at Aline, wanting to offer some kind of comfort but knowing he could do nothing in front of her men. She watched unflinching, her back straight and her eyes never moving from the sight. Her face was ashen and devoid of all emotion, and this unnerved Hugh more than he could articulate.

She looked small and fragile standing amongst the soldiers. Hugh imagined how easy it would be to take her into his arms and steal her away from such brutal sights.

The executioner dropped the axe, ending Hennessey's torment, and his corpse was dragged away.

Aline stood before the assembled men, pale-faced. Hugh saw her hands were trembling. In a clear voice she announced that the journey to Tegge's Eyot would begin at first light.

'We have been betrayed by one in whom the High Lord placed trust and he has paid the penalty, but we still have one enemy to face. Tomorrow we move against Duke Stephen and take retribution for his crimes.'

Amid a rousing chorus of cheers the camp became alive with activity. The nobles knelt before Aline. Each swore his loyalty, then left the execution ground to issue instructions to the troops, leaving Aline finally standing alone. Only Hugh lingered, watching from a distance.

Needing to reassure himself of her wellbeing, Hugh drew Aline to one side, turning her away from the bloodstained ground.

'However well deserved the death, it never becomes easier to witness it. Are you all right?' Hugh asked gently.

A look of anguish crossed Aline's face so briefly that had Hugh not known her well he would have missed it. She collected herself instantly and her eyes hardened. The sight cracked something inside Hugh.

'Of course I am all right. I am not weak, Hugh. Did you doubt that I could watch my enemies die without crumbling?'

Hugh opened his mouth to respond, then closed it again as he realised the truth of her accusation. 'I know you aren't weak, but you don't have to pretend to me,' he said. 'A sight like that could turn the strongest stomach. There is no shame in admitting that. Your men will not think anything less of you.'

'My men have shown me more respect today than ever before,' Aline said bitterly. 'All it took for that to happen was one death—one brutal show of torture.'

'Hennessey deserved to die for his actions,' Hugh said passionately. 'His death warrant was signed the moment he attacked you. I wish I had killed him myself and spared you that responsibility.'

'I wish you had. He should not have died like that. No man should. I could have stopped it with a word. I could have commanded him to be beheaded instantly. But I chose not to.' Aline closed her eyes, blinking away the tears that sprang suddenly to her eyes. 'How does that make me any better than Stephen?'

Hugh gripped Aline by the hands and stared deep into her eyes. Her tears fell freely now, her long lashes glistening. Hugh put a hand to her face and gently brushed away a stray tear with his thumb. He longed to kiss her again as he had last night, to drive the pain from her heart.

'You are nothing like him, Aline, because now you are flaying yourself alive at the thought of it. He would never do that. Too long ago he stopped listening to his heart, if indeed he ever did, and no one checked his nature.'

Aline stepped away and studied him in silence. There was a look of guardedness in her eyes that Hugh had not seen since the early days of their journey to Roxholm. It burned him to think that she still did not trust him. What more could he do to convince her of his loyalty? he wondered.

'*You* tried to watch over him,' she said finally,

with a small smile that caused Hugh's heart to leap. 'Never doubt that. You cannot spend the rest of your life holding yourself accountable for his actions.'

Aline smiled at him again and put her hand on his arm. Hugh's skin became alive to her touch.

'I did not thank you for what you did this morning—saving me from Hennessey's attack,' she said. 'I have said so many times that I don't need a protector, but yet again you were there to prove me wrong.'

'I would do it a thousand times if you would let me,' Hugh said, unable to keep the passion from his voice.

Aline's eyes widened as he spoke and Hugh realised how much he ached to hold her. To distract himself from the thought he dipped his head to look at where the scar on his chest lay. The wolf attack and the journey to Roxholm seemed a distant memory now.

'I was repaying the debt I owed you after you saved *me* from a different sort of animal.'

Aline placed her hand over the scar. Hugh wondered if she could feel the way his heart fluttered to her touch. Her grey eyes were serious as she held his gaze.

'And now the debt is settled, what will you do?' she asked.

Hugh looked at her in silence, unable to answer. Did she expect him to leave now she was safe? Did she want him to go? He couldn't bring himself to ask.

Unexpectedly Aline smiled. 'There will be a feast tonight. I will be expected to attend. Will you come with me?'

Hugh's throat tightened. 'It will be an honour,' he said gruffly.

'I will have servants bring you clean clothes,' Aline said. She smiled and wrinkled her nose. 'And the means for a bath.'

Hugh watched her depart, her soft laughter a song in his ears.

The camp was quiet as he made his way to his quarters, with most men engaged in their own business, so the voice that spoke from between the tents caused Hugh to jump.

'A word, please, Sir Hugh.'

Godfrey moved in front of the doorway, the expression on his young face stern and his shoulders set.

'There are two things you should understand. Just because you came to Lady Aline's aid today it does not mean you are trusted or liked. Also, I don't intend to apologise for my treatment of you yesterday. I believe it was entirely justified under the circumstances.'

From its abrupt delivery, the speech had obviously been prepared in advance. Hugh felt a

prickle of satisfaction that his rival had felt the
need to rehearse his words. His rational side
whispered that he would have done the same
under those circumstances, but nonetheless a
stab of jealousy went through him.

In the end his better nature won out.

'Your actions need no explanation. In fact
your loyalty does you credit,' Hugh said, his
voice calmer than he felt. 'I would have done
the same if the situation were reversed.'

Godfrey looked taken aback at the lack of hostility his words provoked. He rubbed his hand
through his golden beard thoughtfully.

Hugh bowed, and before Godfrey could respond brushed past him into the tent.

Chapter Twenty-Three

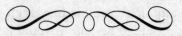

A large marquee had been transformed into a makeshift mess hall. Groups of men sat eating, their degree of importance signalled by their proximity to the highest table, where Aline sat with Godfrey and the other nobles. Hugh had not appeared and she kept slipping her eyes to the doorway, anxious that he might have decided not to attend.

Determined not to dwell on the man, Aline began to walk between the tables with an assured step, talking with confidence and provoking glances of admiration and oaths of loyalty from all she spoke to. No one who watched her would be able to say she was failing in her role, and no one would know how she had to force each smile to her face.

Her eyes fell on Hugh as soon as he entered the tent and her pulse raced. Not only had he bathed, he had trimmed his beard close and brushed his hair back into its familiar loose waves. The wool tunic he wore clung to his torso, drawing Aline's eyes to the shape of the muscles beneath. A rush of longing flowed through her veins as she remembered the way her hands had moved over that taut flesh as he lay on his bed the night before.

He sought her out and his face broke into a wide smile, his eyes lighting up. Aline's hand shook as she walked to greet him and led him to a seat at her right hand. Godfrey glared at Hugh with open hostility and Hugh bristled visibly. It was understandable, but Aline frowned at the sight.

'Aline, I don't understand. Just why is this man here?' Godfrey asked angrily. 'When I found you he was... Well, I had reason to believe he was intent on doing you ill. He should be under guard, not roaming about the camp freely, but you release him from his bonds with no explanation and now you invite this stranger to dine with us!'

'He isn't a stranger to me,' Aline snapped. 'I will not allow this behaviour,' she said sharply. 'Not tonight of all nights. I will not have fighting amongst friends.'

Both men stared at her. Godfrey's eyebrows shot up in surprise at her tone, but Hugh's eyes flashed with approval.

'Aline, you've changed.' Godfrey patted her hand kindly. 'You must have suffered great distress over the past few weeks. What you have endured would test the strongest man. No one would blame you if your mind were confused.'

Hugh was watching her carefully, his eyes keen.

'I am not confused, Godfrey,' she said haughtily, drawing her hand back. 'How could I have lived through the past weeks and not changed?'

She became aware that the surrounding men had ceased their conversations and were listening intently. Hugh was watching her, a smile on his face, and she raised her head higher, confidence surging through her.

'How can you trust that he isn't a spy?' Godfrey asked. 'He is no longer entitled to call himself "Sir," from what I understand. He's no more than a commoner.'

'I have made my feelings clear,' Aline said sharply. 'Tomorrow how many of these men will die because of what I must command them to do? I cannot bear the thought of so much bloodshed, and tonight my heart aches too much to watch people I care about attacking each other.'

'Sir Godfrey asks a fair question, my lady,' Hugh said placidly. He turned to Godfrey. 'The answer is that I can no longer remain loyal to my former lord after everything he has done. I would rather spend my days as a peasant than live as a lord under his rule.' He raised his voice so all could hear. 'Lady Aline, let me join your army tomorrow to fight against Stephen.'

No! Aline wanted to shout out in protest, the thought of Hugh fighting sending knives of terror through her.

Hugh pushed his chair back and strode to the centre of the room, all eyes upon him. He paused while the ripple of surprise died away. 'You all agree that Stephen must die for his aggression and the dishonour to Lady Aline? It is my responsibility and my right to see he is brought to justice, but I cannot reach him alone.'

There was an uproar that pounded like drumbeats through the room.

'Why should we let you?' Godfrey asked, and shouts of agreement filled the room.

'For too long I believed that serving Roxholm meant supporting Duke Stephen, but I was mistaken. My allegiance should always have been to my province, not to him. If I can be held responsible for anything it is for standing by him for too long. I intend to atone for that tomorrow.'

'Yes.'

Aline's voice rang clear, silencing the assembly. She felt light-headed as she raised her head and met Hugh's eyes.

'Yes, you may ride with us, Sir Hugh.'

She stood and with shaking hands raised her goblet to the assembled men. She wished them good fortune and inclined her head to receive their response, then left while her legs would still hold her upright.

Torches had been lit and a brazier was glowing by the time Aline returned to her tent. The room was stifling, and heady with the scent of sandalwood smoke, after the cool air outside. Her head ached, and despite the fur-lined cloak she had slung over herself she shivered. Even so, she imagined that had there been a hundred furs surrounding her nothing could thaw the ice in her bones.

Whilst in the presence of her men she had succeeded in remaining in control of her emotions. That she had not shown weakness publicly was a source of pride, but now she was alone and unseen her strength was ebbing.

A light flashed briefly behind Aline's closed eyes as the curtain across the doorway was parted. Even without looking Aline could sense it was Hugh, just from hearing him move across the space between them.

'Aline, am I intruding?' Hugh asked softly.

She burrowed her head further into to the pillow.

Hugh came closer. 'Talk to me, please,' he said.

Aline felt a hand on her shoulder and the weight of his body as he sat on the bed. Her skin prickled at his intimacy.

'Thank you,' he said. 'For what you said just now. I will not fail you, I swear.'

'I'm sorry for what Godfrey said.' She swallowed down a sob. 'I should never have asked you to sit with them. It was thoughtless of me!'

'No, they're protective of you, and I cannot blame them for their suspicion,' Hugh said.

She could feel the heat from his body as he moved closer.

'I'm so tired.' Aline sighed wearily. 'I want all this to be over.'

'It will be soon. Stephen dies tomorrow,' Hugh promised, his voice husky. 'I swear he will never hurt you, or anyone, ever again.'

The possibility of Hugh's death struck Aline again like a blow to the chest. 'I don't want you to fight,' she burst out.

'Would you care if I died?' Hugh asked. 'Would you mourn for me?'

'How can you even ask that?' Aline cried, standing up and staring at him.

Hugh stood to face her. His next words were almost as much of a shock as his earlier declaration had been.

'Because you are back with your Godfrey now. Why should you care what happens to me?

'Do you think I love Godfrey?' Aline asked in surprise. The idea seemed nonsensical and she had to stop herself from laughing aloud.

Hugh looked down, scuffing the rugs with the toe of his boot. The gesture seemed at odds with the confident figure he usually portrayed and Aline's heart gave a flutter at the thought of his jealousy.

'When he found us by the river I saw the rage in his eyes. What he did to me I would do to any man I thought would harm you. I assumed his feelings were the same as mine.'

Aline folded her arms. Though she tried to glare at Hugh she could not prevent a note of softness creeping into her voice. 'Godfrey is very dear to me. I have known him almost my whole life. His was the very first marriage proposal I refused.'

Hugh's face lit up. 'You refused him? Why?'

In the torchlight Aline was struck again by how handsome Hugh was when he smiled. She smiled back, her heart fluttering. 'Because I don't love him, of course. I told you once—no man has managed to capture my heart.'

Hugh took a step towards her. Aline felt weak, the need to touch him almost unbearable.

She knew she should tell him to leave, or leave herself. She knew she was going to do neither.

'No man?' Hugh asked, his eyes glinting as he moved closer.

There was barely a hand's width between them now.

Aline shook her head. 'I never wanted any man before. Not the way I wanted you last night.' She reached up and put her lips close to his ears. 'The way I want you still.'

With a growl of desire Hugh took her face between his hands and kissed her with a passion she had never encountered. At his touch Aline went weak. Tremors of excitement raced up and down her spine. No kiss she had ever experienced had created such delirium.

Sure her legs were about to give way, she leaned in towards him, her arms sliding around his neck before he could pull away. His powerful arms snaked around her waist and he lifted her off her feet, crushing her against him. Aline's head spun. She looked into Hugh's eyes and recognised the same intense desire she felt.

Hugh pulled away abruptly, releasing her from his embrace.

'Why…? What…?' she began.

'Oh, my lady, I want you more than I can ever say,' he said tenderly, the formality sounding like an endearment, 'but do you realise what this means? What we are about to do?'

Aline's hesitation lasted only seconds. She could no more stop than she could live without her heartbeat.

She curled her fingers in Hugh's hair and tugged him close again. He planted soft pecks across her cheeks, the soft hairs of his beard tickling her face. His tongue gently traced the silky curve behind her earlobe and she gave a sigh. She arched her back, her hips and breasts brushing against the length of his body, and she felt him harden in response. Hugh moved his fingers to begin to work at the ribbons at her shoulders, taking his time to undo each one, his eyes never leaving hers. He eased the dress off, leaving only the light chemise. In the sudden blast of cool air Aline shivered.

Hugh must have interpreted this as fear, because he paused again. 'We can still stop,' he murmured in her ear.

In response Aline kicked off her shoes and slid her hands under the cloth of Hugh's tunic, exploring his smooth torso. Her nails grazed the firm curve of his lower back and he growled deep in his throat, his eyes widening with animal hunger. He pulled the shirt over his head and let it fall to the floor. Aline reached out a hand, brushing her fingers lightly over his chest.

This small act seemed to send Hugh into a frenzy because he scooped her into his arms as though she weighed nothing and strode to the bed. He knelt and laid her lovingly down on top of the covers. She feared for a moment that he was going to leave, so she tugged him forwards until he joined her. They lay entwined, kisses becoming faster and harder, hands and mouths exploring curves and undulations.

Hugh rolled onto his back and with a few deft wriggles kicked off his boots and shrugged out of his breeches. Aline giggled unexpectedly at his ungainly movements and he twisted to look at her over his shoulder, a suggestive glint in his eye that caused her stomach to roll over. He lay down next to her and began teasing her chemise downwards until she was fully naked, dropping kisses onto her skin as it became available. He tugged the blanket across, cocooning them both.

The heady scent of Hugh's skin made Aline's head swim as he began to nibble gently at her earlobe. Her heart beat faster as she inclined her head to allow him easier access to the soft hollow of her neck. He stroked his hands gently over the swell of her breasts, lightly brushing his thumbs across her nipples, which hardened to his touch. She ran her hands lightly up Hugh's back, grazing him again with her nails. Hugh's eyes closed and he gave a low moan.

Aline twined her legs around his and pulled him closer, fingers clawing at his waist.

'Now. Please!' she begged urgently.

But Hugh would not be rushed. He took her breast into his mouth, sucking gently. By now Aline could barely contain herself; every touch sent her into further delights. Hugh's fingers circled her breasts, stroked her sides, lightly ran across her flat stomach and down further, until finally they reached their intended destination. She whimpered as his fingers brushed the soft hair, stroking gently between her legs, sending her spiralling into a whirlpool of pleasure. She writhed beneath his caress, clinging to him in a futile attempt to stop her head spinning. This was too much!

She reached out and brushed her hand against his most intimate part, feeling his hardness increase under her touch. Hugh moaned, then clasped his hand around hers and guided himself towards her. She tensed in readiness for the pain she had heard would accompany the first time.

'It will not hurt, I promise,' Hugh whispered, as though he had read her thoughts.

She curled her arms around his waist and impatiently pulled him closer.

There was a brief feeling of discomfort as he entered her, moving with a slow intensity, but the delicious friction of each stroke sent waves of pleasure through every part of her body. Then she was caught in the rhythm of Hugh's movements, echoing the rise and fall of his body with her own. A delicious pressure was humming through her body. Aline's breathy gasps grew faster, her nails digging into his buttocks.

Hugh covered her mouth with his lips as he moved inside her. She wrapped her legs around his legs, lifting her hips and arching her back to draw him closer. Hugh's urgency increased and the ferocity with which Aline pulled him in lit wild fires deep inside her. Layers of intensity piled one atop the other, lifting her up and drawing her down.

They cleaved together, stroking, kissing, clawing, biting, until Hugh could hold back no longer. He cried out, deep and guttural, as tremors racked his body. Aline's bones were flooded with liquid fire and she collapsed limply beneath the equally exhausted man.

They slept in each other's arms until the torches burned to nothing and the night turned to day.

Chapter Twenty-Four

The sky was barely light as Aline woke to the movement of Hugh slipping from the bed. The morning chill infiltrated the space he had vacated. She burrowed under the covers as a blast of cold air hit her naked body. Eyes closed, she lay for a moment, storing the memories of the previous night before they slipped away.

It had been a revelation; she had never suspected it was possible for her body to respond in such a way to a man's touch. Today her limbs felt as fatigued as if she had been on horseback for hours, and the delicious feeling of rawness inside her brought a flush to her cheeks.

Hugh had found a table with a jug and wine goblet laid out. He drained the goblet and filled it again, then carried it over to the bed and sat on the edge, shivering slightly in his nakedness. He offered the wine to Aline with a wide smile of such warmth that she felt a heave of lust deep inside her. Her eyes flickered over his body and she looked away shyly, struck by the enormity of what they had done. She pulled the covers up close around herself, as though they were a shield.

The smile left Hugh's face as he saw her solemn expression. He shook his head firmly. 'I will allow you no regrets today, Aline, no shame. I've wanted you for so long, but whenever we have got close you back away like a frightened doe, or try to tell me it does not mean anything. I won't accept that now. We both wanted to do what we did last night. You desired me as much as I did you.'

'Yes!' Aline cried, lifting her eyes to his. 'Yes, I desired you. For once in my life I wanted to know what passion truly was. To feel desired for myself—not for the wealth or power I represent.' Aline slipped her hand into his. 'I do not regret it for a moment, but it can never happen again and we can never speak of it. No man would have me if they knew what I have done.'

'No man *will* have you,' Hugh growled, his eyes fierce. 'You belong with me—you always have done.'

A pang of sadness twisted Aline's heart, greater than she had ever felt before. 'We both know that can never be. I am not free to choose my own path in life and my councillors will never permit me to marry for love. A woman's position is worlds apart from a man's. You can bed anyone you want without repercussion, yet because of one rash act my reputation will be in tatters if anyone finds out.'

'No one will find out,' Hugh said tenderly.

He climbed back into the bed and pulled Aline into a tight embrace. She nestled into the crook of his arm, knowing there was nowhere else she would rather be.

'I want you to understand you are not just some woman I have bedded. I know I can never have you, but when I am blind and in my dotage last night will still feature in my dreams—if I have the fortune to live that long.'

His eyes glinted as they roved over her body. A fresh swell of arousal made Aline shiver as she recalled his arms holding her steady as waves of pleasure carried her to the edge of delirium. She put her hand to his chest, tenderly stroking the bruises that adorned his chest, her fingers curling in the dark hair that covered the taut muscles.

Hugh sighed appreciatively, then kissed her thoroughly and for a long time before breaking off to stare at her seriously.

'I won't expose you to such censure. The sun is rising. I have to be gone before anyone thinks to look for me.'

Hugh's words burned in Aline's ears as he

slipped from under the sheets and began to move around the tent, locating his clothes. Aline sighed and rolled onto her side. She watched the way Hugh's muscles rippled when he lifted his arms to draw the tunic over his head. She told herself that Hugh was strong and an able swordsman—however, the time was coming when he must face combat, and the knowledge burned like a brand into her heart.

Hugh finished pulling on his boots then stood, running a hand through his tangled locks.

'You look sad, love. Don't be.'

Aline sat up, hugging her knees to her chest. 'I cannot stop thinking of what lies ahead today. I don't think I could bear the pain if you died.'

Hugh sat on the edge of the bed, drawing her head onto his chest with one hand while the other ran light fingers along her spine. Through his tunic she could feel the hard muscles beneath and hear the strong, steady rhythm of his heart.

'That is precisely why Stephen will not stand a chance against me,' he reassured her. 'When this is all over I will come back to you. How could I die, knowing you are waiting here?'

'Waiting here?' Aline could not hide her surprise at his assumption. 'But I won't be waiting here. I shall be with you at Tegge's Eyot!'

'What?' Hugh's voice was incredulous.

'Did you think I would not lead my people against our enemy?' Aline asked in surprise.

Hugh pulled away from her and sprang to his feet. 'No! It is too dangerous for you. Aline, I will not allow it!'

It took a moment for Aline to register his meaning, so unexpected was his response. She climbed from the bed, dragging the sheet with her. She wrapped it about her body and faced him, hands on hips.

'*Allow?* I do not think that you are in a position to "allow" me to do anything, Sir Hugh!' she exclaimed hotly.

Hugh drew a sharp breath. 'I am "Sir" now, am I?' he asked, his voice edged with a coldness that sent shivers of misery through Aline. 'And for what? For trying to keep you from danger?'

Aline's cheeks flamed at his words and her lip curled. Hugh watched her warily, his stance reminding Aline of an animal ready to flee a hunter at any moment.

'You have no right to command me to stay or go!' Aline ranted. 'I went to bed with you, but that does not mean I gave you control over my destiny. You are not my guardian or my husband, with the right to control me!'

Her voice was harsher than she'd intended and Hugh jerked his chin as though she had struck him physically. She instantly regretted the words as they left her lips.

Hugh's mouth twitched down at the corners. 'Of course you are correct, my lady. I would not presume to have such a claim on you,' he muttered. 'Perhaps it is best if I leave.'

He bowed and walked to the doorway stiffly, his hands bunched into fists at his side.

Aline gasped in distress. 'No!'

At the sound Hugh stopped, stood for a moment with his back to her. When he turned his face was thunderous. They stood unmoving, separated more by their words than by distance.

'No,' she repeated.

Her voice was little more than a whisper and she feared that if she had to force the word any louder her voice and composure would both crumble.

Hugh moved towards her, his expression transforming from anger to tenderness, and though Aline wanted to hurl herself into his arms she held her hands up, a barrier between them.

'Please don't leave like this. I'm sorry, Hugh. I don't want to quarrel with you. But do not command me to stay here while you go to face Stephen,' she said. 'I am High Lady of the Five Provinces. I will not send my men off to die for me and then wait here in safety. If you cannot or will not accept that then we have nothing more to say to each other.'

Hugh stuck his shoulders back and lifted his chin. 'It is not my place to stop you, however much I wish to protect you. There are no lands or wealth I can display before your council that could win me your hand. I can never play a part in your life. But do not expect me to be happy about you risking death. Now, if you will excuse me, I have to go and prepare for battle.'

He turned and walked from the tent.

Aline watched him depart, then threw herself back onto the bed in despair, her mind assailed by impossible decisions.

A thin rain started to fall as Hugh walked back to his own tent, the greyness mirroring his mood perfectly. He was not sure if he was more furious with Aline for her refusal to see sense or for her taunt about husbands. He knew he had nothing to offer her. Stephen had taken everything and left him a shell, filled only with his love for someone far beyond his reach. He should have killed the bastard when he had the chance! A boiling rage flared within him and he smashed his fist against the tent pole.

'Please, sir, you must come with me.'

A herald was loitering nearby. He led Hugh to the armoury, where the quartermaster provided him with a mail shirt, a thickly padded surcoat and a broadsword. Hugh hefted the sword in his hand and was surprised at how heavy and cumbersome it seemed. He had not realised until that point how much his body had been weakened by his ill treatment. He should have been training for his battle with Stephen. Too late now! He sighed deeply.

Walking back out into the drizzle, Hugh felt a further sense of isolation. People passed him by with scarcely a glance. He had no men of his own to command, nothing to do now but wait.

As he stood buckling his sword Godfrey walked up to him.

'I saw you leaving Lady Aline's tent at first light,' Godfrey said darkly. 'What were you doing in there?'

It was on the tip of Hugh's tongue to tell Godfrey to mind his own business, but half a truth was better than an outright lie. The young man cared about Aline almost as much as he did. Perhaps he could be an ally now.

'I was speaking with Lady Aline,' he answered. He frowned as he added, 'She intends to come to Tegge's Eyot and I was trying to persuade her otherwise.'

'And you failed?' Godfrey asked. His forehead wrinkled into lines of worry. 'If you knew her at all you would know that once she has made her mind up she rarely changes it—especially not if she is ordered to do something,' he said.

A horn blew, loud and shrill, calling the soldiers to assemble. A burst of colour flashed amid the crowds: Aline's skirts. Hugh and Godfrey stared at her, momentarily united in their concern. Hugh watched her movements keenly, drinking in the sight of her and fixing her image in his mind as though she was an amulet. He knew Godfrey was watching him but he no longer cared.

'I don't like you, and I don't trust you, but for some reason Lady Aline seems to hold you in high regard,' Godfrey said sternly. 'I don't know what you have done to convince her of your worth, but know this: if at any point Aline comes to harm because of your actions I will kill you. Slowly. Over a number of days.'

'Thank you for your warning, but there is no need, Sir Godfrey,' Hugh said, narrowing his eyes. 'Anyone who attempts to harm Aline will have killed me already, since that is the only way I will ever cease protecting her.'

He saw in an instant that if he wanted to safeguard Aline there was only one possible course of action and the start of a plan began to form in his mind. He stalked off towards the assembling troops, leaving the younger man to follow in his wake.

Aline was standing by a horse when he arrived. Her hair had been plaited thickly and coiled into a net at the back of her head. Over her dress she wore a waistcoat of thick leather. Slung over the saddle were a crossbow and a quiver full of bolts. Despite his dark mood Hugh smiled at the memory of her standing over him in another place and time, her eyes flashing fiercely as she held a bow to his heart.

'We aren't going to be shooting wolves, my lady, and if you think a scrap of leather will protect you from swords or arrows you are mistaken,' he said grimly, folding his arms.

'Thank you for your advice,' Aline said coldly, drawing back. 'Unless you have anything else to say I suggest you find your horse. I have made my decision and there is no point delaying any longer.'

Her face twisted with misery and a knot formed in Hugh's throat at the sight. He wished he could unspeak the words.

'Then, as this may be the last chance we have to speak, please walk with me for a moment,' Hugh asked.

She hesitated and Hugh feared she would refuse, then she dropped the reins and walked out of sight of the watching men. Hugh followed, and when she stopped he reached for her hands and trapped them tightly between his own.

'Please reconsider. I don't intend to insult you by asking you to stay here. I only want to know you are safe,' he whispered. He bowed his head and kissed slowly and deliberately along the ridge of each of Aline's knuckles. 'The thought of you being within Stephen's reach again is enough to drive me to madness,' Hugh continued.

He pulled her closer. She did not resist as he folded his arms around her, though she did not return his embrace. He held her tightly, still wounded by the harsh words that had passed between them but drawing strength from their closeness.

'I am not scared of death,' Hugh said softly, his forehead touching hers, 'but the thought that I might die and he would take you, and I could do nothing to stop him, terrifies me more than I can say.'

'I am not scared to die either,' Aline replied. 'If I thought I could kill Stephen myself I would do so, but I know I cannot. I am too weak—as I discovered to my cost before.'

A look of intense anger crossed her face.

'When I think what he did to my grandfather, how he has hurt so many people, I feel consumed with hate. The idea of what he planned for me terrifies me, too. That is why I need to see him die. I have to be there to know he is truly dead.

And if I asked *you* not to fight, would you stay behind?' Aline asked. 'Of course you wouldn't.'

Hugh stared into Aline's eyes, full of determination and fear. 'If your mind is made up then please do one thing for me. Stay at the back of the troops. I don't want my mind to be distracted with worrying about you when I should be fighting,' he said bluntly.

He could not bear to see the look on her face at his harshness, so without a backwards glance he returned to the gathering, his eyes searching for Godfrey. He knew what he had to do.

Chapter Twenty-Five

Tegge's Eyot. The name sent shivers down Aline's spine as they neared the island. All too clearly she could picture the desolate outcrop in the midst of the churning river. She had visited the old fortress once as a child and spent an afternoon investigating the ancient granite seats and weathered throne, running her fingers along the carved faces and letters. The crypt, with the skulls and bones of past High Lords, had given her nightmares for weeks. She had never returned, but the memories had stayed with her ever since.

At some point in the past the island had been a setting for tournaments: a place for men to display their strength, win fortunes and settle old scores. Aline and her brother had laughingly played at sword-fighting in the high-walled arena. Now the thought that real blood would once again be shed on the dusty earth floor chilled her bones. Not for the first time her throat seized at the knowledge that men were ready to die in her name, and that many would do so.

Aline rode halfway down the trail of men, accompanied by Godfrey and Hugh. Though her intention had been to lead, their combined protest had convinced her she would be safer there. She allowed them this one concession to keeping her safe. The two men had been riding together since they left the camp, talking intently. Hugh's face was solemn and his brow creased, though they did not appear to be quarrelling. Aline's spirits rose to see that the two of them appeared to have reached an accord.

She glanced across at Hugh. His waves of tangled hair were pulled back and tied at the nape of his neck. Like all the soldiers in the procession he wore a thigh-length hauberk of fine chainmail. Unlike the others he wore no tabard bearing colours, only a leather surcoat buckled loosely. The significance was clear to Aline: he was an outcast now and showed no allegiance to anyone. Not for the first time she found her heart torn in two at the thought of what he had given up.

Hugh must have sensed Aline watching because he turned and stared at her. Despite the gravity of the situation Aline felt her heart flutter like a caged bird. She vowed that whatever else happened today this man must not die.

Hugh turned back to Godfrey and spoke again. Her friend cast a look in her direction, then nodded brusquely.

The procession drew to a standstill when the trees began to thin. They were getting close to the open fields that surrounded the bridge to the island. All around them the men were laying down their weapons and gathering into huddles to share flagons of wine.

Hugh dismounted and held out his arms to Aline. He had not spoken to her since she had rejected his final plea, but as she climbed from the saddle he moved one hand to the centre of her back, holding it there perhaps a moment longer than was decent. It took all her resolve not to throw herself into his arms in front of everyone.

She declined all offers of food and drink, knowing that the knot of terror in her throat would allow nothing to pass, and paced back and forth across the clearing, unable to find peace. She felt as frustrated as a caged bear and just as helpless. The men sat eating together and she knew they were watching her anxiously. Let them! She did not care about hiding her agitation, and walking was better than weeping.

'We should move out soon,' Godfrey said. 'With luck we will have another few hours of light.' He turned to Hugh. 'That should be time enough to find Stephen and do what you have to do.'

What you have to do. Aline frowned, wondering about the meaning of Godfrey's words and infuriated at the thought of them keeping something from her. She intercepted a look between Hugh and Godfrey, something akin to acknowledgement or confirmation. She stalked back to her horse and swung herself into the saddle, leaving the men in discussion. Movement in the undergrowth caught her attention. She'd raised a hand, about to cry a warning, when a dozen men wearing the colours of Roxholm leaped from behind the trees with swords raised.

Hugh drew his sword and launched himself forwards with a bellow. He cut two down where they stood. Two more came from the right. With a calmness that took her by surprise Aline reached for the crossbow. Her bolt caught an attacker full in the chest as he ran towards her horse. Aline looked into the face of the dying man and a feeling of nausea overwhelmed her. He was barely older than she was.

She dropped the bow and slipped from the saddle to kneel by the fallen man. Her blood pounded in her ears and she feared she might faint. Hugh had stopped fighting and was staring down at her, his eyes filled with compassion.

They began moving at the same time, meeting in a powerful embrace with arms locked around each other.

'I killed him.' Her voice rose with shock. 'I just—' She broke off, her throat full of sorrow.

Hugh held her tightly until her shaking ceased. 'Nothing can prepare you for battle,' he said softly. 'No matter how many training exercises you do, and however well you wield a sword or bow, you cannot anticipate the reality. Do you understand now why I wanted you to stay behind?'

Aline wrapped her cloak tightly about herself, regret coursing over her that she had been too proud to obey him. 'I wish it were finished.' She sighed wearily. 'I cannot bear the thought of any more bloodshed. How many more have to die today?'

Hugh took her by the shoulders. He glanced once at Godfrey, then fixed her with his blue eyes. 'There will be no need for bloodshed, and I will end this,' he said. 'Godfrey is going to lead a detachment to secure the area. When we get to Tegge's Eyot I intend to call a truce. I'm going to challenge Stephen to a duel.'

At first Aline did not understand his words. She stared at him uncomprehendingly, but then, as her brain pieced together what he had said, her knees began to shake.

'No!' she cried, clutching him by the shoulders as though she could prevent him leaving.

Hugh waved an arm around at the ranks standing silently watching. 'Whom would you choose instead?' he asked. 'Which of these men deserves to die in my place? How many lives is my life worth?'

Aline looked at the floor, knowing there was no answer to his question, but the thought of what he was planning sent fear coursing through her veins.

Godfrey strode up to Hugh and clasped him by the shoulder. 'Are you ready?' he asked. 'We will give you a half-hour start.'

Aline thought back to the two men riding together, their heads bent in discussion.

'How long have you been planning this?' she asked accusingly.

'Since I realised there was no way of preventing you from coming,' Hugh said simply. He gestured to the bodies littering the ground. 'You need to trust me when I tell you a battlefield is no place for a woman. You fought well just now. I know you can shoot. But how would you fare against ten men? Against a hundred?'

Aline tore away from him angrily. 'And were you going to tell me? Or let me wait to discover it from other mouths or when I saw your corpse? You speak of trust, but you did not even have enough confidence in me to tell me of your plans. How can I ever trust you?'

'You can trust me not to expose you to danger, however much you protest that you are happy to expose yourself to it,' Hugh answered, folding his arms sternly.

'You don't have the right to decide for me what is safe and what is not,' Aline raged, her face flushing.

'Perhaps not,' Hugh replied. 'But I have the right to decide where I choose to take you, and I have the right to challenge Stephen.' He exhaled deeply and folded his arms. 'This is about more than avenging you, as important as that is. I cannot stand by and allow the Duke to continue his reign. I have nothing left of my former life: my lands are forfeit and if I return to Roxholm my life will be, too. If I defeat Stephen then I will claim his title. I have to do this to have any chance of a future.'

Misery tore into Aline's belly. She glared at him, digging her nails into her palms to stop herself crying. 'And you kept all this from me? Then, if that is your decision, when this is over we shall never see each other again.'

Hugh winced at her words. 'If that is what you wish, my lady, then that is how it must be.

I would rather risk earning your hatred for ever than see you die in battle.'

He mounted his horse and wheeled about to address the company, his voice firm and clear.

'I am the last remaining blood relative of Rufus, the previous Duke of Roxholm. I intend to end Stephen's rule and claim the title of Duke. If I win there will be no one who can say I did not do so justly. I ask now, all of you here, that you will aid me in this.'

A loud cheer went up from the troops.

'Good,' Hugh said. 'Then there is no time to waste.'

The rest of their journey to the island was un-interrupted. Aline and Hugh rode silently, side by side. Aline's head was bowed, and whenever Hugh stole glances at her he could not help but notice how her hands trembled. He could understand her resentment at his secrecy, but the thought of seeing her no more wounded him to the core of his being. If he survived he would think about how to win her forgiveness, and if he didn't... He gripped the reins tighter and tried to push that thought to the back of his mind.

The assault had ended by the time Hugh's company arrived. Godfrey's men must have been efficient, or the waiting army unprepared. There were fewer bodies than Hugh had feared.

The young knight and his surviving men were at the river-edge, resting after their exertions. Sharp knives of envy tore Hugh's stomach as Aline jumped from her horse and hugged him tightly.

'You did well,' Hugh said, patting the younger man's arm.

'Most surrendered,' Godfrey explained. 'I think that no one wants to die for the Duke.'

Two dozen or so soldiers sat back to back. Their arms and legs had been bound together and they wore grim expressions as they contemplated the fate that awaited them.

Hugh dropped to one knee by the group and spoke to one of them. 'Do you recognise me? Do you know who I am?' Hugh asked.

His answer came immediately as the man gasped, a look of joy and disbelief on his face.

'My lord, we will surely win now you are here!'

'I'm not here to fight for Stephen,' Hugh said. 'Tell me where to find him. He belongs to me!'

The man nodded his head towards the island. 'He's at the stone circle. He won't leave the throne. He sits there, declaring himself High Lord.'

'How many do you think remain loyal to him?' Hugh asked.

The man shook his head and shrugged. 'Not

many, I would imagine. There is talk that he has gone mad.'

With a nod at Godfrey's herald Hugh strode to the water's edge. The herald reached for the horn on his belt and blew it loudly. Three long blasts rang out around the island. An expectant hush fell over the assembled men. From somewhere in the distance came answering notes, joined by a further blast from elsewhere. Slowly figures began to appear around the island.

'Lay down your weapons, all of you!' he demanded. 'I call a truce. I am here to challenge Stephen.'

'Sir Hugh, have you taken leave of your senses?'

The speaker was a knight Hugh had little fondness for.

'You take it upon yourself to make this decision without any consultation of the council. Do you expect us to stand by while the fate of our province is decided in this way?'

'You stood by and did nothing while the High Lady was held captive in our city. Why change now?' Hugh snapped, his temper rising. 'You knew Lady Aline was there, and under what circumstances. Our province has been dishonoured by your inaction—because of our tolerance of Stephen's misdeeds as much as by what he has done. By laws older than any of us here, I have the right to do this by my birth.'

By his side Aline stood firm, her face pale. She still had not spoken to him since their arrival. He spoke to everyone but knew in his heart the words were meant for her.

'There is much we have to atone for, all of us.'

Aline turned to face him. Hugh could not tell what she was thinking but her eyes tore into him.

'Summon your men,' he instructed the knight. 'Bring everyone, no matter whose side they fight on. I want everyone to witness this.' He turned to Aline and held out a hand. She brushed it away as he knew she would.

'I'm coming with you,' Aline said, her voice fierce and her jaw set. She gave him a look of challenge, as though daring him to try to stop her. 'If it is your right to challenge Stephen, it is equally my right to witness his end.'

A cold sweat trickled down Hugh's back as he weighed his chances of preventing her going. A rush of love enveloped him, almost knocking him sideways. The woman he had fallen in love with would never change her mind, or she would cease to be that woman. Surrounded by her men she would be safe, even if he could not guard her himself.

'Very well, my lady, if you insist.'

* * *

Together they walked towards the island. Hugh took a hard look at the bridge spanning the river between the mainland and Tegge's Eyot. It was wide enough for perhaps eight men to fight alongside each other and was roughly the length of ten carts. The river churned underneath the arches, sending spray across the stones. With no walls at the side a slip would mean a tumble into the icy water and almost certain death.

He thought again of Aline fearlessly hurling herself from the riverbank, and the panic he had felt believing he could not save her. He held her arm tighter, reassuring himself more than her.

As though reading his thoughts, Aline sighed with exasperation. 'I am not going to jump, Hugh, don't worry. I won't fall either. When will you understand I do not need to be treated like a child or a fragile maiden, capable of nothing more arduous than needlework or dancing? After everything that has passed between us, don't doubt me now.'

'I don't doubt you. I just want you to do as I ask,' Hugh said honestly.

Her eyes widened at his words and she studied him closely. 'I will not forget that you kept your intentions from me, nor forgive you,' she said coldly. 'I will stand by your side and face

Stephen with you, but I still have not changed my mind. Once the battle is over I am leaving.'

The soldiers of Leavingham had pushed further forwards and the gates to the old keep lay open. The men now guarding it saluted as Hugh and Aline walked through into the courtyard.

'Spread the word that I am here,' Hugh commanded. 'Gather as many you can find who will support my claim to the title.'

With a feeling of anticipation growing in his belly Hugh watched the three men run off together, yelling their message. He looked around, his eyes wary for signs of danger. Stephen's men had been camping in the walled courtyard and the debris of daily life littered the ground: abandoned tents, discarded cooking pots and fire pits. Other than these lifeless forms the courtyard was deserted.

'Where is Stephen?' Hugh wondered aloud.

'I know where he'll be,' Aline said. She crossed the courtyard and walked through the great gateway as though in a dream.

Hugh unsheathed his sword and followed, anxious to keep her close.

They turned a corner and came upon an imposing archway guarded by four sentries wearing Roxholm's colours, their pikes held menacingly forwards.

'Let us through or cut me down,' Hugh snarled.

The men exchanged glances, then lowered their weapons. Hugh stepped through the arch into the grassy area beyond. Twelve seats set in a horseshoe shape faced a large stone throne. On the throne sat a man, a sword in his hands. Aline halted as she saw him, two bright spots appearing on her pale cheeks. She looked at Hugh, her eyes wide with unspoken fear.

'I'll keep you safe, I swear,' he said. 'You have nothing to fear now. Wait here.'

He stepped past her and walked to where the figure sat.

At Hugh's approach the man looked up, his face transforming into a mask of pure hatred. Hugh set his shoulders and glared back.

'Hello, Stephen,' he said.

Chapter Twenty-Six

Stephen leaped to his feet with his sword out at arm's length. His lips curled in derision but his hands shook visibly, causing a shiver of satisfaction to travel up Hugh's spine at the sight. Hugh had barely enough time to unsheathe his sword before the Duke hurled himself forwards. There was a sliding wail of metal as the two weapons met. The shock of the blow reverberated up Hugh's arm as Stephen's sword flew from his hand. It slithered across the marble floor and came to rest by one of the seats.

Every muscle in Hugh's body ordered him to strike Stephen down and his hand tightened on the hilt of his sword. Rage coursed through his veins, goading him to do it quickly, to put an end to the man cowering before him.

An urgent voice behind him shouted, 'No! You don't want to do it this way!'

He lowered his weapon as Aline ran to his side, breathlessly.

'You! You can't be here!' Stephen's voice rose to a shrill howl as he stared at Aline. 'How did you survive the river?' He turned to Hugh, a cruel smile on his face. 'Do I have you to thank, cousin, for returning my bride to me?'

At Hugh's side Aline shrank back. Hugh's arm twitched involuntarily as he yearned to draw her close. A blinding rage swept over him at Stephen's words, coupled with fear that Aline might even now believe the lies. He hefted the sword again.

'Aline will never be your bride,' Hugh spat harshly. 'She belongs to no one but herself. I am here for you, Stephen.'

Stephen gave a low moan of terror, raising his arms to shield his face.

'I survived the river, and everything before that, because I had a good man to aid me,' Aline said scornfully. 'A better man than you could ever understand how to be.'

Hugh felt his heart lurch at her words.

Stephen's jaw dropped open. 'Somebody kill them both!' he screamed.

'Sit down,' Hugh barked.

Unexpectedly Stephen's knees buckled and he sank back into the throne. His face reddened and his eyes bulged in fury.

Hugh stared back, lowering the sword but not sheathing it. His loathing for the man was so strong it seemed almost tangible, coalescing into the wind that blew around them, so sharp he could almost taste it.

Rapidly the arena began to fill. Men from both sides huddled in groups, eyeing each other with cold, suspicious looks. Satisfied that enough people were present, he turned to Stephen, who was slumped in the throne, a grim expression on his face.

'Stephen, son of Rufus, you are responsible for the murder of the High Lord, the kidnap of Lady Aline of Leavingham, the ruin of our province and other misdemeanours too numerous to list.'

More men had arrived and Hugh began to spot familiar faces in the crowd: men he had trained, friends he had drunk with, nobles he knew well.

'This man is not fit to rule!' Hugh shouted. He looked across the crowd, his eyes flashing rapidly from face to face. 'Those of you who would accept me as your Duke lay down your weapons. I want no more blood spilled today.'

A ripple of shock spread through the crowd, accompanied by cheers and considerably fewer shouts of protest. There was a clattering as swords and pikes were dropped. Many men fell to their knees.

'No more blood?' Stephen spat, his voice thick with undisguised contempt. 'What has softened you, cousin? Your loyalty died the instant you set eyes on her, didn't it?'

'It didn't die soon enough,' Hugh answered harshly.

Stephen swore under his breath, casting a look of hatred at Aline. Unconsciously she moved closer to Hugh. He held a hand out and she slipped hers into it, their fingers interlocking. She smiled at him faintly—friends again, however briefly.

'I should have killed you while I had the chance and taken her before your blood stopped pumping. Maybe I still will,' Stephen spat. 'The people will never accept you as Duke.'

'Look around you, Stephen. Why have they not hacked me to pieces in your defence?' Hugh waved his arm across the throng of men listening intently to the exchange. 'You have a point, though, cousin. I want nobody to say I took the throne without just cause and legitimacy, so I intend to win the title by fair means. Cousin, I formally challenge you for the title of Duke of Roxholm.'

'On whose authority?' Stephen sneered.

'He acts on the authority of the High Lady.'

Aline spoke loudly enough for the whole gathering to hear. She walked up to Stephen, back straight and head high. As quick as a flash she brought her hand round and delivered a slap to Stephen's cheek that rang out loud. The Duke recoiled with a cry of astonishment.

'I would slaughter you like a dog for what you have done, if the choice was mine alone,' Aline said scornfully, 'but Sir Hugh has more honour. Now, without your army to protect you, do you have the courage to face Sir Hugh, or are you the cowardly worm I take you for?' Her eyes sparkled and her expression was victorious.

Hugh cheered inwardly at her words. He had been wrong to try and stop her coming; he knew that now. A shadow of regret passed over his heart that he had been so determined to shield her that he had sacrificed the closeness they had shared. He swore that if he survived he would find her and tell her.

'So the abductor becomes the champion?' Stephen sneered, his eyes narrowing. 'I never took you for a romantic fool, Hugh. Do you think that by doing this she'll let you into her bed?' He leered at Aline.

Hugh's heart soared as a burst of love shot through him. Images of their lovemaking rose unbidden in his mind and a warm glow enveloped him, renewing his strength. He could tell Stephen everything that had passed between them, could throw that defeat in his face, but he knew he would not. Those memories were theirs alone.

'What do you propose?' Stephen asked.

'We settle this the old way. It seems appropriate in this setting. Succession by combat. We fight to the death.'

The expression on Stephen's face made Hugh's heart sing. It changed from disbelief to anger, before finally settling on fear. His eyes rolled back in his head and his lips twitched wordlessly.

Hugh brought his face close to Stephen's ear. 'Your death will be clean and quick, I promise you that.'

Stephen crossed his arms and spoke in a voice dripping with spite. 'I agree to your terms. I bested you before and I can do it again. We meet in an hour, as soon as the sun has crossed the river.'

After that the protocol of combat had to be observed. Nobles from both sides crowded round to organise a selection of weapons, or hurried off to arrange rooms. Aline stood to one side, silently watching. Hugh noticed that Stephen didn't take his eyes from her. He longed to enfold Aline in his arms, to drive out the anxiety in his belly, but she turned away as he caught her eye. She had clearly not forgotten the vow she had made.

Hugh walked over to one of Roxholm's no-

bles—the knight who had questioned his announcement. 'Give me your word that, whatever
the outcome of today, no harm will come to Lady
Aline and Stephen will not be allowed to rule
unchecked.'

The man nodded and clasped his hand across
his breast. 'I swear that Roxholm will attempt
nothing regarding Lady Aline.'

Hugh breathed a little more easily. He realised
with a start that Aline had moved closer and had
been listening intently. He smiled at her reassuringly. 'You'll be safe, Aline. Whatever end I
face it will come easier to know that.' Her eyes
brimmed with tears as he spoke and, not wanting to embarrass her, he walked away.

'Come with me, please, Sir Hugh.' A soldier
stood to attention, then motioned Hugh to follow.

'Where are you taking him?' Aline's voice
was full of alarm and she hurried alongside.

'It's part of the tradition of combat,' Hugh told
her reassuringly. 'It allows the fighters to prepare for the ordeal, and ensures neither tries to
flee before the fight.'

'Do people try?' Her voice was hopeful.

Hugh stopped walking and faced her. 'Some
do. If they cannot face the thought of death.'

She laid a hand on his arm and looked up into
his face. Hugh tensed. Was she about to plead

with him not to fight? He did not think he could face having the same argument once more.

Instead she smiled, and in her eyes Hugh saw pride and something more. Something he dared not even name—had not dared hope to see again.

'But not you,' she said.

Her words ripped through Hugh's heart. For a moment he wavered in his decision. What use were titles and land without her by his side? Let someone else dispose of Stephen. The moment passed as soon as it had arisen. He had come too far now to turn back.

'After everything that has led me here? Nothing could be further from my mind,' Hugh said gravely. He cast a final look at her and followed the soldier into the keep.

It was the slowest hour of Hugh's life. At one time Tegge's Eyot had housed a permanent garrison, but owing to many years of peace it had been stood down over a decade ago. Now the rooms were barely furnished, with mildewed tapestries and carpets. Hugh lay back on a lumpy bed and stared at the ceiling.

Now he was facing what could be his final hour he felt oddly calm—or maybe it was simply exhaustion that numbed his senses. If he died today he would be alone, with no comforting arms to hold him at the end. But Aline was safe. He had achieved that much at least. He closed his eyes and tried to summon her face, but it slipped from his mind like mist, leaving only a vague sense of longing.

A knock at the door woke him from his day-dream. The hour was not yet up, surely?

He swung himself off the bed to see who it was.

Hugh was halfway from the bed when Aline entered. Her entire body tingled with longing. The briefest flicker of amusement crossed his face, then he looked at her sternly and she fal-tered.

'A vigil is supposed to be a solitary affair, Aline. Though it does not surprise me that you disregard the conventions.'

She looked at the floor, embarrassed. 'I couldn't stand the thought of you being here alone. I came to keep you company, but if you would prefer mc to leave…?'

'There is no one I would rather have by my side as I wait. I am glad you came,' Hugh said tenderly. 'I know we must part, but I would hate to do so as enemies.'

Aline's lip began to tremble. She wanted to hurl herself into his arms, to beg him to change his mind, but she knew it would be futile. The time had long passed for that.

'You aren't my enemy,' she whispered. 'Never believe that.'

Hugh's expression softened. He held his arms outstretched towards her. Aline shook her head, knowing that she was hanging on to her composure by a thread.

'I don't need comforting,' she said resolutely.

'Maybe not,' Hugh said, 'but at this moment in time I do.' He pulled her into his arms before she could protest.

At his touch, flames ignited inside Aline. She reached her trembling hands around his broad back, but instead of the warm, supple flesh she'd anticipated beneath his shirt her fingers met cold iron links. She raised shocked eyes to meet Hugh's. Visions of his death flashed before her eyes and her head swam. Aline wanted to scream against the treacherous thought that went through her mind: *this is the last time we will do this.*

Hugh's face was solemn, and he answered her thoughts with a sad smile. 'It's hard to believe this is the same day I woke in your arms,' he whispered softly.

They held each other silently, tightly. A wave of sadness threatened to overwhelm Aline at the thought, and she pressed tighter into Hugh's embrace, wishing she could feel the warm contours of his body instead of the chill metal. She breathed in deeply, remembering the first time she had caught his scent: leather and horses and something uniquely *him* that took her breath away.

She clutched on to Hugh, her lips seeking his. He met her kiss hungrily, his hand cupping the back of her head, drawing her closer. She melted against him, all her resentment melting away at his touch.

There was a hammering at the door and a voice shouted that the hour was up. Aline froze.

Hugh took hold of both her hands and when he spoke his voice was low and grave. 'Aline, promise me now that whatever happens you will stay safe. Do what Godfrey says. I have assurances, but if you are in any danger I want you to run.' He put his head close and spoke into her ear. 'If it is my fate to live I will come to you, I swear. If I don't—'

'Don't say that! I don't want to hear it,' Aline interrupted urgently.

'If I don't,' Hugh repeated firmly, taking her face between his hands, his ice-blue eyes boring deep inside her, 'then I want you to always remember that I love you more deeply than I ever thought possible.'

Tears coursed down Aline's cheeks but she no longer cared. 'We haven't had enough time.'

Hugh's expression was so tender it almost broke Aline's heart.

'My time with you has surpassed anything I could have dreamed of, and I would not exchange that for a hundred more years of life.'

He kissed her softly and a sob welled up in Aline's throat. She forced it down and shut her eyes. Hugh kissed her lightly on each closed eyelid, his touch soft and brief as a feather.

'Stephen is waiting,' he said.

'You don't have to do this,' Aline whispered, her voice faltering, barely able to look at Hugh.

'Yes, I do,' he replied, a faint smile on his lips.

Hand in hand, they left the room.

The sun had crossed the river and long shadows covered the ground, turning the world grey. As the sentries escorted Hugh and Aline to the combat ground Godfrey joined them. He pursed his lips at the sight of Aline's red-rimmed eyes and looked accusingly at Hugh, then his eyes drifted to their hands still intertwined. He raised an eyebrow at Hugh, who stared back boldly, refusing to relinquish his hold.

'As the challenged man, Duke Stephen's has the right to name the weapon. He has selected short swords,' Godfrey said.

Hugh chewed his lip thoughtfully, aware of Aline watching him anxiously. He usually favoured a two-handed broadsword, but with his

344   *Falling for Her Captor*

arm still weak the choice of single-handed blades
might be the only way he could hope to survive.

'My lady, I know I have surrendered the right
to ask, but I want you to leave the island,' he said
to Aline, his voice as light as he could make it.

'You don't want me here?' Her face twisted
with betrayal.

He reached a hand to her face and caressed
her cheek. 'It is no slight upon your courage,
but if I am going to die I don't want you to witness it,' he said firmly. 'Don't remember me in
that way.'

He expected her to protest, but instead she
bowed her head in agreement.

'Thank you,' he said. He lifted her hand to his
lips, the formal gesture seeming appropriate for
the situation. He drew Godfrey to one side. In a
low voice he muttered, 'Give me your word that
if I die you will keep Aline safe.'

Godfrey regarded him carefully. 'I think you
had better make sure you *do* survive. I can promise to keep her out of harm's way, but I have no
means in my power to mend a broken heart.'

The words nearly dropped Hugh to his knees
as the young knight walked to Aline and, with
an arm around her waist, guided her from Hugh's
sight, possibly for the last time.

Hugh walked alone to the arena, where the
remaining knights and nobles stood beside Ste-

phen. With a salute to the crowd both combatants entered the arena. Two short swords, their blades the length of a man's arm, were stuck into the soft earth in the centre, three strides apart. The gates were closed and excitement rippled through a crowd eager for blood to be spilled. The trumpets sounded and both men lunged for their weapons, all other thoughts lost amid the need to survive.

Chapter Twenty-Seven

As soon as she'd crossed the bridge Aline regretted her decision. She almost ran back when a sudden fanfare filled the air, ending as abruptly as it had started. Cheers and roars, and the discordant clang of steel upon steel drifted across the water on the wind.

Why had she agreed to wait? She paced back and forth, ignoring all Godfrey's pleas for her to sit. Since she had left Hugh every minute had been torture as she gave free rein to her imagination. He died in her mind at least once a minute, and she had to bite down on her lip to stop herself from screaming.

The wind changed and she could no longer hear the battle. How could time pass so slowly? Her hands shook at the thought that Hugh might already be lying lifeless or dying. She should never have abandoned him.

'Come with me,' she said abruptly.

'Where?' Godfrey asked.

Aline rolled her eyes in disbelief that he could not know. 'Back to the island, of course. I have to be there.'

She set off at a run, not caring if he followed, heading straight to the arena. Crowds of men were gathered side by side, regardless of allegiance as they watched the conflict, hiding the events from her sight.

Aline rushed forwards, but a hand at her elbow pulled her back.

'Aline, you shouldn't see this,' Godfrey said.

She tried to shake him off but he held tight.

'No—listen to me,' he insisted. 'You gave him your word. Sir Hugh needs no distractions. If he sees you're here what will that do to his concentration? If he loses, then—'

'He won't lose!' Aline snapped. Godfrey's words stung her but she saw the truth in them. If Hugh failed because of her presence she would never forgive herself. 'Lend me your cloak, please. I have to witness it, but I won't let him see me.'

Godfrey stood silently and Aline feared he would refuse, but he gave a reluctant sigh and unfastened the buckle at his neck.

'He's a brave man, Aline.' Godfrey smiled. 'I'd almost say he deserves you. *Almost.*'

Aline threw his cloak over her shoulders,

drawing the hood close over her face. With Godfrey staying close by, she pushed her way to the
front.

Aline had seen combat before, but only for
show and competition. Never before had she seen
a fight between two men who truly wanted the
other dead with all the strength in their hearts.

Both men were bleeding where the swords
had delivered glancing blows to their legs or
arms. The weapons met again and again, peals
of metallic sound ringing out above the cheers
of the watchers, setting Aline's teeth on edge.
It seemed impossible that they could maintain
their pace for much longer and she forced herself to watch, willing all the strength she possessed into Hugh.

The two men were close together, their
swords locked between them. Feet sliding in the
dirt, they twisted round, teeth bared with effort.
Stephen brought his foot down heavily on Hugh's
ankle, causing him to cry out in pain. Aline felt
her knees buckle, and it was only the crush of
bodies that stopped her sinking to the ground.

Hugh drove his fist against Stephen's jaw. The
Duke howled as he threw himself backwards
and, taken by surprise, Hugh struggled to hold
his balance. He landed heavily, the sword skitter-
ing from his grasp as he crashed to the ground.

All thoughts of secrecy forgotten, Aline screamed his name in anguish.

Hugh landed hard on his arm, the chainmail painfully scourging the skin beneath. The sword flew from his hand and landed beyond his reach. He hurled himself towards it, changing direction mid-fall, but he was not close enough.

Above the shouts and boos he heard his name: one female voice full of despair that chilled Hugh to the bone.

Aline!

His head whipped around in disbelief, searching for her in the crowd. Now he saw her—a glimpse of pale hair beneath a hood, a face twisted in torment and clear grey eyes bright with alarm. For the briefest second their eyes locked and Hugh floated on euphoria. Until then only the pain had been real, only the fight had mattered. Now he remembered why he had to win. His reason to live was standing there.

'So she's here,' Stephen crowed, walking over to him, sword over his shoulder. 'I wonder how she feels to see her champion cowering in the dirt, about to lose his head?' Stephen continued, his eyes shining with glee. 'And how ironic that after all these years it is another woman who is your weakness. Think on *that* at the end, cousin!'

'My strength,' Hugh spat. 'Not my weakness. Not. At. All!'

Pulling himself to his feet, he hurled himself at Stephen, bearing the Duke to the ground before he had time to raise his blade again. Stephen twisted round, bringing the weapon between them, his face contorted with exertion as he struggled to his feet.

Gritting his teeth, Hugh gripped hold of Stephen's wrist, sidestepping to pull him close. The short blade quivered upwards as both men wrestled in a deadly tug-of-war. From somewhere far away Hugh was aware of shouting, but none of that mattered now. His world was filled with one thought alone: he could not lose this fight. Not now Aline was here.

At the limit of his endurance, Hugh gripped the sword with both hands. Slowly the blade turned away from Hugh's chest until it was facing towards Stephen. Hugh's arms screamed, and his elbow was sticking out at an unnatural angle. A further twist in the wrong direction would dislocate the joint, but to loosen his grip now would mean death.

The tip of the blade scratched Stephen's neck and a bead of blood sprang up. Shock lit Stephen's face. He loosened his grip—not much, but it was all Hugh needed. Visions of Aline filled his eyes and he drove the blade home.

Stephen slumped forwards, his expression one of disbelief. Hugh caught him in his arms, the sword falling to the ground. He sank to his knees under the weight of the dying man as the last of his strength left him. As the Duke's corpse fell to the ground Hugh crumpled into a heap alongside.

He could hear the crowd roaring, but the sound seemed to come from far away. His limbs felt numb and cold, though the fire that burned through his wounds was excruciating. His chest felt weighted under rocks and breathing was too painful to bear.

A sense of relief flooded his aching body as he allowed himself finally to rest, knowing Aline was safe. Now he could let go and drift into oblivion one last time.

Aline's world fell slowly away. When the two fighters crumpled to the ground she refused to believe her eyes. The blade had plunged into Stephen's throat, not Hugh's, so why did he lie there, unmoving? With a heart close to breaking she waited for him to stand, to proclaim his victory and claim his title, confident that he would at any moment.

When he did not move her confusion turned to a dread greater than she had ever felt before, constricting her chest so she could barely draw breath. A scream built inside her: a discordant wail of loss she knew would never cease. All that escaped her lips was a low, keening moan. She felt too numb even to cry.

'He can't be dead!' Aline's voice was strangled by the panic that gripped her throat.

She looked at Godfrey, hoping for some reassurance, but he didn't speak. Godfrey shook his head, his face a white mask of uncertainty.

Aline turned away from the scene. Her head told her there was nothing to be done, but her heart ached with such longing to be close to Hugh, to touch him one last time. Without knowing how, she was walking on legs of ice round the edge of the amphitheatre.

'Aline, don't!'

Godfrey's voice echoed in her ears as she forced her way through the crowd. His cloak caught around her legs and she tore it from her shoulders, hurling it away. Shouts of surprise filled the air as the men recognised her. As if parted by some unseen hand, they stepped aside to allow her through. Some fell to their knees, others shouted her name, but she ignored them all.

A gathering of noblemen and knights stood by the entrance to the arena.

'Open the gate,' she ordered as she reached the battleground. 'Let me through!'

Their faces registered surprise, changing to sorrow at the desperation in her voice.

'Let me through. Now!' she repeated.

They sprang to obey, tugging at the great gates. One of the knights, old and dark-haired, took hold of her arm gently, speaking words she barely heard. She shook him off without a glance in his direction and walked into the arena.

The two opponents looked like broken dolls, thrown down in boredom by a careless child. Stephen lay on his back, his sightless eyes staring at the darkening sky. Hugh had fallen half onto his back, one arm over Stephen's chest, the other twisted out beside him. Blood oozed from his calf, where Stephen's sword had sliced the flesh, soaking into the dirt beneath. His face was turned to the side, his dark waves of hair a curtain hiding him from the world.

Aline took three faltering paces towards him, then stopped. She bowed her head, wrapping her arms tightly around her chest in an effort to crush the ache from her heart. She stumbled forwards as though in a trance and sank to her knees beside the bodies. She reached for Hugh's hand, limp and yet still warm.

'High Lady.' Someone stepped towards her. 'The Duke is dead. You have nothing to fear any longer.'

'The price was too high!' she screamed at the sky, her grief refusing to be silenced any longer.

The hand in hers twitched slightly—only a slight pressure but there all the same.

Aline's head jerked down. Incredibly, she saw the almost imperceptible rise and fall of Hugh's chest, hardly daring to believe it was true. Hugh's head moved slightly and he drew a juddering breath. With a sound that was half laugh, half sob Aline hurled herself across his body and flung her arms around his neck, burying her head in his chest. Now, at last, her tears began to fall.

Hugh groaned as the weight of her body—slight though she was—knocked the breath from him and she pulled away, fearful of injuring him further. His arms wound weakly around her, drawing her close again.

'I told you to leave me,' he chided, though his eyes were warm. 'Will you ever begin to do what I ask you?'

'I couldn't stay away. I saw you fall. I thought you were dead. I thought…' Aline sobbed as she held him tightly but she smiled through her tears.

'Does this mean you are still going to speak to me?' Hugh asked, his lips twisting. 'Or have you come to bid me farewell?'

'Farewell?' she asked, confused.

Hugh stared up at the sky. 'You told me we

would not see each other again after today,' he reminded her. 'I wondered if you were intending to leave as soon as the duel ended.'

Until that point she had forgotten the harsh words she had spoken to him and her stomach churned.

'I should never have said that. I was angry and resentful and I did not mean it,' she said, her voice cracking with emotion. 'If you had died I don't know how I would have lived,' she murmured, her voice shaking. 'I'm not strong enough without you.'

Hugh stroked the tangled hair back from her cheek. 'Yes, you are. You are the strongest woman I have ever known. Everything you have been through you have faced with courage and dignity. I was so consumed with thoughts of keeping you from harm I lost sight of your strength. You will be a wonderful High Lady. Live well and be happy, Aline.'

'I can never be happy without you!' Aline cried. She drew back to look at him. 'You are the only man I have ever loved—the only one I will ever want. If it was in my power to choose I would never let you leave me.'

Hugh's eyes crinkled and unexpectedly he smiled, his face handsome in the fading light. 'You are High Lady and, if I know you as well as I think I do, you have the determination to do anything you choose.'

Aline stared at him, puzzled, then the implication of his words sank in and a bubble of joyous laughter burst from her lips. She idly wondered what the watching men must think to see their High Lady sprawling in the dirt, embracing a bloodstained warrior, then she realised she did not care and flung her arms around him again.

'Help me to stand, please?' Hugh asked.

She took his arm and hauled him upright. Her arms were firm around his waist but the chainmail was heavy. He almost fell, but by now others had rushed forwards to catch him, lifting his arms around their shoulders. Aline relinquished her hold willingly. She intended to have him back in her arms before long.

The knights of Roxholm and Leavingham entered the arena and knelt before Hugh and Aline in an impromptu show of allegiance. Godfrey knelt with a wink and a grin on his face as he looked from Aline to Hugh.

When the men had finished Hugh turned to stand before Aline. His eyes brimmed with love, desire, and so many emotions Aline could not yet read—but she wanted to spend the rest of her life learning. She wondered what he saw in her expression, hoped he could see the love she felt for him.

'Aline, I have wasted so much of my life on misguided loyalty and a code of honour I never believed in. I will spend the rest of my days atoning for the things I did to you. I offer you my loyalty and my life.'

With difficulty he began to sink to his knee, but she stopped him with one flash of her eyes. He hesitated midbow and met her gaze with the raising of an eyebrow.

'No, Sir Hugh. You need never kneel to me,' Aline said. 'There is nothing to atone for. I forgive you everything.'

Her voice betrayed only the slightest tremor. Only one who was very close or knew her very well would spot it. She took him by the hands, her fingers burning at his touch, and drew him to his feet. When he was standing she turned to address the assembled people.

'This man is the rightful Duke of Roxholm. Let no one say otherwise. He has won his title fairly. He is honourable, courageous, and loyal.'

The roars of approval prevented her from continuing. She gave him a shy, private smile before holding up a hand to still the voices.

'More than this, I have given him my promise and my heart. He is the man I choose as my husband.'

She laughed with exhilaration at the ripple of amazement that ran through the crowd, the whoop of joy from Godfrey's direction and the cheers from the knights. She looked at Hugh. He was smiling from ear to ear.

She leaned close, overcome by unexpected shyness, and whispered, 'If he will have me, of course.'

Tears of joy sprang to Hugh's eyes. He lifted Aline's hand to his lips then, throwing caution and protocol to the wind, pulled her close. His arms enfolded her in a powerful embrace, his lips finding hers waiting eagerly.

Her heart bursting with love, Aline wrapped her arms round his neck, meeting his kiss passionately.

She was finally truly his.

Epilogue

The stars were out and the air cold by the time they returned to the camp. The soldiers from Roxholm accompanied them, there being ample room for all the troops. Fires were lit and a whisky barrel produced, adding to the merriment. Men were sent to hunt, and at last the air was filled with the tempting scent of roasting meat. As the moon rose high the camp came alive. Someone produced a whistle, someone else a makeshift drum, and a loud chorus of ribald songs filled the night air.

Aline excused herself from the company of nobles and sat alone by a small fire, staring into the flames. She waited patiently for Hugh to return from having his wounds tended to. There was no need to hurry; they had all the time in the world.

Finally he appeared at the edge of the camp, his arm around Godfrey's shoulder for support. His face creased into a broad smile as he spied her and the two men made their way across the field. The young knight helped Hugh to sit before giving Aline a broad grin and vanishing into the throng of soldiers.

'Hello,' she whispered as Hugh shuffled onto the bench alongside her. She took his hand and softly moved her thumb in circles over the bandaged wound on his arm.

'Your stitching was neater,' he observed with a smile. 'All armies should have a fine lady to embroider their cuts.'

Aline studied his face in the firelight. He looked pale and weary, and fresh bruises were forming.

'It hurts to move,' he grumbled good-naturedly in answer to her unasked question. 'I ache in places I did not know it was possible to feel pain.'

She burrowed closer to his side and planted a kiss on his bruised jaw. Hugh sighed softly but Aline knew it was not from pain. She repeated the gesture and he turned his head to meet her lips with his own.

When he finally drew away his eyes were sad. 'You know I have to leave tomorrow?' he said softly, regret clear in his voice. 'I need to go back to Roxholm. There is so much I have to resolve.'

'I know, but you'll come back. And you're not going tonight. We have our whole lives to be together, so what do a few weeks matter?'

'Should we build a new castle?' Hugh asked jokingly. 'Somewhere between both our lands? Or shall we spend summers by the sea and winters in Leavingham?'

'I like that plan,' Aline told him, visions of years to come with this wonderful man playing through her mind.

She leaned against him as they listened to the music and stared up at the stars. No mention had been made of where Hugh would sleep, but when he began to yawn she waved him off with a smile, not bothering to watch the direction he took.

For a while Aline spent time walking among the men, talking with them and listening to their tales, but all the while her eyes returned to the spot where her heart pulled her. Finally satisfied that her duty was done she took her leave of the company, slipping between the curtains into her tent.

She was unsurprised to discover Hugh was there. He was snoring gently as he lay asleep, wrapped in cloaks of fur, his face serene in the light of the torches.

Aline bent to remove her boots and stockings, then unwound her hair and ran her fingers through it, feeling the knots of tension begin to dissolve. She unlaced her dress and let it fall to the floor alongside the pile of Hugh's discarded garments. A coy smile played at her lips as she snuffed the torch before removing her underclothes, too. Slipping naked into the bed, she pulled the furs round her, pressing close to Hugh's body for warmth.

A shift in his breathing told her Hugh had awakened. His eyes remained shut but his hand reached out and snaked into hers. She smiled, flutters of anticipation curling in her belly. He rolled towards her, wrapping his free arm around her shoulder and tugging her close. She came willingly and nestled into the warm contours of his frame, a shudder running through her at the touch of his skin against hers.

She wriggled her legs underneath his, warming her bare feet between his calves. Her hand moved to his chest, stroking the fine hair and supple skin, her fingers brushing lightly across his nipples. Hugh sighed with pleasure and Aline felt the heat of arousal growing within her. She began to work her fingers lightly in small circles down the firm muscles of his torso.

'Take pity on me, Aline,' Hugh implored in mock supplication. 'I intend to spend my life making love to you but I've fought one battle today. I fear I'm incapable of another conquest!'

Aline stifled a giggle at his plea, her heart skipping a beat at his words. She pulled herself onto one elbow to grin at him, letting her breasts press against his chest.

'Do you promise me a whole lifetime, my lord? In that case I will excuse you for tonight.'

She planted a kiss on his lips, then lay back down, her head finding space in the hollow between his neck and shoulder. Hugh wrapped an arm around her, his fingers curling into her hair as it flowed over her shoulders.

They lay without speaking, listening as the last noises of the camp began to die away. A pleasant drowsiness crept over Aline and she sighed in contentment. It struck her that in this man's arms, wrapped in furs, there was nowhere she would rather be. Reaching her mouth to Hugh's, she kissed him again, parting his lips with her tongue.

Hugh burrowed his hand deeper into the silken fall of her hair, cupping the back of her neck as he tugged her close. She pressed her body closer to his with an appreciative sigh and kissed him harder. He ran his fingers down the length of her spine before rolling himself over to cover her body with his own. Aline arched her back in pleasure, tilting her hips against him.

As Hugh's kisses became fiercer, and his touch more urgent, Aline recognised with pleasure that he did not intend to wait after all.

* * * * *

MILLS & BOON®

Why not subscribe?
Never miss a title and save money too!

Here's what's available to you if you join the
exclusive **Mills & Boon Book Club** today:

- ✦ *Titles up to a month ahead of the shops*
- ✦ *Amazing discounts*
- ✦ *Free P&P*
- ✦ *Earn Bonus Book points that can be redeemed
  against other titles and gifts*
- ✦ *Choose from monthly or pre-paid plans*

Still want more?
Well, if you join today we'll even give you
50% OFF your first parcel!

So visit **www.millsandboon.co.uk/subs**
or call **Customer Relations** on **020 8288 2888**
to be a part of this exclusive Book Club!

SUBS_2014

Snow, sleigh bells and a hint of seduction

Find your perfect Christmas reads at
millsandboon.co.uk/Christmas

MILLS & BOON®

Why shop at millsandboon.co.uk?

Each year, thousands of romance readers find their
perfect read at millsandboon.co.uk. That's because
we're passionate about bringing you the very best
romantic fiction. Here are some of the advantages
of shopping at www.millsandboon.co.uk:

* **Get new books first**—you'll be able to buy your
  favourite books one month before they hit
  the shops

* **Get exclusive discounts**—you'll also be able to buy
  our specially created monthly collections, with up
  to 50% off the RRP

* **Find your favourite authors**—latest news,
  interviews and new releases for all your favourite
  authors and series on our website, plus ideas for
  what to try next

* **Join in**—once you've bought your favourite books,
  don't forget to register with us to rate, review and
  join in the discussions

Visit **www.millsandboon.co.uk**
for all this and more today!